Hello Mr Beckett

by

CARRIE McGOVERN

Copyright © 2023 by Carrie McGovern

All rights reserved.

No part of this publication may be reproduced, distributed, or transmitted in any form or by any means, including photocopying, recording, or other electronic or mechanical methods, without the prior written permission of the publisher, except as permitted by copyright law. For permission requests, contact info@carriemcgovern.com

The story, all names, characters, and incidents portrayed in this production are fictitious. No identification with actual persons (living or deceased), places, buildings, and products is intended or should be inferred.

Published by Embrace Publishing

Book Cover Art by Lauren Osbourne

Edited By Helen Bowman from In The Detail

ISBN – 978-1-7384973-1-7

Dedication

I dedicate this book to my husband, again, because he said I had to.
Whatever!

Chapter One

Megan

I put the key in the lock and turn, apprehensive of what I'll be met with on the other side of the door. I push it open and peer in. There's no sign of anybody and I don't get that prickly feeling on the back of my neck when I'm not alone. Walking through the hall, I put my bags on the floor and make my way into the living room. It's been a weird day at work, which is happening a lot more these days, and I don't need more grief when I get home, which I usually get.

There's something afoot at work because the bosses have been acting weird, well weirder than usual anyway. The head count of normal people in the office has dropped by 25 per cent, as Emma has left us for her dream job. That leaves Beth and me with Penny from accounts, Maureen from finance, who looks like she's permanently chewing a wasp, a handful of upper management and then, of course, the drivers.

Penny is lovely, but we don't have that much in common, although her geriatric friends are probably as crazy as mine. Okay, so geriatric might be a bit of a cruel label to land them with, but they are all nearing retirement age. And don't we all know it, we get a daily run down of *what I'm going to do when I retire*, and the list is extensive.

Beth is one of my best friends. She is my ray of sunshine in this drab and dreary office. Beth and Emma were the only ones who were actually nice to me when I first joined as an apprentice. Though they did tease me relentlessly about being naïve. They still do actually. Beth has taken over the role of mother hen with us all. She has two kids of her own, who she is permanently trying to micro-manage, and a husband who is really lovely but gets roped into all kinds.

I'm not sure whether I'm classed as the extra child or the little sister, but my friends are my family and I love them dearly. Especially now I constantly do things that my parents disapprove of. Not that I could see them much, even if I wanted to, because they jet set all over the world, reliving the fun they never had because they were tied down by a child. Or that's how I've interpreted it.

We are heading out tonight for one of our girls' nights down at the Dog and Swan pub. Emma and Lizzie will be there too. Emma was one of my work gang, but she moved on from our skanky office and is now a marketing manager for some big company. She's absolutely smashing it. Although we were really happy for her when she got new job, we were also envious that she had been able to escape. Especially for me as I joined our office as an apprentice and haven't yet managed to escape. That was over a decade ago.

There was whole load of drama recently when she got together with a younger man, Ben, who moved to live with her and her boys. She was the talk of the office. Mainly because no one has anything else interesting to gossip about.

It all happened when we had a *girls' night on tour* weekend in Edinburgh. One of our group of mismatched friends, Sammy, lives the champagne lifestyle up there, with her well-paid job and beautiful flat. She is amazing, although she'll not be here tonight. We don't see her that often, but when we do, we all know it will be a night to remember. Or not, as the case may be. We met Ben and his group of friends that weekend and we've never really been able to shake them off since. And like I say, Emma is now living with one of them.

Then there's Lizzie. She's a force to be reckoned with, curt and to the point. She is like the voice of reason, sometimes a little bit harsh, so if you are feeling a bit delicate and don't really want to hear the truth, then don't ask Lizzie. Lizzie has two children the same ages as Emma's boys. I think that's how they initially met. She is separated from the kids' Dad, or so we think, because some days they are well and truly split, and other days Jonathan is hanging off her every word and following her around like a puppy. Which is funny given he's a pretty buff and good-looking authoritative type.

I cautiously walk through the flat and I feel my anxiety levels rise. Darren is usually here when I get home, especially when I'm late, like I am this evening. I search each room looking for him. I have my excuses for being late already cued up because I know the interrogation is looming. I just nipped to the shop to pick up a pint of milk for tomorrow morning's coffee and I missed the next bus. But whatever I say, I'm always in the wrong.

I've lived with Darren for about two years, probably a bit longer, and it started like a dream come true. I couldn't believe that he wanted to spend all his time with me. But as time has gone on I'm feeling more anxious about the whole situation.

My friends don't like Darren and they've made that perfectly clear. They see his behaviour towards me as controlling rather than protecting. Lizzie is especially vocal about it, so now I keep some of the things he does to myself. They'd think I'm stupid for still being with him if they knew the half of it.

When we first got together he put a tracker on my phone to keep me safe, so if I ever needed him he would know where to get me. But now it just makes me super conscious of what I'm doing. It's not to keep me safe, it's to keep an eye on what I'm doing.

I shout out that I'm home, but there's no answer. I'm not sure whether it makes me feel better that he's not in or more on edge because he could come back at any time. This situation could go one of two ways. Either something has happened to him, or, most likely, he's pulling one of his mind game tricks. He will go incommunicado for a while, either make me worry about where he is, or blame me for not contacting him. He'll say he didn't receive any messages and he'd been trying to contact me this whole time. This is all because he knows I'm going out with the girls and he doesn't like it one bit.

This could be the final straw for me. His overbearing *protectiveness* is now outweighed by his stalking and nasty tendencies.

I conclude the flat search. Whatever I do now, however this eventually plays out, I'm going to be in the wrong and I'll have to beg for his forgiveness. At the minute that just isn't going to wash with me. But for now I'll play his game. I send him an additional message to the 14 I have already sent, asking how he is and reiterating my plans for tonight. I take an *accidental* screenshot to prove it. The girls will be here to pick me up soon, so I start to get myself ready.

Our local haunt for our girls' nights out is the Dog and Swan pub. It's a far cry from the sophisticated places that Sammy takes us to in Edinburgh, but it's familiar and safe. We are already two drinks in when our late arrival rushes in, looking stressed and flustered – not her usual self at all.

"Sorry girls." Emma plonks herself down on the sofa next to Lizzie. "You would not believe what's been going on over the last few days!" Emma has had her fair share of drama over the past 18 months. It was a bit touch and go for her relationship with her boyfriend Ben.

"Are you going to enlighten us then?" Lizzie, as always, is straight to the point. She's the strong, confident type and takes no shit from anyone, especially Darren. She's the only person that Darren is scared to answer back or try his manipulation charms on. She always picks me up from my front door so that Darren can't try to ruin my night out, which is his usual MO.

The girls have been trying to convince me to leave him pretty much since I moved in. I seem to always get to the point where

I feel that enough is enough, and he turns on the charm and becomes the ideal, perfect boyfriend. But I now realise that the sweetness only ever comes after the arseholeness.

"So, we had a little surprise this week." Emma starts. "We have an addition to the family."

"You're pregnant?"

"God no!"

"You've got a puppy?"

"Again, no!"

"Well, are you gonna tell us or is this some kind of twisted guessing game?" Lizzie is straight to the chase.

Emma gives Lizzie the wide eye warning. "Alright! Ben has a daughter!"

Well I certainly didn't see that coming. She continues. "We got a call from one of his old fuck buddies to say that, not only did he have a daughter, but she was already two years old and critically ill in hospital."

"I bet that went down well with Ben," Beth chips in.

"He was fuming. We had to take an emergency trip up to Scotland."

"And is she okay?" I ask.

"Yeah, they thought it was meningitis, but it was just a bad viral infection."

"So who's the mum?" I think that's the question on everyone's lips.

"She's called Charlotte. She's actually really nice. Down to earth. I really felt for her and Ava."

"And how do you feel about that situation?"

"Well it was kind of a shock, but I knew Ben would eventually want kids and I wasn't gonna be able to give him them."

"Or want to!" Lizzie feels exactly the same as Emma about having more children.

"Well exactly. The thought of giving birth again." She shudders. I know Emma had a bad birthing experience and her kids have been a bit of a handful, so I guess this is the best of both worlds.

"Bloody hell Emma, you really like living on the edge. What a change from this time two years ago," I say, thinking about the situation with her ex constantly taking advantage of her kind nature.

"I know, right!"

The chatter carries on and we take our turns to go to the bar. Mitch, the landlord knows what drinks we want without even asking – an indication that we come here quite a lot. He also asks after everyone's kids and pets, as if he absorbs all the information that is chatted about in his pub. He must be great at quizzes because he remembers every unique detail about people.

Everyone has had a laugh and we are just the right side of drunk when Steve, Beth's husband, drops us all back home. The partners of our little friend group are very protective and take it in turns to pick us up and drop us at home, to make sure we are all safe. As soon as I get out of the car, the anxiety flushes through my body, wondering what interrogation I will face once I get in, or whether Darren will be back yet. Steve waits for me to unlock my door and head inside before giving a wave and leaving.

The flat is deadly quiet again. I have messaged Darren a few more times but with no response. I walk into the darkened living room and I know immediately that I'm not alone. I feel him before I see him. He's sitting in the chair in the corner, the air thick with tension.

He flicks on the lamp above his head which illuminates his face but not much more. He's acting like he's in some kind of gangster film, and it's not the first time. He pulls this trick every so often and it's getting a bit old.

"Where do you think you've been?" He sounds like a really bad vintage movie villain, from the films my dad used to watch on a Sunday afternoon.

"You know where I've been, I told you. The real question is, where have YOU been?"

"How dare you! No messages, no calls, no nothing! You don't give a shit!" He's fizzing with anger, the tension just radiates off him.

"I did message you. Many, many times in fact. Plus you knew I was going out!"

"I was planning on taking you out for dinner."

"Likely!" I say just under my breath.

"What the fuck did you say?"

"Well when was the last time you took me out anywhere? And you decide to take me out, just as I'm not here to ask."

"We can't all live the high life like your mate, married to a sugar daddy." He's referring to Emma and Ben, who has his own successful business. He's jealous because he hasn't got the motivation or skill to do something like that himself.

I roll my eyes and turn away but before I know what is happening, I feel the restriction around my throat. My hand goes straight to my neck to claw at his hands. I'm lifted off my feet, back flat against the wall. My heart is racing so much it feels like it will burst out of my chest.

I keep clawing at his hand, the lack of oxygen has me seeing stars and I can feel my limbs lose sensation. Panic sets in and I desperately pull at his hand, digging my nails in enough to draw blood. But still his hold remains.

He still hasn't uttered a word, his eyes wild, his face a mask. Now I don't have enough air to get any words out. I'm pushed up on my tiptoes and his face is so close to mine. He's snarling and I can feel his hot breath – a mixture of alcohol and contempt. Just as I think this could be the last thing I do, he lets go and I drop to the floor, my limbs too weak to hold me up.

I fight to get enough capacity in my lungs to speak. "What the fuck?" It's all I can muster.

"Don't you fucking dare!" He slaps me hard across the face and I feel the heat, then the sting on my cheek.

We stare at each other, both stunned. The silence only lasts for about 30 seconds, but it feels like a lifetime. It's clear that nothing can ever be the same again.

It's me who breaks the stand-off. I shakily get to my feet and make my way out in silence, grabbing my bag from the hall as I go. The door closes behind me and I begin to walk. He's never followed through on his threats before. Emotionally destructive yes, but not physically. Something has snapped in his head. Maybe he didn't think I would answer him back and realised his old tricks have run out of steam.

Before I know it, I've walked for miles in a numb kind of trance, not feeling the rain soaking through my clothes, goose bumps covering my body. I have no memory of how I got to the house I'm now stood in front of, but I raise my hand to knock on the front door. It takes forever for the lights to go on inside and I finally hear movement inside. The door is opened by a weary-looking Steve, followed close behind by a pyjama-clad Beth.

"What the fuck happened?" Steve never swears. He opens the door fully and ushers me through the entrance hall. My feet are on autopilot as I make my way inside and before I can register what is happening I'm wrapped in a dressing gown, towel in one hand, brandy in the other and sitting on the front room sofa.

Chapter Two

I open my eyes and it's not the light streaming in from the window, nor the two small faces, about three inches away from my nose that hit me first. Instead it's the searing pain below my eye socket and the throb coming from my neck that overwhelms me.

"Morning Aunty Megan," Poppy says, as I lift my lids and try to focus. "Aunty Megan, your face looks weird."

"Did you have a fight in the pub like Uncle Max did?" Jonah pulls back a little, sizing me up. "Did you walk into a lamp post?" He narrows his eyes and does that cartoon stereotype thinking face. "Did an elephant escape from the zoo and…"

"Guys, leave Aunty Megan alone and come and get your breakfast," Beth insists.

"It was an elephant, I knew it! Parents always change the subject when you get it right." Jonah fist pumps the air and walks off into the kitchen, with the air of arrogance only a six-year-old can have. Poppy is still staring at me, so close I feel like she is inspecting me like I'm a museum exhibit. She jumps when her name is called and runs into the kitchen.

"Good morning to you two hooligans too!" I shout back and I hear the faint sound of them giggling. Beth walks back in with two steaming cups of coffee, hands me one as I pull myself up and sits next to me on the sofa I passed out on last night.

"Are you gonna tell me what happened?"

"Same old shit. Except this time I stood up for myself and he just lost it. I have never seen him like that before." The realisation seeps in and I dread to think what could have happened. "He had me by the throat, and then slapped me round the face when I dared to question his actions."

"Shit!" Beth's eyebrows pull together. I expect she's seen this coming for a while, so it's not much of a surprise to her. "So what now?" My friends have stopped trying to cajole me into leaving Darren. They know better because I always go back to him, mostly out of a sense of loyalty, pity and maybe a bit of love. But not this time.

"I need to leave him, but I've got nowhere to go." Then the panic starts rising through my body, my hands turn clammy. I feel like I might vomit as I think of all the things that keep me tied to Darren. "Oh my god! What am I gonna do?" I don't know whether to cry, scream or do a runner.

I'm pulled out of my intrusive thoughts by the sound of the doorbell. The feeling of panic rises again. What if he's come for me? I'm not sure what would be worse, him coming back to finish the job or coming to beg for me to go back to him.

Steve has answered the door and I can hear a few different voices coming from the hall. One by one they filter into the living room, coming over to hug me or ask if I'm okay.

"So you invited the whole lot of them?" I say to Beth with distain. I thought I might be able to keep my humiliation to just a handful of people. Beth shrugs as the room fills up.

There's Emma and Ben, hand in hand, then Lizzie and Jonathan, trying to make it look like they aren't totally besotted with each other. Seven adult bodies not quite knowing where to put themselves. To add to the chaos, Jonah runs in and launches himself at Ben, while Poppy hides behind Beth's legs.

It's just all too much and I excuse myself to the bathroom so I can freshen up and fight the overwhelming urge to run. Plus, there's one more person to tell. I sit on the toilet, lid down, and bring up my contacts list. I find the name Shelley and type out a quick message. As soon as it's sent I turn my phone off. I don't need another interrogation right now.

Eventually, once I've washed my face and cleaned my teeth with a squeeze of toothpaste on my finger, I head back down to face the music. As I enter the room it falls silent. They've obviously been discussing my situation.

It's Jonathan that starts the inquisition, his police training kicking in again. I don't quite know what he does. He doesn't wear a uniform, but he has an air of importance about him.

"Can you tell us, in your own words, what happened last night?"

"He was sitting waiting for me at the flat. Sitting in the dark. Flicked on the light, all Godfather or whatever, started going on about me being out and not telling him. I'd been messaging him, and getting no response, all day.

"I just couldn't be arsed with his game of gangster, so I called him out on it." I take a deep breath before I go into the rest. "Out of nowhere, he had me up against a wall by my throat." I look around the room for their reaction. Jonathan is still as calm as when he started but both Emma and Beth look like they're about to burst into tears. I hope they can keep it together, because once they go, that'll be me blubbing and I don't know if I'll be able to stop. Ben clenches his fists but is distracted by his phone which keeps buzzing. He leaves the room to answer it. Steve is just shaking his head as if he can't believe what I'm saying.

"Then he hit me in the face," I say, pointing to my swollen eye, "and I walked out, came here."

"So, what's your next move?" Jonathan continues. "What do you want to do now?"

"I don't know. I need to leave him, but I have nowhere to go."

"You will always have somewhere, Megan. We've got you." Emma's kind eyes look back at me.

"Stay with us for a few nights." Ben has walked back in. "I've got you a place sorted already, it just needs some furniture." Wait, what? Before I can even get clarification on what he just said, he leaves the room to answer his phone again and Jonathan pulls my attention back to him.

"Megan, we can get him charged with assault. That eye looks pretty nasty."

"No. I don't want to see him again."

"The thing is," he starts, "we need to get all your things out of the flat. If he's there, I think it will get messy and I'll have to arrest Ben and Steve for murder." I scoff at the thought of Steve having any kind of a violent streak, but looking at him now, he looks like he's primed to kill.

"But if I ask some of the lads to come over, take a quick statement, he could be out of the picture for a few hours, courtesy of Westgate Police Station."

I look around the group for some kind of indication of what the right thing to do is, but nothing is forthcoming, so I just shrug acceptance. Jonathan takes that as the permission he needs, and leaves the room to call someone. The rest of the group fusses over me.

The police were here for just over an hour taking details. The rest of my friends have rallied around sorting bits and pieces, while I have been in a trance-like state.

Jonathan escorts the officers out of the house with a pat on their backs, and a request for any updates. Emma has a change of clothes and some toiletries ready for me. Beth is staying with the kids while I travel in the car with Steve to the flat. We are at the front of a convoy of three cars, parked a few streets away from the flat. As we sit, I bite the cuticles on my nails and there is an unnerving quietness about the vehicle. The silence is broken by the ringing from Steve's phone.

"Yes gotcha!" He hangs up and turns to me with a small smile before starting the engine to move towards our destination – the place I shared with Darren.

The car comes to a stop outside the building that has never quite seemed like home. It's only now that I really see it for what it is – a cold, empty place. Even if there were any good memories they are outweighed by bad, and even more so tainted by the events of the previous night.

I get out of the car, not really wanting to go inside. I don't want to face the fact that for the last few years I've been living a lie. A lie I told to my family, my friends, and most of all, to myself.

Jonathan comes up next to me and takes the keys from my hand. It's as if he can read my mind. He gives me a quiet smile of reassurance and heads to the door, flanked by the other men. The girls hang back with me.

"They will check the coast is clear," Emma says, breaking me from my thoughts.

"All Clear!" Ben shouts from the doorway.

Lizzie turns to me and puts her hands on my shoulders as if she's gonna give me a pep talk.

"Right Lady, pull yourself together! We need to get in and out as quickly as possible. Emma is gonna pack your clothes, I'm gonna to do the kitchen stuff and the boys will start moving anything bulky. You need to point us all in the right direction. Start by letting them know what furniture you are taking. Anything too big and we'll need to rethink it. Okay?"

Always straight to the point is Lizzie. I think she missed her vocation in the army to be honest. She's still staring at me and I realise she's waiting for an answer.

"Okay! Not much of the furniture is mine, just the bedroom dresser."

"That can go in my car." Ben has joined us to get instructions from Lizzie.

"And there's a little armchair in the bedroom too!" Ben gives me the thumbs up and heads back inside.

"I have loads of boxes in my car, let's get them out and start packing." I want to give Lizzie a salute but my brain isn't sending any signals to my limbs. Emma comes up behind me and gently moves me towards the car.

The time goes by quicker than it has over the past 24 hours, and I keep checking in with Jonathan to see if he's had any updates while we are packing. I'm a big ball of anxiety and I've been very little use to the others, except for saying yes and no to what things need to be taken.

I hear a car pull up outside and my heart begins to race. A flush of dread washes over me until Ben shouts an *all clear* from the door. It's not just me who visibly relaxes at the statement.

"Megan, there's someone here for you," Ben follows up. Oh god I hope it's not my parents. We haven't spoken in a while, mainly because they didn't like me living with Darren, and told me the fact at any chance they could get. I don't think I could handle an *I told you so* today. I head to the front door reluctantly and, as I poke my head out to confront the outside world, I see a tall figure getting out of the car.

Oh my god, he's here! He straightens up and turns towards me, time slowing down until I see his full face. He really is here!

My body goes into autopilot as I head out of the door and run up to him. I wrap my arms around him as if he's a long-lost relative. He envelops me with his big frame and rests his chin on the top of my head.

"You came!" I say into his chest with a smile. Then my face drops. "Why did you come?" That's when the tears start, and I know I'm not going to be able to get any more words out. It's as if the barriers that have been holding me together are suddenly released, and every emotion I have floods out at once.

"Because you needed me!" He says it as if it were obvious. Sean pulls me away from his body so he can study my face, the darkness of his mood shows in his eyes. "You know I have to kill him now, don't you?"

He wraps me up in his arms again and I feel him talking more than I can hear him. He walks me away from the flat and bundles me into the car, plugging my seatbelt in before driving away. Leaving our friends to do the rest of the job, while we head back to Emma's house.

"Talk to me!" Sean breaks up the multitude of thoughts running through my head. "You don't need to tell me what happened, I've already been filled in. Tell me what you're thinking."

"Honestly, I don't know where to start." The good thing about talking to Sean is I don't need to put any guard up or filter out any thoughts. I can just vomit up a lot of different verbal detritus and he seems to be able to pick out the stuff that needs the most focus. This is why he has been my confidant since we met. We gelled somehow, we just get each other.

"Just let it all out."

"For a start I feel humiliated. I feel like everyone thinks I'm an idiot and deserve everything I get. Then I think what the fuck do I do? I have no money, no home. I can't go back to my parents. I can't put all this on my friends, they have their own stuff to think about and deal with." I take a deep breath, knowing I'll probably start again with everything that's going around in my head. "What will he do when he finds out I've left? Will he come after me, will he ever just leave me in peace? I'm not sure whether the police will make him back off or make him even more pissed off at me and try and hurt me again."

It takes a few moments for Sean to compute everything before he speaks.

"Firstly, that's bollocks, your friends are fighting your corner because they love you unconditionally... well, almost. Secondly, he won't dare come anywhere near you, I'll make sure of that. Thirdly, you must have money, you have a decent job."

I let out a sob and I know what I'm about to say next will really test him. "Come on spit it out, no secrets!"

"My wages go into his bank account so we can pay the bills."

"Oh fuck!"

"Please don't Sean, I feel stupid enough as it is."

"But I've seen you pay for things when you are out."

"I get an allowance on a prepaid card." I wince as I say it. I didn't really question it at the time, it seemed reasonable. We were strapped for cash. We transferred money onto a card each week so we could budget better. The rest stayed in Darren's bank account to pay the rent and bills and things.

"So you don't have access to that money? No card or anything?" I just shake my head and the tears start to roll down my face in a silent cry. "How did he transfer the money? Was it online?"

I take in a few shaky breaths and manage to get some words out. "Yes, from his laptop."

Sean immediately goes to the screen on his dashboard, bring up a number and dials. Within one ring it is answered with a quick acknowledgement.

"Mate, you're on speaker, but are you still at the flat?"

"Yeah, what's up?" Ben's voice echoes through the car.

"Is there a laptop there? In the living room?" He looks towards me and I nod.

"Let me check." We can hear him walking through the flat and moving things around. "Yes, it's here."

"Grab it and bring it with you."

"Sure. We're almost finished actually."

"Great, leave a few taps on once you leave, will you?"

Ben sniggers, "Lizzie is already on it!"

They hang up with no goodbyes just as we pull into the driveway.

Chapter Three

"Honestly there is nothing going on with me and Sean," I reiterate for what feels like the hundredth time. But I can tell by the girls' faces that they don't believe me. It's true though. We have been in contact for a while now. We all met on the night Emma met Ben, Sean is Ben's best friend and works with him. Our friendship really started when he gave me a lift home, after he and Ben gate crashed our girls' night at the Dog and Swan. Darren pulled one of his usual tricks with one of his friends spying on us. He had sent me a photo of me and the barman, which was completely innocent, and started with accusations.

Sean took me home and made sure Darren didn't see anything. He wanted to stay in touch, but I knew full well that Darren would check through my phone, so he suggested I put him in my phone as Shelley. And since then, that's what he's been known as. Even sending flowers to the office under his pseudonym, when I was feeling down. But no, there is nothing going on, he has taken the role of big brother, if anything, and right now that's exactly what I need.

Talking to him comes easy. I stopped talking to my friends about my situation when I knew they would just beg me to leave Darren. Sean just listens to me without judgement and raises my spirits when they are down. But I can also see that this could look like a romantic affair, with all the sneaky texts and phone calls, flowers and presents. And then him showing up like a knight in shining armour.

Everything from the flat is now in Ben and Emma's garage for a few days and the whole dysfunctional family of friends are congregated in the living room for a debrief.

"Megs!" Sean tries to get my attention. He's not doing me any favours by calling my Megs. My friends know there are only a handful of people who can safely call me that. I look up and give him a questioning look. "Do you know the password?" He has Darren's laptop on the table and is trying to get access. I shake my head. "It's actually a number. What about your birthday? He looks back at the screen. And looks back up to me. "It's not that!"

"Try his birthday," Lizzie shouts over. "He is a narcissist after all!"

"Try 04-04-94," I shout back.

"Bingo! Come here and let's get this shit sorted out." I go over and sit with him at the dining table and have a look at the laptop. I'm not sure what we are looking for because I was never allowed on it.

"Let's look through his browser history," Sean says, with a smirk on his face.

"Do we have to?"

"Yep, just so you can see what a loser you have walked away from. You deserve more than this."

He brings up the list and it's just porn site after porn site. I screw my face up in disgust.

I have no objections to porn, but there's just something sleazy about keeping it a secret from your partner, let alone the descriptions in some of this history. But Sean spots something in the list and points. It's his online banking, he opens up the page.

"Tut, tut, tut, Darren, not so bright are we. He's left his passwords populated and he doesn't have two factor authentication. Idiot!"

"So you can get straight in?"

"Yes. And look there." He points to the screen at the payments. "That's your wages going in." He points to another line. "And these are payments to gambling and porn sites!"

"So, he wasn't spending my money on rent and bills. He was fuelling an addiction!"

"Yep. Let's try get this money out!" He looks in the list of authorised payees. "Any there yours?"

"No. But that one there," I point to a line, "is the card my allowance goes on." I search around in my bag for my purse. "I don't usually have the card, but I remember now, he gave me it the other day because my Google Pay was playing up." I pull the card out of my purse and hold it up.

"Excellent!" I watch him transfer the whole amount, which is only £476.15 on available funds, onto the account and he takes the card off me. "Write down the pin number on this." He gives me a pen and the back of a used envelope. Once I scribble the numbers down, he takes it off me and goes over to Ben. They talk for a few moments before Ben leaves and Sean joins me back at the table.

"Okay, let's look at what else we can do!"

"I'll leave you to it, I don't want to see any more."

"Good idea, plausible deniability!"

I have no idea what that means so I just shrug. But Jonathan's ears have obviously pricked up. "Anything I should know about?"

"Absolutely not. Walk away Jonathan, walk away…" Sean throws the comment at him. Then he stops and looks up. "Actually, she needs a bank account. Could you help her set one up?" Jonathan nods and gestures for me to go with him.

I'm so glad Sean is here, everything just seems so much more manageable when he's around.

Chapter Four

What a mental few days it's been. I took a few days off work, mainly so I didn't have to explain the black eye, which is currently more yellowish and I'm able to be cover it with make-up. But also, I needed to sort out where I would be living.

As well as being best friends, Sean works for Ben at his property development company. When he got together with my friend, the only way they could see it working, with her having two teenage boys, was for him to move down here from Edinburgh. Sean wasn't happy about it, but he knew it was the only way his best friend back would be back to being whole again. Since Ben has been working here, he has taken on a few projects locally and has a satellite office, which Sean works out of from time to time.

One of those projects was to take a street of run-down Victorian terraces and transform the whole place. He's not had them very long, but they've managed to complete two of the houses already. On the outside they still look like a tidied-up version of their old selves, but inside they are beautiful and modern.

Apparently, one of the houses has always been earmarked for me to rent. My friends could always see my relationship going south in some way. So, I have a new address to set up bank accounts and so on, I just haven't quite moved in yet. The place is bare white walls with a mixture of grey wooden flooring and carpet throughout the house. They need the house furnished to take marketing photos, so I have been staying with Emma, and helping Ben order in the furniture.

We have slowly moved in some of my boxes and I'm here, sitting in the nearly empty house waiting for the delivery men to arrive. Sean has been my absolute rock these past few days. He's worked out of the satellite office for a few hours but made sure I haven't been left on my own. He's sat on my bed chatting until I've fallen asleep. In fact, now I think about it, this is the first time I have been alone in days and it feels weird. But it's nice not to have noise and humdrum around me for once. I suppose I better get used to it, living on my own again.

There's a noise at the front door and it swings open with a bang. "Hi honey, I'm home!" Sean shouts from the door. Idiot! But I smile because he makes everything seem that little bit better. He struggles through the door, his arms laden with bags and boxes.

"What's all this?"

"I got a few things."

"A few? What kind of things?"

"Things you don't have."

"Why?"

"Erm, because you need it?" His face is quizzical with a touch of annoyance, like it's obvious why he's doing it.

"But I can't afford it!"

"You're not paying for it!" He gives me the look that tells me not to argue with him. "Look, we've got," he starts to pile the boxes up in front of me, "a toaster and kettle, a sandwich maker and a coffee machine."

"I don't drink enough coffee to warrant a machine!"

"Oh that's for me!"

"You're moving in too?" I was only joking but he looks very sheepish.

"Well, I thought maybe I could help with the rent and bills, so that when I need to be down here, I have a place to stay."

"You thought, did you?" I fold my arms across my chest and plaster a look of annoyance on my face.

"Okay, sorry. Bad idea." He looks down at his feet. He knows that after the way I was treated by Darren, I really don't need to be told what is best for me and how my life is going to be led, especially without being asked beforehand.

I slowly start to smile, because actually it is a good idea. Ben isn't currently charging me rent, but he'll have to at some point. And then dealing with bills, with the way they are rising month on month as well, is going to be a nightmare. But the thought of a part-time house mate, one that is actually my friend, seems like a good compromise.

"Well maybe it might actually work, as long as you don't get under my feet and you don't boss me about."

"Great. Because I already ordered a bed for the spare room." I narrow my eyes at him. "They are from the company! The house comes furnished." He shrugs.

"I bet it doesn't really. I bet you and Ben have cooked this up together to make me feel less pathetic."

"Stop that! You're not pathetic, you were just taken advantage of because of your kind nature."

"You mean because I'm naïve?"

"Maybe a little, but that doesn't necessarily have to be a bad thing."

"Is that because I'm not an old cynic like you?" I give him a look of challenge. "When are you gonna find yourself a nice girlfriend anyway Sean?" He gives me a stern look. I have crossed a line. This is a no-go topic for us and I shouldn't have pressed that button. I don't know why he's so closed off exactly, but I get glimpses into it when his guard is dropped. "I'm sorry, that was uncalled for."

He looks me straight in the eye, weighing up whether my come back was disproportionately harsh. "Okay, you're forgiven, but don't let it happen again." He roots through another bag and pulls out something else. "This one is from me."

He places the small, white, rectangular box on the worksurface. I'm absolutely speechless. "It's a new phone. It means you don't have to wipe the old one in case there's more tracking software on it that we didn't find." He looks at me, waiting for me to say something. I pick up the box and shuffle the lid off to find a brand-new phone. It's probably the latest model and makes my current one, that Sean still has confiscated, look like a

Nokia from the turn of the century. "New number, new start, because I don't trust that arsehole not to pull anything stupid."

"You really shouldn't have." I look down at it in wonder, tears threatening to escape.

"But I really wanted to. I need to know you're safe."

"Thank you!" I close the distance between us and wrap my arms around his waist. He hesitates but eventually wraps his arms around me, letting go of the tension in his shoulders.

He is so much taller than me and makes me look like a child. He's not usually a touchy person. This is only the second time he has accepted a hug from me. The first was the day they all helped me move out of the flat. Either he's softening up, or he just knows I need the contact. Either way, I am grateful.

"Get off, you soppy woman!" And he's back! He pushes me off him and I just laugh. "Let's get this phone set up."

The darkness is setting in now and I look around my new home. It's an absolute mess of boxes, plastic wrapping and polystyrene bits. But it's my new safe place, all warm and cosy. The delivery men dropped off the new furniture earlier, and then Sean and I jumped in the car for a trip to a home furnishing store for plates, cups and cutlery. It's amazing what stuff you take for granted when you have to leave and start afresh.

The house is small but perfect. The front door opens onto a generous sized living area, with a corner sofa and a fireplace, that follows through to a compact but well-functioning kitchen.

The boys made sure they designed it so it would function well, but with space enough to enjoy the rooms.

There is a very compact toilet and shower room that backs onto a tidy little garden. The houses didn't originally have a garden, just a yard, but they felt the place needed somewhere you could enjoy on warm nights. There's nothing better than sliding your toes through cool, soft grass on a summer's day.

Upstairs there's a luxurious family-sized bathroom and two generous bedrooms. It is technically a three-bedroom house, but with most of these types of properties, the third bedroom, the box room, lives up to its name because you can literally only fit two large boxes on the floor. I've decided this is going to be a closet-type changing room.

Even though we are currently the only house on the street that is occupied, there is a constant hum of noise from the builders, who are lovely and always say hello. Sean is very security conscious, so we have cameras on the doorbell, cameras covering the property, and also the street. He told me it was because there are a lot of building supplies that they need to keep an eye on, but I know some of it is to keep me safe. It allows me to relax when Sean is back in Edinburgh. I have an app on my new phone that shows me who is at the door. It's very handy when I'm upstairs getting ready and I need to know whether it's worth jogging down the stairs, half dressed, to answer the door or not.

It doesn't look like I will have many evenings alone in the near future, because the girls have set up some kind of rota to keep me occupied. They haven't said as much, but from the requests for a cuppa and clothes advice and whatever, the coming week in jam-packed with visitors.

I am just waiting for reality to bite though. This can't be my life. I can't have just been handed this without any comeback, can I?

I asked Sean earlier, whether Darren had made any contact, but he won't say. He asked me what would be better? Knowing that he hadn't even realised I had gone, him throwing a fit and issuing threats, or not knowing either way. He has a point, but I'm still not clear on what the answer to that question is. So instead, I make my excuses of being tired and full of takeaway and head upstairs to my new bedroom, with new crisp sheets and the faint smell of paint, and I lock myself away with my own thoughts.

Chapter Five

My alarm goes off and I moan as I pry my eyes open. It's my first day back at work since the incident with Darren. Sean went back to Edinburgh yesterday. He tried to delay it, but I know full well that he has meetings all this week because I heard him on the phone to the office. I need to stand on my own two feet sooner rather than later.

It takes me a minute to realise that it's not my alarm, but that my phone is ringing. I scramble to answer it. "Hello?"

"Megan, are you ready?" It's Beth, sounding all Mumsy.

"Shit! I'm on my way." I hang up. The clock on my phone says 8:39am. I start work at nine o'clock and somehow I missed my alarm. I jump out of bed and rush for the bedroom door but manage to half trip over my slippers and four throw cushions that should be decorating my new bed.

It takes approximately 12 minutes to clean my teeth, wash my face and pull on the least crumpled clothes that are draped over my bedroom chair. The gods must have been looking down on me after all, because the bus pulls up at my stop just as I'm a few metres away. And today we have the nice bus driver who waits for me, rather than just driving off, catching the edge of a puddle and soaking me through. Trust me it's happened before.

I get into work five minutes late and I don't think people have noticed. As I pass Beth's desk and slide into my chair, she gives me a wide-eyed look. I click the switch on the computer and take a big, deep breath. I don't want to give my boss anything else to moan about, especially when he's been in such an arsey mood lately.

Penny turns to me as I'm sorting my desk out. "Megan, hey I tried to message you the other day, but the message didn't deliver."

"Oh, sorry Penny, I have a new number. I lost all my old numbers, so I was waiting to see you to give you it in person."

"I wanted to tell you about something, but that idiot has been circling all morning. I think we're gonna get called into a meeting or someone has died or something. I'll tell you after."

"No problem." As soon as my machine fires up, which takes an age because it's ancient, there's the ping of a companywide email, requesting we all attend a meeting in the boardroom. We don't actually have a boardroom. Our haulage company isn't that sophisticated. I know without even looking that both Beth and Penny have rolled their eyes and its now a toss up to which one will make a comment first.

"Staffroom for this meeting then?" Beth is the winner and says what everyone else is thinking.

It takes a good 15 minutes for everyone to gather in the staffroom. People are taking the opportunity to make themselves a drink and catch up on some office gossip. But our boss is looking more and more ashen by the minute.

Today he is sporting a half tucked in shirt with brown trousers circa 1992, that clearly haven't fitted since he bought them. His shirt is crumpled with stains down the front and he has the look of a man who drinks and smokes to excess but still classes himself as a *catch*.

"Could I have everyone's attention, I have some quite uncomfortable news." He takes a breath, I think it's all for effect. "With the cost of living rising and the price of fuel sky high, the business hasn't been sufficiently buoyant of late. And with the downturn in the global financial situation..."

"...and the continual mismanagement..." Penny chips in under her breath, which was quite audible to everyone and warranted a glare from the boss. I nearly spit my tea all over Beth.

"...the business needs to refocus its resource strategies to become more agile in a proactive dynamic global market."

"Has Cyril been reading the Financial Times again?" Penny leans over to us, this time she doesn't try to hide the comment. Cyril is not as dynamic as his words suggest, but he keeps heading off to business development conferences all over the country. The company doesn't get any better, he just uses over-complicated words to tell us the situation is shit.

He gives her the glare again and continues. "That means we will need to reduce our staffing levels."

There's a collective *WHAT?* from half the staff and a disbelieving gasp from the other half.

"And where will these reductions be coming from exactly?" Penny doesn't look particularly shocked.

"Well I have assessed the distribution of resources across the company and the only expenditure the company can tolerate is from the Admin Pool."

The blood drains from my face and I go a little light headed. I can't lose my job now! I've just moved house and I'm only just surviving as it is.

"But you didn't even replace Emma when she left," Beth says. "So, the pool only consists of myself, Megan and Tammy, who is now only part time anyway, and we are doing the work of four full time staff. We can't lose anyone else."

"Well we can't lose the drivers, can we?" he responds.

"What about finance?" I answer, and Maureen gives me the biggest glare. But I think because Polly is nearing retirement age, that reduction has clearly been factored in.

"I don't really have the answers right now to your questions. But if you could send them to me in an email, I will address them individually."

"By address, does that mean ignore them because he doesn't know how to open Outlook?" Penny is on a roll today and Cyril leaves the room without another word. We all make our way back to our desks.

As I take my seat while having a mild nervous breakdown, Penny wheels her chair round to my side of the desk. "Well that went well! We all have to suffer because Cyril is shit at his job?" She looks at me for a while, seeing that I'm trying to calm my nerves in order to have this conversation. "Anyway, that actually fits really well with what I had to tell you."

"Eh?" I have no idea what she's talking about.

"I knew something was brewing, the way he's been going on like a prize prick. And I was talking to Anne the other week about it." I still have no clue what she is going on about. "Anne works in that big place in Newcastle, some techy-bio-science something or other, as the PA to the CEO. But she's retiring, and her job will be up for grabs. It seems they are looking outside of the company to fill the role." I'm still not following.

"I thought it would be ideal for you. It's long hours because CEOs, especially the men, are very time demanding. But because you don't have a young family, it would suit you more than it would Beth."

"You think I should apply? I mean would I even have a chance?"

"You'll have as good a chance as anyone else."

"Thanks Penny, you might have actually saved my life. What do I need to do?" I feel like there might be some way out of this hole.

"I'll send you her details. Just contact her and tell her you're friends with me, that'll get you a shoe in! She owes me one for losing a signed copy of that book I told you about from my favourite author."

"Thanks Penny, I owe you one!" I give her a big hug and she looks a little shocked for a moment.

I turn back to my screen and she wheels herself back to her desk. The day doesn't get much better as everyone is reeling from the news and not an ounce of work gets done, although its only really me and Beth in the firing line, everyone knows that's only the tip of this particular iceberg. Even with great management, it would be a struggle to keep a company like this afloat.

Chapter Six

After another rollercoaster of a week, I'm sitting exhausted on my sofa with a glass of wine. The conversation about the job with Anne, Penny's friend, went well. The company is Beck Industries, some big Biotech company on the Quayside in Newcastle. The job is a personal assistant to the CEO, who I Googled and identified as Marcus Beckett, an older man in his early 60s. So now I'm having a mild meltdown about my CV, which was basic when I first wrote it, over a decade ago. I'm toying with the idea of not going for the job and just becoming a waitress, or even lap dancer. Shaking the thoughts out of my head, I pick up my phone and call the person I know can definitely help with this situation.

"Hi trouble," he answers straightaway.

"Hey, I need your help."

"Don't you always?" I frown as I realise he must be really fed up of my needy phone calls. He makes it sound like a joke but, in fairness, I've been a bit of a burden. He's done everything from buying me a new phone, to getting me somewhere safe to live.

"Sorry!"

"I was joking. What do you need?"

"Okay, not sorry then. I need help sorting out my CV, and you being an uber efficient business man, I thought you could help."

"No!" he says straight out. "It's HOT efficient business man!"

"Whatever!" I smirk, he's proper full of himself. "Where do I even start?"

"How about, once I finish up here, I'll come down and we can go out for dinner and we can work on your CV? Have you got a laptop?"

"Erm no. I was gonna ask at work if I could borrow one, but if they even have any, it would be so out of date they'd use a hamster wheel to power them on."

"Doesn't matter, I'll sort something. I'll be there about seven."

"Right. I'll see you then."

· ♥ · ♥ · ♥ · ♥ · ♥ ·

It's been a pleasant evening with Sean, eating dinner at our local Italian restaurant. I tried to pay but he was having none of it. He's lent me a laptop to use, but it looks like it's brand new, and he hasn't put a return date on it, so I think he may have bought something else for me. We thrashed out the CV, starting from scratch. There were only one or two tantrums from me, and a handful of death stares from Sean. After that the weekend was a whirl of cleaning, making up more furniture and many visits from my friends for one reason or another. I know the actual reason each time was to check that I was coping with my new life.

It's Monday morning and I've been quite productive. Maybe not in the job I'm actually paid for, but productive none-the-less. I have sent my CV to Anne at Beck Industries and immediately got asked to attend an interview. Which is great but also terrifying. It's in a few days, so the amount of time I have to panic and rethink my options is particularly limited.

I got in touch with Emma asking to borrow some interview-appropriate clothes and I've emailed Cyril to tell him I have a doctor's appointment for that day. I quoted *ladies problems* when he started asking questions – that shut him right up.

My head is a whirl of a hundred different thoughts. I never expected to be dealing with an interview this quickly. So, just like I always do, I called Sean and he interviewed me over the phone and gave me loads of tips. He even suggested the kind of answers they would be looking for. All those tips and answers have currently escaped my head, which now feels like it is stuffed full of marshmallows.

I'm standing on the Quayside looking up at the imposing building in front of me. It's a mix of glass, sandstone and brick, and takes over the skyline. My anxiety levels are bordering on mental breakdown. I wipe my sweaty hands down my skirt and stress that I look like a mess. My cream blouse is wrinkled, and the flouncy bow is out of shape. When I left the house my hair was immaculate – up in a nice and tidy, tight bun. Now there are bits pulled out everywhere. Public transport has a lot to answer for. I need to put learning to drive on my vision board. Who am I kidding? I don't even have a vision board.

I take a deep breath and give myself a little pep talk. I need to get through this interview. I need to get this job, because I know full well that I'll be the one getting the boot from the haulage firm. I'm the easy target. I know there are legalities that Cyril needs to jump through, but it's always the case that if you're the one they want to leave, they make it happen.

I push through the revolving doors and head into the foyer. The atrium is high, light and airy. You can see all the balconies right up to the top floor. I spot the reception desk and make my way over. There's an elegant woman sitting behind it. She's sitting so straight you'd think she was attached to a pole. She has a headset on and keeps answering the phone without picking it up. I stand in front of her, waiting to be acknowledged. When I think she's finished on a call I open my mouth to speak and she answers another call, putting the person on hold while tapping on her computer.

"How can I help you?" she eventually looks at me with a tight smile. It takes me a few moments to realise she's talking to me.

"Erm, yes. I'm here for an interview." She looks at me deadpan and I start raking through my bag trying to find information about the job. "It's with Anne." She continues to stare at me as my eyes flit from side to side trying to search my brain for any more information she may need.

"What's your name?" she asks, the expression on her face not moving in the slightest.

"Megan, Megan Scott."

"Anne you've got a Megan Scott at reception for you." Even as she speaks her gaze remains static. I'm not sure whether she's talking to me or not. "She'll be down in a minute, take a seat." I think that was aimed at me. I make my way over to the colourful, informal seating area.

I look around the building. Up at the tiered floors of this building and around at the smart looking people who have probably got their shit together, coming and going. Do I actually fit into this place? It seems completely out of my league. I may look the part today, but can I keep it up? How will they feel when they find out I'm not a qualified professional? I've not been to university, I was brought up in an ex-mining village in the backend of nowhere, I barely scraped through secondary school. The most sophisticated I get is drinking a mojito on the occasional night out.

"Megan?" I look up, pulled out of my self-deformation by an older-looking woman, grey hair in a neat bob and glasses strung round her neck.

"Yes, that's me."

"Hi, I'm Anne. I'll take you upstairs."

I stand and follow her to a bank of lifts. Once the doors close, Anne turns to me gives me a broad smile. "There's no need to be nervous Megan. It's going to be myself with Lauren and Amy from HR interviewing you. We want it to be as informal as possible. Mr Beckett is in a meeting, so he won't be joining us."

I let out a breath of relief and smile back at her. "So you are friends with Penny then?"

"Yes, we've been friends for a whole lifetime. We went to school together. I bet she's told you how I lost the signed copy of her favourite book." She rolls her eyes.

"She did mention it."

"For the record, I did replace the book. I also took her to a convention in London to get it signed again, where she also met, got a hug from and had a photo taken with her favourite author. But no, she never mentions that bit does she?" I laugh. These two are funny.

"No she didn't, but she does keep going on about all the fun you are gonna have when you all retire."

"I can't wait! Don't get me wrong, I love this job, but I just can't be at someone's beck and call all the time." She smiles at her little pun on the company name. "Be under no illusions that this job is going to be an easy ride. It really isn't. It's long hours and hard work. Especially dealing with the men round here. But you just train them to do things the way you want, and it all works out well."

"You mean they train you?"

"Absolutely not! You have to run the show here. They just don't realise it."

We arrive at the door to the conference room, before I can ask her any more questions.

・♥・♥・♥・♥・♥・

The interview went a lot smoother than I thought it would. The questions were easy enough, after Sean's coaching. And after those they just wanted to get to know me a bit.

Now I'm sat alone at a table outside the bar opposite the offices, with a large glass of wine. I think I have deserved it. I sit and contemplate the direction my life has turned since that fateful night when everything changed. There's a light breeze and I sit and watch a few boats travelling up and down the river. The ripple of the water has a comforting effect.

My phone buzzes and the screen lights up with Sean's name. He's no longer Shelley, as I no longer have a need to cover up who I am communicating with. He's the only one who knew about the interview, which saves the humiliation if I don't get the job.

"So? How did it go?" No pleasantries from Sean, he's always just straight to the point.

"I think it went well. But you can't really tell with these things can you?"

"When do you find out?"

"They have a few more to interview so maybe the start of next week."

"Where are you now?"

"God Sean, I feel like I'm still in the interview."

"Sorry, I'm in between meetings. I just wanted to quickly check in before I head to the next one."

"Okay, I'm sitting having a glass of wine in the bar opposite their building."

"Good for you! Got to go." And before I can say anything else he's gone.

Chapter Seven

Sean

I'm debating what to do with this bloody phone. I took it off Megan the day she left that piece of shit and replaced it. I knew he would try to contact her, and even if she constantly blocked him, he'd find a way. Also, I wasn't sure that he hadn't put other surveillance apps on there, this way he thinks that she's still picking up his vile messages. I've turned off the location, so he doesn't suspect that someone else has it.

I had a feeling that he'd send nasty messages, he's an arsehole like that, but I was not ready for the extent he would go to get a reaction and I'm totally out of my depth. She asks about it every now and again, but I just kind of skirt over the fact. I downloaded all the photos she had, so she was happy enough. Well for now at least.

I message the one person I know can help me.

> **Me:** Mate, I need your expertise, it's about Megan

> **Jonathan:** Alright Sean! I'm actually up your way, does this need to be done in person?

> **Me:** Probably best

> **Jonathan:** Right I'm free in an hour or so, we could meet half way. I'll msg time and place

> **Me:** Cheers mate

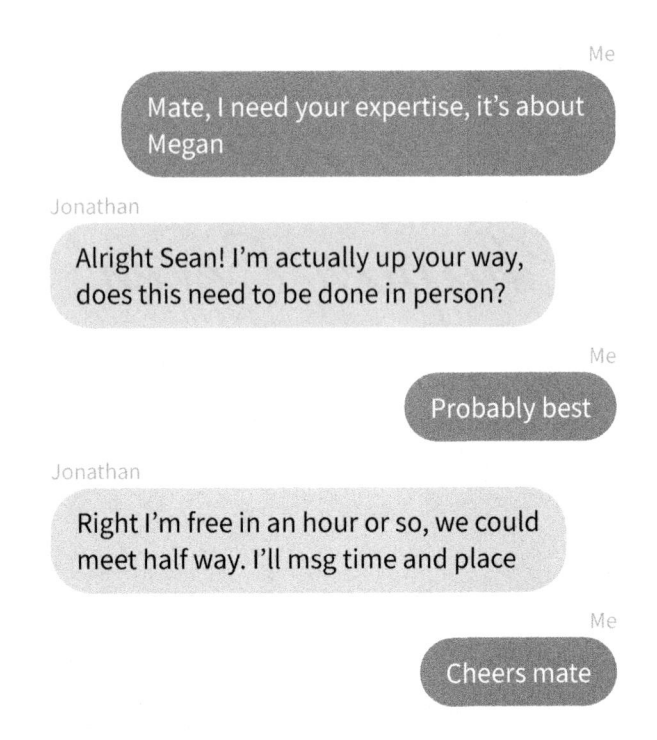

After a few minutes Jonathan sends me a pin to where he wants to meet, it's some industrial estate about 25 miles away. If I didn't know he was a cop, this would be super shady. I close down the document that I've been working on for the past two hours, but got no further with, and gather my things, the traffic will be heavy at this time of the day, so I best set off now.

It's dark and there's a light drizzle coating the windscreen as I sit, parked in the empty carpark of an industrial outlet, everything is closed and it's kind of eerie. A set of headlights glare through the droplets as a car turns in and parks facing me, blinding me for a moment until the engine is killed.

I get out and slam the door shut, making my way over to the white Audi and open the passenger door and get in. "Well this looks all kinds of dodgy."

Jonathan Laughs and holds out his hand, "Alright mate, good to see you."

I shake his hand. I like this bloke, there's something about him, he's no bullshit, straight to the point. He doesn't say much but you can tell he has everyone's back. "You too, except I wish it was for something a bit more tasteful and a bit less dark and sinister. I feel like I'm in some crime drama right now."

"Welcome to my world. So, what you got for me?"

"Megan's old phone." He pulls an inquisitive face. "Yeah I kept hold of it just in case something happened."

"And has it?"

"Well that's what I'm anticipating. Take a look at this." I hand him the unlocked phone and he takes it and scrolls through, the screen illuminating his face, his expression impassive.

As soon as he sees it, his eyes widen, and he shakes his head. "Fuck!"

"Exactly!"

"This is definitely a section 4, or malicious communications at the very least, but if he were to act on these threats, it becomes a whole new ball game. Have you told Megan?"

"No, I didn't want her to be scared and stop living her life, but I think we're walking a fine line. I want to keep herself safe, but not stressed."

"So I'll need to take this in, keep an eye on it, verify that it is coming from him, then I'll give it to another team to investigate."

"What do you think they'll do with it?"

"Depends who's leading, but they'll probably bring him in for questioning at the very least. I'll try get the heads up for when that happens."

"So how do we play this with Megan, seeing as I'm not always down there?"

"Well if I find out anything, you'll be the first to know."

"Right, I'll just jump in the car and come down if anything happens."

"Well I better head off. Maybe we meet up for a pint when you're next down?"

"Yeah, maybe we can then talk about something other than that prick." Jonathan laughs and I open the car door and rush back to my car, trying to avoid getting wet. The question is do I tell Megan or not? I'm still in two minds, maybe wait to see what the police say first, no news is good news.

Chapter Eight

Megan

This place is as bustling as ever – the Dog and Swan at its finest. The smell of beer and bodies fills the air. It's another girls' meet up and the first since that fateful day. I'm a little bit apprehensive. Darren and his friends come in here from time to time, and I feel a little bit sick at the thought of coming face to face with them. This should be a celebration, but the cloud of his presence hangs over it. But why should I change the way I live because of him?

The call about the job came in earlier on this week. Anne rang me herself to congratulate me and give me a start date. I spoke to Cyril. I didn't tell him I had another job to go to, and he was more than happy for me to take voluntary redundancy and leave at the end of the month, which is two weeks away. The compensation wasn't a lot, but it was enough to not have to worry about the next few months of bills and to enable me to buy a new, professional wardrobe.

I see the girls sitting in our usual seats and wave. I walked over by myself this time, as the new house isn't far. This place is definitely my local now. They all stand one by one and give me a massive hug.

"I got your usual," says Lizzie.

"Great, thanks." I take a big swig of my fruity cider. "I've got some news," I say, and everyone turns my way. Beth already knows, I couldn't have the rest of the office finding out before her. She grins up at me and gives me a thumbs up. "I've got a new job!"

"Ah Megan, that's amazing. You've finally escaped." Emma looks over at the others and her smile drops. "Sorry Beth! But yay Megan!"

"That must be a relief. Well done you!" Lizzie says. "Are you gonna fill us in on the details?"

"Yes, its PA position for a big firm in Newcastle."

"Nice!"

"I'm so proud of you Megs. But also, so, so sad that you'll be leaving me in that hovel." That's the only down side of moving jobs. I'll be leaving my work family behind.

"So, what's your boss like?"

"Well I've not actually met him yet. He's an older guy. I've googled him. I've met his current PA who's retiring and she's going to be holding my hand for the first few weeks."

"Did Cyril follow through with the redundancy package?"

"Well, yes. He had to really because he told the whole company that one us the three of us would be made redundant, and

I wouldn't have got this job if he hadn't made that announcement. I did forget to mention the new job when I told him about the voluntary redundancy. I knew he'd try to find a way of backing out, just to save himself a few pounds. And this way I can buy a new wardrobe of suitable clothes and pay everyone back for all the help they've given me.

"Don't think I didn't realise that Ben doubled the money that went into my new bank account and hasn't charged me rent." I look to Emma and she just shrugs. "So that means the next round is on me."

"We're not gonna argue with that," Beth says with a little grin.

I stand and make my way over to the bar and am greeted by Mitch, our favourite friendly barman. "Hiya Mitch."

"Megan, congratulations!"

"Are you some kind of undercover detective Mitch? How do you know these things?"

"You should know by now…I keep my eyes and ears open." He gives me a broad smile. "This is for you to celebrate with." He hands over the Dog and Swan equivalent of champagne. "I'll bring the glasses over."

"Ah thanks Mitch!" I smile at him and then feel a dark presence next to me, too close for comfort. A low baritone voice makes himself known with a little cough-come-throat clearing.

"Are you Megan?"

I turn to look at him. He is a tall hulk-like man, dark toned with a wiry beard. I can't place whether I have seen him here before. His face is pulled taught, not a hint of a smile, his features grim.

"Erm..." I stutter, trying to get some words out while a foreboding feeling flashes over me. I'm on high alert.

"Did you date Darren Pritchard?" And now I understand this reaction to the stranger. A wave of panic sweeps from my feet all the way up my body. But before I can get anything out, Mitch steps between us, using his body to shield me.

"Mate you need to leave." He manoeuvres him towards to door. "I don't want you harassing my customers." The man tries to object but Mitch is very insistent, and I'm still stuck to the spot. Mitch shouts to Lizzie as he exits the bar and she's beside me with her arm around my shoulder in a flash. Very unLizzie-like.

"You okay?" she asks, her tone softer than usual.

"He was asking about Darren."

"Oh." She takes a deep breath and moves to stand in front of me, like a parent does when they have important news for a child. "There's something I need to tell you." I can't get any words out, so she carries on. "You know Sean took your old phone? Well he gave it to Jonathan last week because Darren had been messaging. I don't know the content of the messages, but they were nasty. Nasty enough to involve the police. They didn't want to scare you. Jon wanted to verify them before logging it officially at the station."

I just stare at her in a state of shock, my mind a mix of emotions, panic and a million questions that I can't seem to voice. Was that man here to carry out one of Darren's threats? Why didn't Sean tell me? At least I would be prepared. Or was I better in ignorant bliss?

Mitch is back, putting his hand on my shoulder.

"Megan, are you okay?" All I can manage is a nod. "That bloke wasn't here to hurt you. I've had a word with him, and it seems as if his sister has hooked up with Darren and he's worried." He rubs his chin as if contemplating something else. "Darren's been in here with his mates shouting his mouth off. I think we should nip this in the bud. He's telling all kinds of lies and it needs sorting. I know this is gonna be hard for you, but I think it's best to tackle this head on. Speak to this bloke and set the record straight."

"I can be there with you for support," Lizzie says. I'd forgotten she was even there, she's not usually this quiet.

"We can go up to the function room for some privacy."

"Wow, the Dog and Swan has a function room? Who knew?" Lizzie tries to lighten the mood.

Mitch shrugs, directing his answer to Lizzie. "It's mainly used for the knitting circle and a handful of meetings. We're not the Savoy, you know." He looks back at me, making sure I have his full attention. "I'm gonna be with you the whole time and you can bring Lizzie."

I answer, but its barely audible. I can't seem to find my voice. "No, just you."

"Okay, give me a minute." He rushes out of the door and is back in no time. I hand the bottle of fizz over to Lizzie and Mitch steers me by the shoulders, guiding me to a door I haven't even noticed until now.

"You!" He points at someone. "You need to hear this too!" I look back and it's one of Darren's friends, Adam. My shoulders tense and Mitch gives me a reassuring pat on the shoulder.

We go up a dark flight of stairs and I can hear Adam following on behind us. As the door at the top of the stairs is opened, the smell of stale air and beer fill my senses. The room is dark, the only light coming in through the windows from the street outside. Mitch flicks a switch and the strip lights buzz to life.

The man from downstairs is sitting on a stool in front of a bar that's like a mini version of the one downstairs. He looks too big for what he is seated on, like a giant Viking.

He looks up and speaks softly. "I'm really sorry if I scared you Megan, I didn't mean to."

Mitch pulls up two stools for us, giving us a good distance from the man so that I don't feel intimidated.

Adam takes a stool nearer to the man. "And what am I doing here?" he asks, his tone dripping with distain, which surprises me because he was always the one in the group that was the kindest.

"I've heard the shit you lot have been peddling," Mitch bites back. "You will listen to Megan's side of the story. And when I say Megan's side, I mean *the truth*! After that, you either cut that shit out or you're barred." Adam rolls his eyes and folds his arms across his chest in defiance. "Shall we start with why you're here, Tom?" He gestures to the giant.

He nods. "My sister has just got together with this lad and from what she said there were red flags all over the place. Said he had an ex," he motions to me, "that went all psycho." I can feel the well of tears ready to burst and the lump in my throat. "I knew that there had to be more to the story, and Tara has started to act... different."

"Megan, do you want to tell him what happened?"

"I…" I don't even know where to start to be honest.

Adam interrupts before I can pull any of my thoughts together. "He told us that you stole money off him and went off with another bloke. Said you turned psycho when he confronted you, and then you made up some shit and got your police mate to arrest him."

"Why don't you tell them what actually happened Megan?" I can feel Mitch getting pissed off with Adam now, the tension fizzing off him, I think one wrong word and it will kick off.

I take in a deep breath. I know it's going to come out sooner or later and the whole world will know what happened that night, so they may as well have them.

"I came home from being here with the girls." I look to Mitch for validation. "He hadn't been answering any of my calls and messages, but he knew I was going out for the night. I came in and he was sitting in the dark waiting for me. He started accusing me of all sorts, but I'm used to that by now." I look over to Adam and give him a nod. "You must know, you all take photos of me when I'm out. Totally innocent situations but at the right angle, they look like something else. You send them to him, so he can torture me over them, accuse me of all sorts." Adam starts to look sheepish. "I'd had enough so I called him out on it. Instead of talking about it reasonably, he held me against the wall by my throat." Tom lets out a gasp and it's then I notice the dampness of my hands sitting in my lap. The tears start to fall, and I take another deep, jagged breath. "Eventually he let go just before I passed out and then he struck me across the face. That's when I left. My friends wanted me to go to the police, I didn't really want the hassle, but I needed to get my things from the flat without him kicking off. So, they took him in for questioning. I didn't press charges.

"As for the money, when we got together, he convinced me that I should put all my wages into his bank account to pay rent and that. I know it was stupid looking back, but you've got to understand he can be very convincing, and the manipulation was a gradual thing. He effectively gave me pocket money each week." I hear a sob. I look around the room and realise it actually came from me. Adam won't even look me in the eye and Tom looks shocked.

Mitch puts his hand on my arm and gives me a clipped smile, encouraging me to carry on. "I found out when I left, he didn't pay rent, his parents did. And he spent my wages on gambling sites and porn. I took what was left of my money out of his account, so I could start again. It's less than £500, so a fraction of what had gone in.

"Should I go on?" I don't wait for an answer. "He had a tracker on my phone and if I stopped anywhere, other that work, I would get an interrogation and constant phone calls, even when he knew I was just getting a loaf of bread or something. He hid or damaged my clothes, so I couldn't go out in them, only saving a few that he deemed fit. And they were only because he was scared of Lizzie finding out.

"I used to cook for him and he would say it was inedible and throw it at me, then order a take away for himself. He said I was ugly and no-one would ever want me, that I was lucky he even gave me the time of day. He said I was stupid, and it was only a matter of time before I was fired from my job, and he wasn't going to be there to support me.

"He accused me on many, many occasions of flirting with his friends, especially you Adam. Said you thought I looked like a slag when I got dressed up and you wouldn't go near me, so not to bother."

"He forced me to have sex with him when I didn't want to, but made out I was just being frigid and, being my boyfriend, it was his right to have sex with me. I also think he has drugged me on occasions to have sex with me, but I can't prove it. Is that enough for you all to get the picture or do you need more to believe me?"

"We do believe you Megan," Mitch says, taking my hand. And that's when the flood gates open and I can't stop the sobs coming out. I cry so hard I think I'm never going to be able to catch my breathe. The relief that they believe me is overwhelming, I didn't even realise I had been holding onto all this emotion. I locked it away, not wanting anyone to know what I went through, not even my friends.

"I think she's been through enough, don't you?" Mitch directs this to the two men and they stand to leave, both whispering their condolences to me. He shouts to Adam as he passes. "You can tell your mate that he's barred, and you can steer clear too if you're gonna put up with that kind of behaviour. Including the threats he's been sending her."

"He's no mate of mine," Adam answers back.

The room has gone quiet, the only sounds are my stuttering breaths.

After a few more tears my breathing begins to stabilise. Mitch hands me a tissue.

"I'm sorry you had to go through that, and I'm sorry I made you relive it."

I shrug. I suppose they needed to know.

"But don't let this define you Megan. Nothing he said to you was true. You are a beautiful, intelligent, strong woman. Now let's get downstairs and celebrate your new job." I nod and we both stand, make our way downstairs and I head for the toilets to clean up my face.

Once all the mascara is cleared up and my red swollen eyes have calmed down, I leave to rejoin my group of friends. I pass Adam and his friends on the way. He looks like he's seen a ghost. Hopefully, I think, that's remorse spread across his face. I know he didn't do those things to me but he's still guilty for not calling Darren out on his behaviour and effectively condoning it.

As I reach the girls they stand up one by one and give me a hug and a kiss. No more is mentioned, and the bottle of fizz is opened with a pop.

Chapter Nine

Today is the day I start my new job. I didn't sleep particularly well with my mind going on overdrive, wondering whether I'm going to survive my first day, let alone anything else. I'm so out of my depth. I have no idea how I made it through the interview, let alone them thinking I was the best person for it.

And now I'm stood, palms damp, trying to pluck up the courage to walk through those doors and face reality. I'm wearing clothes similar to those I wore for my interview, so I get the lay of the land before I commit to any kind of style. My hair's pulled into a tight bun, as I don't want to stick out any more that I already do. Looking up at the imposing building, I straighten my skirt, take a deep breath and push through the revolving doors.

Looking round the foyer it seems familiar, yet new, like I dreamt the last time I was here. I find the stone-faced receptionist. She's still ramrod straight and as elegant as before, bright red lipstick the only colour she wears, and I make my way towards her.

"Hi." She doesn't even acknowledge I am in front of her, let alone that I have spoken. "I'm Megan, it's my first day."

"Good morning Beck Industries, how can I help? Yes, I'll put you through to his office straight away."

She still hasn't looked at me and just keeps on taking calls. I clear my throat to get her attention. I actually want to slam my hand on the desk and say, look at me, I'm right fucking in front of you. She meets my eye for a split second and is back to ignoring me.

I hear someone approach me from behind, and a voice makes me jump. "Good morning, Martina."

"Good morning, Mr Henry." The surly reception says, a fake smile on her face. So she's not deaf, just ignorant.

"I'm here to see Mr Beckett." I say, curtly.

A smirk pulls on her face. "I'm sorry he isn't available, you'll have to come back another time." This woman is a complete bitch! I step back from the desk and root around in my handbag for my phone. I find the number I'm after and it starts to ring. "Hiya Anne, it's Megan. I'm downstairs and the receptionist won't even acknowledge me."

"I'll be right down."

I fold my arms across my chest and glare towards the desk, but there's still that emotionless face. There's a click-clack of footsteps across the hard floor and Anne appears. While the receptionist gives me the *evil eye* for daring to take matters into my own hands.

"Morning Megan, we'll get you a pass sorted first of all." She looks towards the receptionist. "Martina, pack it in! Just because you didn't get the job, stop being so bitter or I'll get you moved to the basement!" The receptionist gives Anne daggers but doesn't say a word. Anne motions to a row of doors and we both make our way towards them.

"What's her problem?" I ask.

"There are many, just ignore her, she'll get over herself eventually." We go through one of the doors and Anne introduces me to the women sitting around a bank of computers. They all greet me in unison. "I'll leave you here to get all your paperwork sorted and your ID badge. The girls will call me down when you are finished." I nod and Anne heads out while I'm left to wade through a ream of paperwork.

After what seems like a full day, the paperwork is finished. My eyes are blurry and I have written my name 847 times. Anne walks in and I stand up and stretch my aching muscles.

"All done?" I nod. "I think maybe we'll leave a tour of the building for another time but there is someone I'd like you to meet first." We leave the room saying our goodbyes, and she gestures over to the lifts. "She's on the fourth floor. Your desk is on the fifth. We'll go and say hello on our way." Anne presses for the lift and the doors open.

We step out onto the fourth floor. There's a balcony, where you can see all the way down to the foyer, and in front, the windows look out onto the river. There are banks of desks around the room put together in groups of six with dividers in between some and not others. As we walk past heads lift up from what they are doing to spy the new girl. We get to an area marked with a sign hanging from the ceiling saying *Finance*.

Anne approaches a desk where a woman, probably my age, is looking through spreadsheets. She doesn't fit into the type of person that works in this office, she's sitting nearly cross legged on an office chair, her hair is made up of long spiral curls that seem to have a mind of their own. She is wearing a black corduroy pinafore dress with a stripy t-shirt underneath.

"Dionne!" Anne says, breaking her concentration, she looks up to us from her screen and smiles.

"Hiya Anne, what can I do for you?"

"I was hoping you could take Megan under your wing for a few days. Show her around, have lunch, that sort of thing." Anne turns to address me. "You don't want to spend all day with me, you need someone more your own age."

"Yeah sure, shall I pick you up for lunch at one o'clock?" Dionne chimes in.

"That would be great." I'm grateful for someone to be my guide and she's so much nicer than the receptionist, although that's not hard.

"Where am I picking you up from?"

"Fifth floor." Anne says and Dionne's eyes widen. "Megan is Mr Beckett's new PA."

"Ah... that explains Martina's extra unpleasantness this morning. See you at one." She gives us a quick wave and turns back to her computer, while we make our way back to the lifts.

The fifth floor may as well be in a completely different building because it looks nothing like the rest of the office. It's all sleek and high end. There's no desks in view as we make our way.

On the previous floor the number of desks hid the big opening through the centre, where you could see all the way down, but unlike the balcony, this is more like a little oasis of green plants and trees, springing up through the floors.

Down either end there are large offices and meeting rooms of different sizes, some with glass walls, others closed off to the world. We walk to the very back of the building, passing break out and kitchen areas that look more like a hotel bar than a coffee room.

We finally arrive at the back, to a huge oak desk that's sitting outside a door with the silver name plate that says, *Mr M Beckett CEO*.

I stand in front of the heavy wooden door, wondering if he will step out at any moment and introduce himself.

"Mr Beckett is currently in a meeting, you will meet him once he gets back. In fact, he should be finished by now." Anne must be able to read minds. She gestures for me to take a seat and stands behind me as I log into the computer. "Your job is to make his life easier. You'll manage his diary, set up meeting rooms, catering and field calls. You may have to take minutes at meetings and send out email notifications, things like that. But basically, anything he needs you to do."

The fear takes over me, I wouldn't even know where to start. My pulse starts to race as I question why I'm even here. "Don't worry, you're not starting from scratch." She takes out a notebook from the drawer. "Here is your little book of everything. Everything you need to know is in here and I'll be helping you for a week or two."

As she speaks I spot someone walking towards us from the corner of my eye. I turn and see he is wearing a navy blue suit with a white shirt and a navy tie. He has dark hair, short at the sides. The closer he gets the more of his feature I take in. He's tall and fills his suit well. He strides with purpose and then I meet his eyes, grey and piercing. I expect him to smile as he gets nearer but his expression is stony. He has got to be the most gorgeous man I have ever seen. My heart races and I can feel my cheeks flushing. I expect him to turn off and go into one of the other offices, but he is heading straight for us.

Everything goes in slow motion. He looks like a model in an expensive cologne advert. But his eyes narrow at me.

It's Anne that breaks my fixation on him. "Hello Mr Beckett! Good meeting? This is Megan, your new PA."

WAIT, WHAT? I eventually regain my composure and stand, holding out my hand to shake his. But he doesn't take it, he just keeps staring, his face like thunder.

"Not a chance," he eventual musters. "A word please Anne!"

"Give us a minute please, Megan." She walks into the office behind him and shuts the door, but I can hear the conversation loud and clear.

"There's absolutely no way. I told you I wanted someone older, preferably a man."

"Well that's just tough."

"I can't work with her."

"You are not your father Myles, now pull yourself together."

They start whispering and I strain to hear the rest of the conversation, but I'm just out of range. Suddenly the door swings open, and he strolls back out and faces me, still with a stony and thunderous expression. He stretches his hand out.

"Myles Beckett, pleased to meet you." He doesn't seem very pleased. I give him a tight smile and take his hand, but as soon as the connection is made he pulls his hand away like he's been given an electric shock. He turns and walks back into his office.

Chapter Ten

Myles

Well, this week has been a total shit storm and it's still Monday. After a completely disastrous meeting about patents and the technology from our competitors biting at our heels, she happened! Megan Scott, my absolutely gorgeous new PA. The specific reason I asked Anne to make sure her replacement was older and preferably male, but apparently there are rules about that kind of thing. But don't HR realise that this could turn out way worse?

I knew I was in trouble when I stepped out of the lift and saw her from afar. She stood up and I could see her curvy body filling out that skirt and the silky sheerness of her blouse that rolled over her chest. Her hair tied up showed off the porcelain skin of her neck.

The only saving grace of Megan being here, was that they hadn't hired Martina. Although I don't find her attractive, she has always had the hots for me and I just can't be doing with that. The work place is for work and should stay that way. Heaven knows, the company paid out hundreds of thousands in compensation claims and gagging orders, after the mess my father made.

Thank the stars my father never tried it on with Anne. Well not that I know of. She is the absolute rock that held this place together when the board took to replacing him. I didn't want the job, but I have never really had any choice in the matter, first born and all. My brother Sebastian, the spare, got off scot-free, picking a career he actually enjoyed, while my law degree is only framed on the wall as a memento of everything I can't have.

Anne has given me a dressing down already, said I was rude when I first met Megan. I was absolutely awful, but it's for the best. We can't be friends. I have kept the door slightly ajar, so it looks closed, but I can hear what they are saying and every so often I get a quick glimpse of her.

I need to focus. Opening my emails, I blow out a breath and rub my hands over my face. It's one o'clock and I have achieved absolutely nothing. I hear another voice outside and see that Megan is leaving. It takes Anne about ten seconds to come in and reprimand me again.

"Myles! You need to give her a chance. I think she has enormous potential, but if you don't make her feel comfortable and help her find her feet, we'll be back to square one."

"Can't you just stay? Forever?"

"Bless you. I love working with you, but my time has come. I need to live my life outside of these walls."

"Fine!"

"You are not your father, Myles. But there are still men like him working here. Men far worse. At least he didn't force anything. You have to stamp that behaviour out, from the top down. I expect you to call them out on their behaviour."

"And you think having someone like Megan will help the situation?"

"I think having a woman as attractive as Megan here will bring them out of the woodwork. You need to protect her."

"From them or me?" She gives me the look she always does when she doesn't agree with me and I have to back down. She thinks I don't know she plays us all at our own game. Everything in the building is the way Anne wants it to be, and not me. "Where is she now?"

"I've sent her to lunch with Dionne from Finance, she'll show her the ropes and tell her who's who. Plus she needs a friend in here." I put my head in my hands and groan. "Give her six weeks. If she's no good, or you just can't work with her, you can look again for someone." She strides out of the door but stops and puts her head back round the door. "But not Martina." God no, that would be a disaster.

Chapter Eleven

Megan

We get in the lift, Dionne presses for the ground floor and the doors close behind us. "What do you think of Mr hot CEO then?"

"Well, he already hates me, and I only spoke five words to him, if that."

"He's the strong and moody type. You'll get used to each other."

"Does he ever crack a smile?"

"Not that I've seen. Well, not a real one anyway." The door opens and we step out and make our way to the other side of the foyer.

"What's the issue with Cruella over there?" I thumb over to the reception desk.

"Ah, she has the hots for Beckett, but I think it has more to do with money and power than anything else. Plus, she applied for your job and didn't get it."

"How is she even allowed to work on reception with her attitude? It doesn't really portray a welcoming image."

"Who knows?" We arrive at some big glass doors that open out onto a cafeteria. Tables are grouped together and it looks more like a fancy restaurant than a workplace canteen. The room then leads its way into an orangery with buckets of light and comfy-looking sofas and arm chairs everywhere.

Dionne picks up two trays, hands one to me and we look through the selection of food.

"You use your ID card as payment. The company gives you a food and drink allowance, and if you go over it, they take the excess off your wages. But to be honest, I eat like a horse and have never had any money taken off me."

"Nice. So at least I don't have to bring in soggy sandwiches."

"Exactly, and it helps them keep upstairs virtually food free too." We pick up some paninis and find a spare table.

You know those people that you meet and just seem to click with? Those who you know absolutely nothing about but feel like you've been friends for years? Well that's how I feel about Dionne. She has a warmth and a kindness to her, but is also quirky and fun.

"So what do you do? I know you work in Finance."

"I'm an accountant. Can't you tell?" A broad smile spreads across her face. She's clearly had comments about her profession before.

"Well no, not really."

"I like numbers, but I also like to be creative in the way I look. They don't often go hand in hand. People seem to think you can either be academically gifted or creative, but not both. I actually paint in my spare time," she shrugs. "It's probably why they don't take me seriously upstairs. That, or the fact I'm a woman and my pretty little brain can't cope with numbers." She rolls her eyes.

"When you say upstairs, do you mean your team?"

"Ah no. My team are great, they know I'm the best mathematician there. I can spot an anomaly at ten paces. I mean the fifth floor. The CFO – Chief Finance Officer – is a prick. He's on some kind of power trip. He makes me take the reports up to deliver them in person, even though he already has them via email."

"Is he just a bit old school, wanting a hard copy?"

"Nope, just a prick! But at least I'll be able to visit you at the same time."

We continue our chatting, telling each other about ourselves and Dionne tells me about the little quirks in the office. The way that some teams, like the marketing team, go out together a lot, but the rest only get together at big company events, usually Christmas. We chat continually until our break is over and we head back upstairs.

Arriving back at my desk, I don't even have time to sit down when Myles comes rushing out of his room.

"Megan!" He stares at me for a few seconds, as if he can't really comprehend that I'm standing in front of him. "I need you to take minutes for this meeting."

I turn to look at Anne, but she's already anticipated my next thought and is handing me a folder with a pad and pen. I grab it and mouth *thank you* to her, and he strides off down the corridor. I have to do a little jog to catch up, which is no mean feat in these heels.

"Have you taken minutes before?"

"Yes, but not for anything very important." I'm having to walk fast to keep up with him. For every stride he takes I need to take three steps. At least I may get fit doing this job.

"Okay, you just need to be brief, a quick outline of the matter, then the decision that was made. Only write any discussion details if it's a real objection, or you think it's important noting." We reach the doors of the meeting room and people are already there, some sitting waiting, others standing chatting while they get a coffee. He points to a chair and nods for me to sit.

I put my notepad down and pull the chair out, when someone speaks to me. He's an older man, maybe late fifties, greying hair at the sides and wearing a designer suit.

"You couldn't get me a coffee, could you?" This would normally seem like a genuine, pleasant command, but something in his tone is dripping with distain, and his smile isn't genuine.

I stand still, contemplating his request. But before I can move, I hear Myles. "Megan is here to take notes, not make you coffee." The man's eyes widen and his nostrils flare, a quick look of anger briefly crosses his face but is masked by a smile. Another woman places a coffee in front of him but rolls her eyes as she goes to take a seat next to him.

Myles comes back with coffee for the two of us, while I'm preparing to take notes. I draw a quick plan of the seating arrangements, so I can figure out who is who later.

"What's that?" He points at the drawing and whispers in my ear, so close I can feel his breath on my neck and goose bumps spread over my body.

"Well I don't know anyone so..." I shrug.

"Okay." He looks around the room. The meeting is for the executive officers and directors, I recognise one to be the man Martina acknowledged in reception. The rest however, I have no idea. "Before we begin can we all just introduce ourselves to Megan, my new PA? It will make her life, and therefore mine, easier if she knows who you all are."

"Daniel Fawcett, CFO, that's Chief Financial Officer, you'll be seeing a lot of me, my office is just down from yours." It all becomes clear who he is, he's Dionne's boss. And yes, he is a prick.

Myles interrupts him. "Alright she doesn't need your life story." There is obviously something going on with these two, but I'm not quite sure what it is. The introductions carry on around the table.

"Imogen Hughes, Director of Marketing." She gives me a warm smile, I'm going to like her.

"Thomas Spencer, CIO and there's Lawrence Owen COO, but he couldn't attend this meeting."

"John Henry, Director of Sales." The man from downstairs.

"Jeremy Waite, Director of Research and Development."

"Sophie Hardcastle, Director of HR."

"Thank you everyone, let's begin with the first item on the agenda." Myles takes over the meeting.

The meeting went by in a blur. I didn't understand any of it, but I got all the actions down. Now I just have to decipher my own handwriting. Everybody files out of the room, leaving just myself and Myles. He pushes his chair out to stand, while I gather my things.

"How was that then?" he asks, with a lighter, more friendly tone.

"Okay. Most of it went over my head though."

"Well, it will do." I expect the follow up to be one stating how I'm *not smart enough to understand*, which I'm well aware of, but there's no need to rub it in. "It is only your first day, after all." He starts collecting coffee cups. "Unfortunately, it is also your job to clear these away." I watch him for a minute. Maybe I have been underestimating him, maybe under that stern look and designer suit, there is something more.

Pulling myself out of my thoughts, I clear the cups to the refreshment trolley, pick up my things and follow him out of the room, down the corridor back to my desk. He doesn't say anything else, and I return to my desk in silence. He goes through his office door and closes it while Anne stands behind my desk with two thumbs up and a big smile on her face. How does she know it went well?

Chapter Twelve

My first full week at Beck Industries has come to an end and it's Friday night – girls' night at The Dog and Swan. I really need a drink and a therapy session with my friends tonight, and with an added bonus, Sean is heading down tonight too. He has a walk-through on the site where we live but could only fit it in his schedule for Saturday morning, so he's driving down tonight and dropping in on Ben while we are out.

I arrive at the pub. I've dressed down in jeans and a blazer. It's funny how things turn around. Before, I would be dressing down at work and dressing up to go out. But the workplace at Beck is so different. The people there are stylish and professional, so I have to be on my A game.

It feels weird not having people decide how I dress, but it's a good weird. First it was my parents, always going on about good impressions and what would the neighbours think, making me change out of the, *that's not a skirt it's a belt*, clothing. And then Darren, who wanted me to look unattractive. I was only allowed to dress up when I was out with the girls so they weren't suspicious of his controlling behaviour. I think I'm rebelling and dressing down for girls' night.

I go straight to the bar. The girls are at our usual table, but I have someone to see first. Waiting patiently, I put a package on the bar. Eventually I catch Mitch's attention.

"Hey Megan, how's it going?"

"Really good actually. I got you something, as a thank you." I hand over the parcel.

"There was no need." He takes it with a shocked expression. You'd think he'd never been given a present before.

Pulling open the paper, like a five-year-old at Christmas, he shakes out the black fabric. "Oh my god, I love it!" He holds the t-shirt against his body. The words *The Best and Most Talented Barman in the World* across the front in white lettering. He lifts the hem of his shirt and pulls it off over his head. Who knew Mitch was toned? He wriggles the new one down his body, his face sporting a wide smile.

"I'll never take it off."

"Please do or you'll stink the place out." I laugh and turn towards the girls.

As they see me, they stand up and give me a hug. Beth hands me my drink and we all sit back down.

"Emma has just been telling us that Charlotte, Ben's baby-mama, has got a new boyfriend and Ben's going all alpha about it."

"Does he really have any right to be upset about it?" I ask.

"No, not really. I mean I'm in Ava's life too, so why wouldn't Charlotte get someone? I think he'll feel better once he meets him."

"He's been bending Jonathan's ear about doing police checks on him," Lizzie chips in.

"Can he do that?" Beth asks.

"I think there was a law introduced where you could check out a potential partner, in case they have a domestic abuse background."

"Was that Clare's law?" Lizzie asks.

"Possibly. So I keep having to talk him out of going up there and forcing the issue." Emma continues, rolling her eyes.

"Have you spoken to Charlotte?"

"Yeah, we get on really well. She really likes this guy and I don't want Ben ruining it for her. But I also want them both to be safe with him because you never know."

We all take a drink. There's the elephant in the room again. They all look at each other, knowing that was the situation for me, not so long ago.

"Tell us all about your first week." Beth breaks the tension. I speak to her pretty much every day, so she knows what has been going on, but the others are none the wiser.

"Well, where do I start?"

"With your gorgeous new boss, obviously." Beth grins at me knowing that this will definitely get everyone's attention.

"I thought he was some older guy?" Emma gives me a questioning look.

"So did I, until he walked down the corridor all gorgeous, brooding sexiness wrapped in a designer suit. Apparently, he took over from his father a few months ago. He is Myles Beckett as opposed to Marcus Beckett, who I thought I'd be working with."

Lizzie raises her eyebrows. "You haven't done anything daft have you?"

"It's me, of course I have. But I think it has gone unnoticed. Actually the job is good, I'm just trying to find my feet. It doesn't help with him being all bossy and stern."

"Isn't bossy in the job description of a boss though?" Lizzie smirks.

"Well yes, but I can't quite figure him out. One minute he's all stern faced and moody, then the next he's all soft and contemplative and nice. But it's early days I suppose."

"How are the rest of the people you work with?" Beth asks, I think she is still bruised by being left behind.

"Well I work on the fifth floor away from all the normal people. But I have made a new friend. She's funny and quirky. I was thinking about bringing Dionne to one of these nights sometime. I didn't want to ask her tonight because I didn't want to sound like too much like a needy new friend."

"Well it's great you have someone to talk to. But let's face facts, she'll never be as good as me."

"She could never replace you, Beth! Anyway, tell us about your mother-in-law."

"Oh god, I'm glad of the escape. Nothing is ever good enough for her. And I'm clearly not good enough for her special boy."

"But you've been married a decade now. Surely she's got over herself?"

"You would think, but no. She called me by his ex's name the other day and whenever she addresses anything to me, it's by my maiden name. Steve just seems to think she's forgetful. I think she's being her usual passive aggressive self."

"Why is she here this time?"

"I don't know. Just to annoy me, I think. It's definitely not to be any kind of help, because it's just like having another child to look after."

I get up from my seat. "It's my round." I make my way over to the bar where Mitch is still showing off his t-shirt. I smile at how much a small gesture has made his day. I pass a group of men and Adam catches my eye and he gestures me over. I roll my eyes, not really wanting to go through this all over again.

"Hey, I just wanted to apologise for the things I did and for not calling Daz out." He looks sincere with his apology.

"It's fine." It's far from fine but I just don't want to engage with him.

"And just for the record, before you started dating, I told him I liked you. He said you were out of my league, which of course you are. I would never have called you any of those names."

"Listen, I just want to forget it all happened. If you keep apologising, then I can't forget it, can I?"

"Fair enough. Can I buy you a drink?"

"No, best not." I'm not sure whether I can forgive him or not, but we are definitely not on *wipe the slate clean with a drink* terms. I signal to Mitch and he mouths *I'll bring them over*, and I head back to my group of friends.

The girls are all animated in their conversation. "What did I miss?"

"The drinks, clearly!" Lizzie says as she looks at my empty hands.

"Mitch is bringing them over."

"You've got him well trained! So, Sienna has a boyfriend." Lizzie informs the group. Sienna is her eldest child. At 15 she is more of a young lady now.

"Is that good news?" Emma asks.

"He's an absolute tool! I mean he's harmless enough, he's just a bloody idiot."

"Are you gonna intervene?"

"No, she'll have to learn for herself."

"How's Jonathan taking it?"

"He's her dad, how do you think he's taking it? Like the world is gonna end! He's going on ridiculous!"

"And how is it going with the two of you? You seemed to be getting on better than ever."

"I don't know. He's stressed about something going on at work. He won't or can't tell me what it is, but he's taking it out on everyone around him, so I'm steering clear for a bit."

"I'll drink to steering clear of stress and workaholic men, for sure!" Emma says. And everyone agrees with that statement. We pretty much all have to deal with those men in one way or another.

The night continues with lots of laughing and tales about everyone's work and home life. Unlike our other girls' nights, I leave looking forward to seeing the man that's waiting for me at home.

Chapter Thirteen

Myles

These past few weeks have been torture. I've really tried to find things wrong with Megan and give myself a reason to get rid of her, but I just can't. She has dealt with everything I've thrown at her. Anne has taken a step back, which only means I have to spend more time with Megan.

I'm still leaving my door ajar so that I can catch a glimpse of her. I have so far interrupted every single conversation she has had with the plethora of men who keep coming up to this floor for one reason or another, just so they can speak to her. It's getting ridiculous and I'm unsure whether I'm annoyed that it might interfere with her work, or that I'm just plain old jealous.

I'm so distracted in normal working hours when she is here, that I've been staying back late more and more just to catch up. But I still get distracted by her empty desk. I am properly messed up in the head.

It's gone 8pm and the building is quiet. There's a tap on my door.

"Yes."

"It is just me, Mr Myles." The slight figure of Kateryna, the cleaner, appears in the doorway.

She isn't really a cleaner, but an accountant, forced to leave the Ukraine when the war broke out. She's working as a cleaner because she doesn't have the correct paperwork and qualifications to work in the UK. All the cleaners here are in the same position. Even if they do have the correct paperwork, they don't want to take on professional jobs because they want to be back in their home country. No one thought the war would last this long, so they are stuck in limbo, only able to do the most basic of jobs.

"What have you got for me today?"

"I have you some Smetannik. It beautiful Ukrainian sour cream cake."

"You know I'll have to go to the gym more now, with you feeding me up."

"You no go to gym, you just work!" She folds her arms across her chest as she chastises me. "When you gonna get good meal?" She's so brutally to the point. Her strong accent makes me feel like I'm being interrogated, but she just cares.

"Are you my mother now?"

"I must be. You time for talking?"

"Always for you, Kateryna!"

"You so smooth. Why you late every night?"

"I'm just a bit distracted."

"Is it new girl?"

"Maybe. She has lots to learn."

"Or maybe she is pretty."

"No. Well, not just pretty. I don't know. I've tried not to like her but she's very... Likable!"

"You like her, you tell her."

"I can't have a relationship with my PA!"

"Why not? You are not your father Mr Myles."

"There's a whole minefield of issues that come with a relationship at work. Anyway, who's to say she likes me. I'm just the grumpy, moody boss." I roll my eyes. My mind wanders back to Megan, the way her hair is always pulled up, showing off her neck. The way she chats to herself while she's working. The smile she has when she talks to someone she likes, but never when she talks to me.

"How's Tomasz doing?" I try to change the subject back round to her.

"He good. He miss home but makes new friends."

"He's doing well at school?"

"He does good maths, like his mother." She gives a broad grin. "His English, not so good." She makes a face and gestures with her arms.

"It's to be expected really, but I'm sure he'll be bi-lingual in not time."

"But what if he settled, then we go back?"

"Kids are very versatile, and he comes from strong, good people."

"This true. I leave you to catch up and dream about girl." She laughs and leaves the office, but she doesn't know how close to the truth she is. Megan has been haunting in my dreams as well as through the day.

Chapter Fourteen

Megan

It's been a tough few weeks at my new job. I don't see Anne much. She's leaving me to it, working from a desk on the ground floor. I have to ring her if I have a question. She says it saves her from butting in, but I think it's because she knows I won't call unless I have exhausted every way around the problem.

My favourite visitor by far is Dionne. We have lunch every day and I'm thinking of inviting her to the Dog and Swan for girls' night in a few weeks. She'll love everyone. She has invited me to a life drawing class. I did ask her how she drew life and she laughed. Apparently, its drawing people in the nude, but I'm not sure that's my scene.

I see her walking up the corridor, a smile on her face, her curls bouncing round her head with every step.

"Well hello there, haven't seen you in a while!" she says.

"You saw me an hour ago at lunch." She shrugs and perches on the end of the desk. But she hasn't sat for long when Myles comes out of his door and looks at her, stony faced as ever.

"You up here again Dionne? Do you actually do any work at your own desk?"

"Hello Mr Beckett. I would actually love to spend more time at my desk. However, my CFO wants constant hard copies of the reports."

"Why?" Myles' eyebrows knit together.

"No idea. I could be finding the answer to world poverty right now, but I'm not. I bet he doesn't even open those reports."

"Can't you just email them to him?"

"I do!" she says, deadpan.

"That's weird."

"Not really." He gives her another questioning look. "It's all about power. He gets me to do this because my time isn't as valuable as my male colleagues'. It gives me less time to be fabulous with numbers, therefore proving to him that I am no better than his boys' club downstairs. Whereas his little band of merry men don't question him about anything and therefore keep him holding the power."

"Bit far fetched, maybe Dionne!" She gives another shrug. She's used to not being taken seriously by a member of the fifth floor.

"Well, I'm going back downstairs. The smell of testosterone is shrinking my IQ! See ya!" And with that, she jumps off my desk and heads to the lifts.

Myles watches her as she walks down the corridor. "Is she always that weird?"

"She's not weird, you're just blind to what really happens." He doesn't argue but looks like he's mulling over what has just been said. With a *hmph* he walks back into his office. The CEO shutters have come back down. For a minute there we got a glimpse at Myles the man and not Mr Beckett the CEO.

The rest of the day is spent typing up minutes, booking meeting rooms and booking Myles' car in for a service. Considering I have no clue about cars, I think I did okay. We'll find out when he goes to fetch it afterwards. It might have a carburettor missing – and I don't know what a carburettor is.

There's been no sound coming from his office all afternoon. He has his door open ever so slightly, and I catch sight of him occasionally. And when I do I seem to stare and have to shake my head to pull myself out of the daydream. He's unbelievably handsome. He has rolled his sleeves up so I can see the definition in his upper arms and I just wonder what kind of body is hiding under that suit.

I wonder if he has a girlfriend, or at least someone that he hooks up with. Of course he has, he is perfection. I doubt he has a girlfriend though. Would I put up the hours he works? He's in before me and he leaves after me. He has no time for a social life.

Movement inside the office makes me panic that he's read my mind, and a hot flush runs up my neck and covers my face. My pen falls off the desk and in my rush to catch it my notebook goes flying. Why am I so clumsy round him? It's not exactly the impression I wanted to make.

"You alright there?" Oh god he knows. He knows I've been fantasising about him. Play it cool Megan.

"Yes, fine. Are you going out?"

"I have that meeting with some investors. You should know, you manage my diary." The heat in my cheeks can't have gone unnoticed. For fuck's sake Megan, pull yourself together.

"Oh yes. Are you coming back to the office afterwards?"

He gives me a look before answering, his features and tone soften. "I am but you'll probably be long gone."

"Do you need me to stay?" Why did I even say that? If he doesn't come back for hours, I'll be stuck on my own with Mr Sleaze.

He ponders for a minute before replying. "No, you must need to get back to your family?"

"No, not really!" Again, Megan, why are these words just vomiting out of your mouth?

"Boyfriend then?"

"Nope, I don't even have a dog to get back to." Stop talking Megan!

"Okay, well get home safely." He turns and walks down the corridor. Just as I'm about to let out a sigh of relief, he turns back round. "So who makes sure you get home?"

"I ring my friend on the way." Seemingly satisfied with that answer he turns away and continues his walk. I get back to daydreaming about my boss... I mean, I get back to work.

· ♥ · ♥ · ♥ · ♥ · ♥ ·

It's four o'clock, and I'm still busy finishing off some minutes, when my desk phone rings. "Hello, Mr Beckett's office, Megan speaking."

"Hi! It's me!"

"Hi me!" I reply.

"It's Myles."

"Hi Myles, it's Megan."

"I know, I rang you!"

"How can I help you?" The sarcasm is dripping off me.

"I've just realised I have a conference this weekend. Somewhere outside York."

"Okay."

"And I need you to come."

"What do you mean?"

"I need you to come with me, as my PA." He's starting to get a little impatient with me, I can tell by his tone.

"But you are going to be in Leeds Thursday and Friday."

"I know, you'll need to get yourself on a train to York on Saturday morning and I'll pick you up from there. You'll also need to call the conference organisers and book yourself into the hotel."

"Are you sure I need to go?"

"Why? Have you got plans? Anne did tell you that you may need to work out of hours." His tone is bordering on anger now. I can hear in his voice that he is gritting his teeth.

And did you take Anne to these conferences? I want to ask but I hold my tongue. "No I don't have plans." I bet he thinks that I just don't want to work, and it's not that. It's that I'll have to see him, with no respite. I'm bound to put my foot in it.

"I'll message you the times and details, but I've got to go."

"Do you have my number?"

"Of course I have your number. I know everything about you Megan, even your shoe size!" He gives a little chuckle, knowing he has got one up on me.

"Goodbye, Mr Beckett!" I hang up. Within a matter of minutes all the details are messaged and I start making arrangements.

I have absolutely no idea how I'm going to navigate this weekend. At least here I have the constraints of his office door to separate us, unlike being trapped in his car for hours.

Chapter Fifteen

Myles

I feel like I'm running on nothing but impatience today. I'm so tired of listening to everyone suck up to me and give me excuses as to why things aren't working the way they should be. I need to get to this conference early, ahead of our competitors, so they don't get the ear of the people who make all the funding and procurement decisions.

But here I am, sitting in my Aston Martin, outside the train station in the pissing rain. Megan is late and I am losing the single ounce of patience I had left. The traffic has been terrible because of the rain and people's inability to drive in bad weather.

I text her again.

Me

> Where are you? We're late!

There's a tap on my window. If I get a parking ticket on top of this, I'm gonna have a fit. I look out of the partially steamed up window to see a very wet Megan.

"I wasn't driving the train you know!"

I get out of the car and take her bag off her. I practically launch it into the boot, while she gets in the passenger side. Her hair is up in a messy gathering on the top of her head, water dripping off her fringe, which is sticking to her forehead. She looks both a mess and absolutely stunning at the same time.

I look her up and down while she wriggles to put her seatbelt on. She's wearing a silver puffer jacket, like something I remember from the 90s. She's trying to get out of it while not taking up too much space. Her white t-shirt is taking the brunt of the water from her dripping hair and her jeans are wet from mid-thigh to her feet. And why she decided to wear pumps in this weather I have no idea.

"There's been some flooding and all the trains are delayed."

I pull out of the car park without a word. Not because I'm cross, which I am, but because I might say something stupid like *you look amazing!*

The atmosphere in the car is somewhere between tense and awkward, but I think that's more to do with me than with her. She fidgets a bit, wiping her sleeve over her fringe to mop up the water.

"So!" I don't know what's meant come after this, I just wanted to break the silence.

"So?"

"Maybe we can try to get to know each other a bit?" She scoffs. "What?"

"You don't seem like the kind of person you *get to know*!"

"I don't know what you mean?"

"Well I've worked with you for a few weeks now and I know absolutely nothing about you, other than you prefer coffee to tea."

"You know me better than a lot of people then!"

"You're very closed." She folds her arms across her chest and looks at me directly.

"That has been said before."

"Well you can't get to know someone without giving a bit of yourself away."

"What do you want to know?" I take a brief look at her.

"With absolutely no indicators, I don't even know where to start." She taps her fingers on her chin. "Okay, do you have a wife... girlfriend... boyfriend... or even a dog come to think of it?"

"No."

"That's all you are gonna give me?" She folds her arms again and looks out of the window. She's probably rolling her eyes too, but I can't see.

"I don't have a wife or girlfriend. I don't really have time for relationships. I had a dog when I was a kid, but I didn't see much of him when I was at boarding school."

"Wow."

"Wow what?"

"Wow, you gave more than a one-word answer."

"Sorry. I'm not used to small talk. What about you, do you have a girlfriend, boyfriend or a dog?"

She thinks for a little bit before she answers. "I am currently single and have no dog. I was never allowed a pet as a child because I was never *responsible enough*."

"Why weren't you *responsible enough*?"

"I don't know. I was never given the opportunity to be responsible for anything, to prove whether I was or even learn how to be."

"Hmm."

"I am an only child and have been handled like I would break at any moment. Everything was done for me. It was all very safe. And when I tried to do anything for myself, I was criticised for doing it wrong. It's only recently that I've been able to take responsibility of anything." I look over to her for a moment to gauge her mood. "It's complicated. I don't have a great relationship with my parents."

"Me either!"

"Why not?" She looks at me, intrigued.

"It's complicated." She rolls her eyes again. "And a long story. maybe something for a different time," I continue and she looks back out of her window, sensing it was just my way of shutting down the subject.

The rain has not given up and the windscreen wipers have a rhythm to them, like it's the car's heartbeat. With only a mile to go, the traffic on the winding country road slows down. Up ahead I see a police car which has cut off the route. Cars are turning around and heading back.

As we get closer to the police car, I wind the window down to speak to the officer.

"Hi, what's happened?"

"The river has burst its banks and flooded the road about 100 yards round that corner," the officer explains.

"I need to be about half a mile that way." I point past the cordon.

"It's closed further down too. It's flooded in two places. You could try going all the way round. It's about a ten-mile detour, and even then, you might not be able to get to where you want."

"Thank you, officer," I say through gritted teeth, as I wind the window back up. He heads back to the dry of his patrol car. I bang my hands on the steering wheel. "Fuck!"

I start to turn the car round and head back the way we came. Megan hasn't said a word and to be honest I had forgotten she was here for a moment. "I need to get to this conference before that fucking arsehole."

"Have you finished having your little tantrum?"

I shoot her a death stare. No one usually dares speak to me like that.

"I have spoken to Sarah, one of the conference co-ordinators, and she said the majority of people haven't been able to get there, not even the keynote speakers. So chill your boots." I'm shocked by the way she has spoken to me, but also how she's taken control has me in awe.

"What now then?" I ask.

"Well, she said there was a little hotel, we must have passed it, called The Star Inn. If we stay there tonight, hopefully the rain will stop and we can get to the conference tomorrow."

I blow out a breath. I hate that she's right. And I'm also surprised that I liked her taking control of the situation. She points out of the window.

"Just there!"

I turn into the carpark that's also starting to resemble a lake.

"There's a higher-level bit, up there. If you park there maybe your car will survive this monsoon."

We park up and I take both our bags out of the boot and follow Megan to the front entrance. The place is very dated, but it looks clean enough. They seem to have been on top of the upkeep, but it has not been modernised.

The sounds of phones ringing greets us, and the flustered receptionist gives us a little smile while she tries to deal with everything. After a few minutes of waiting, Megan goes around the back of the reception desk and picks up the phone.

"Hello, The Star Inn, how can I help you?" She sounds like she's always worked here. "Yes, the road has been blocked. It's unclear whether you'll be able to get to us, I'm not sure it's worth the risk. Can I take your name please?" She looks to the receptionist, who hands her a pen and a pad, whilst still dealing with her phone conversation. These two look like long term colleagues. Does my team work this well together? I don't think they do. There's too much back stabbing. "I'll make sure your reservation is cancelled. No I'll make sure the cancelation fee is waived. Thanks, take care."

Wow! The receptionist is still talking to an irate customer and Megan just keeps answering the ringing phones. After another ten minutes or so, the receptionist, who I know from her name badge is called Cara, has finished her phone call.

"I'm so sorry about that. Thanks so much for helping out."

"No problem. I'm Megan and this is my boss, Myles. We are hoping you have rooms? We were meant to be staying nearby but the road has been closed off."

"Let me just check. We were fully booked, but I don't know who is still going to make it, and there are also people who haven't been able to leave."

The phone rings again and Megan answers. "Hello, The Star Inn, how can I help you? Erm Megan, who is this? Ah no I'm just helping Cara. Hang on." She puts her hand over the mouthpiece to speak to Cara. "It's Billy. He says he can't get in for his shift."

She rolls her eyes. "At least he has a good excuse this time. Can you ask if he's heard from anyone else?"

"Hey." She goes back to the phone. This woman is amazing. How have I not quite seen it before? "Have you heard from anyone else? ... Okay, I'll let her know. Bye!" She looks at Cara with a pained expression. "He says he rang most of the afternoon shift to see if they could get him in, but Chef and Davey had been turned away by the police and he couldn't get hold of the others."

"Oh god. The day receptionist can't get in either. But the other night shift left already so they didn't get stranded. I'm here almost on my own." She looks back at her computer. "But there is one room available, maybe there will be another one once we see whether anyone else can get here."

"Well, don't worry, we'll help you out. Don't stress," Megan says, putting a comforting hand on the woman's arm. A woman she only met fifteen minutes ago.

"Thanks so much. It's room 12. If you put your things there until we sort something else out and come back down for a drink on me." She hands Megan the key and we make our way up the sweeping staircase, wide enough for multiple people to pass.

The walls all the way up hold what look like old photos and paintings of the building. The place is period and quaint. We make it to the top and turn to follow the corridor, passing doors until we see number 12.

Pushing the door open, both our faces drop. It's not only just one room for the two of us, it's one very small room with a double bed and not much room for anything else. Fingers crossed we get another room sorted out, because being in such close proximity to this woman is only going to cause a whole heap of problems.

Megan turns to me with a grimace on her face. "Do you think I could get a shower and change my clothes? I still feel really damp." I try not to, but I can't help but look her up and down. I wonder what she looks like under those clothes, what she would feel like?

"Yeah, sure. I'll just leave my bag and head downstairs for a drink." I head for the door but hesitate. I need to say something, but I'm not sure what. "Megan, you were great back there."

"Was I? I didn't really do anything." I stifle a laugh. Her brows knit together and that's when it hits me. She has no idea how amazing she is.

"See you downstairs." I open the door and leave the room and make my way downstairs before I say anything that might incriminate me.

Reaching the reception area, I see that Cara is still flustered. "Hi. What's the update on the situation?" I ask her. Her face drops. "I'm not here to complain, I'm here to help."

The relief spreads across her face and she looks down at her notebook. "Well I've been doing a ring around of customers and staff. I couldn't get hold of one couple, but other than them, the rest have cancelled. So the good news is I do have another room for you."

"Well we can sort that out later. What about staff?"

"Jeff, behind the bar," she points over at a well-stocked bar area, with pub style round tables and chairs in front, "Maria from housekeeping, and myself. We are the only staff in. There's no kitchen staff at all. So I don't know how we'll feed everyone. We can't exactly order in takeaway." The phone starts to ring and she excuses herself to answer it. I use the opportunity to look around the room.

Beside the bar is an open fire with chunky sofas and arm chairs. It looks like it would be cosy on a cold night. There's a door with the sign *Dining Room*, next to one with the sign *Staff Only*.

"That was the last customer cancelling."

"Right. Get locked up then. We shouldn't be getting any more people now and you can leave your post."

"Good idea." She comes around the desk, Closes the outside door and bolts it, then does the same on the inside. "Next is the food situation."

"Shall we go into the kitchen and see what there is?"

"Follow me." She heads off towards the *Staff Only* door.

Inside is an area that leads one way to the bar and another into the kitchen. We go through to the stainless-steel room that is, thankfully, spotless and ordered. "Let's see what's in the fridge. Chef sometimes prepares things for the next day." She opens the door to the huge cupboard fridge, laden with fresh produce, containers and on one shelf some catering trays that are labelled and dated.

"Excellent. I'll give him a call."

"We have food then?"

"Yes, seems enough here. We can bulk it out with a bit of salad and some chips, maybe."

"Awesome. I'll gather everyone together in the bar and we'll tell them what's going on." She nods and I make my way back out to the bar. First, I text Megan and ask her to come down as soon as she's ready.

"Jeff!" I shout behind the bar and he appears. "Can you gather all the guests into the bar area so we can update them all please."

I look up when something catches my eye. There she is, gliding down the staircase, her hair damp and pulled up into a messy pile on her head. She's wearing joggers and a cropped jumper. Something that should look dressed down and ordinary, but on her looks amazing. I can't take my eyes off her as she reaches the bottom of the stairs. She looks up and her green eyes glisten, her shy smile reaches up and grabs my chest.

· ♥ · ♥ · ♥ · ♥ · ♥ ·

Everyone has been fed and is in good spirits. We are sitting round the real fire in the bar area. There are not enough seats to go round, so Cara is pulling chairs through from the dining room. Megan is sitting on the arm of my chair.

I go to stand up. "You sit here."

"No. I'm okay here." My brows knit together. "What?"

"It must be really uncomfortable." She shrugs. "Then sit on my lap." The words come out of my mouth before I have chance to register what I'm saying. "Sorry I wasn't trying to be creepy. I just wanted you to be comfortable."

She looks right in my eyes, trying to search them for the truth. I think I'm telling the truth, but I just can't get my head straight while she's about. She moves to sit on the edge of my knees, trying not to put any weight on me. "That can't be comfortable either!"

"You will complain when you realise how heavy I am."

"I bench press at least twice your weight, I think I'll cope."

"Fine!" she huffs and positions herself properly on me. I place my hands on the arm rests so I don't touch her. Okay, this was a bad idea. My dick really loves her sitting here, especially as she's wriggling around. Oh god! And to top it all off, she smells amazing. I'm trying not to put my nose on her neck and inhale her.

"Stop wriggling!"

"I'm not!" She wriggles again, and I let out an audible moan.

The conversation is flowing around us, and Megan is getting involved. Apparently, the newly married couple, Emily and Tom, are telling everyone about their honeymoon disaster, and the older couple have been telling us about their grand kids.

I'm only half engaged with the group because the other half of my mind in firmly with Megan, watching her every little movement, listening to her laugh that warms my insides, the smell of her shampoo bursts when she moves her head.

"So how long have you two been together?" I'm suddenly 100 percent in the conversation around me. Emily is the one asking, but it seems that she has the full attention of the group.

"Erm..." Megan begins to answer.

"Not long. A month or so," I answer, and she turns to look at me, wide eyed.

"Not long enough to be coming on a mini-break." This from the older lady, Maureen or Muriel, her name is.

"We aren't on a mini-break. We were meant to be at a conference together, but the road to it was closed and we ended up here," I continue.

"We work together." Megan chips in and does another little wriggle. I simultaneously want her to stop and keep moving. I know this is going to start a group interrogation.

Out of nowhere there's a click sound, and all the power is cut. The only light left comes from the embers of the fire that is almost burnt out. The group is full of chatter about what's happened and what to do next. Megan makes a move to get up but I pull her firmly back down on my lap and whisper in her ear. "You don't know where you are going in the daylight, let alone the dark, just wait a minute."

Cara and Jeff head into the staff entrance and appear holding four big torches and a handful of candles.

"Maybe this is the universe's way of telling us it's time to go to bed. Candles may be a fire hazard," Cara continues, "but we have them just in case. Jeff and I will help people to their rooms if they want to go up."

"I've got a torch on my phone, we'll be ok," I say as I move Megan up and take her hand.

"Goodnight, everybody," Megan says as I pull her towards the stairs, my phone lighting the way.

We get to the end of the corridor and stand outside room 12. "All your stuff is in here, so you may as well keep it. Cara gave me room 14 which is next door. I'll grab my case and head to my room."

She looks up at me for a few moments, not giving anything away. I'm so close I have to stop myself leaning down and kissing her. Instead she turns, unlocks the door and walks in. I follow her in and pick up my bag.

"Goodnight then."

"Goodnight," she answers as if it's not actually what she wants to say.

I need to leave before I do anything stupid, so I turn and head out of the door, closing it firmly behind me. I stand with my hand still on the door handle. I'm not sure whether I'm relieved or disappointed.

Chapter Sixteen

Megan

My body tingles and my back arches off the bed. I can feel him all around me. I can smell his cologne mixed with his manly, earthy scent. Lips touch my neck and continue, kissing, licking and biting down my body. I feel his weight pressing me into the mattress and my legs wrap around his waist. Oh god this feels so good. I need him. I want him. The kisses make their way back up my body and he positions himself fully over me. The room is dark, I can only see the outline of him and not his actual features.

There's a knocking sound I can't quite place. It starts to take over my senses, getting louder and louder.

My eyes open and I gasp. The room is bright, and the sound is a knocking on my door. The realisation hits that I've just had a sex dream about my boss. Oh god! How am I even going to look him in the eye now.

"Megan! You awake?" It just had to be him didn't it?

"Just a minute!" I shout back and pull the covers back and swing my legs out of bed. I give myself a little shake then straighten out my sleepwear. Possibly not the best thing to be wearing when you open the door to your boss – a tight vest top and tiny sleep shorts.

I open the door and he looks me up and down. Crossing my arms across my chest, I feel a bit exposed under his scrutiny.

"I'm heading downstairs to help with breakfast, if you want to come?"

"Yeah, I'll just get myself dressed and head down. I take it the electricity is back on."

"Yeah, it clicked on about 4am."

"You were awake?"

"I don't sleep much. I'll see you downstairs." And with that he's off, no explanation about his comment, but I know it's something I'm going to wonder about.

I get myself washed and dressed and head downstairs. I was able to get a bit of charge into my phone battery and I have several messages from Sean and Beth. I send them both quick replies, otherwise they'll end up sending out a search party. Both are particularly overprotective.

Pushing through the kitchen door, the smell of food and coffee take over my senses. Cara is half out of a walk-in fridge and Myles is in chef whites, piling sausages into a catering dish.

"Oh my god. Not only out of a suit but in chef gear. I HAVE to get a photo of this." He looks up just as I snap a quick photo. I snap again as he smiles at me – something I don't see often and

I know that Dionne will need proof to believe it. "What can I do?" I say, putting my phone away.

Cara comes fully out of the fridge. "Morning Megan! Could you possibly put tablecloths and cutlery out?"

"Yes, sure." I turn to Myles. "You look good in the kitchen!"

"Better than in a suit?" I just shrug and walk out to the dining area. I thought that Myles in a suit was the most gorgeous thing I had ever seen. But I realise that this, right here, is the real Myles and I'd choose him any day over Mr *Designer Suit* Beckett.

Everyone is gathered for breakfast in the dining room. The toasting machine is on, the giant silver roasting dishes are laden with sausages, bacon and eggs, amongst other things. I am circulating, asking what everyone wants to drink, then I head back into the kitchen.

"Everything is out and everyone is here. I just need to do some coffee," I say to a rather hot looking Myles.

"I can do that."

"You've done your fair share. I just need to find the teapots." I look around the kitchen and spot them on a shelf on the opposite side. I look back to Myles as he watches me. "What are you still doing here? Go and get some breakfast, you deserve it."

"I'll wait for you." I give him a quizzical look. What's he avoiding? I know he doesn't like small talk but still!

I put the teapots down on the counter top and grab his arm, pulling him reluctantly through the kitchen and into the dining room. "Sit yourself down here." I push him down into a chair. "Now would sir like tea or coffee?"

He rolls his eyes. "Coffee... please!"

"Coming right up!" I leave him with Matt and Eric, to collect the drinks.

Placing coffee and tea pots on each table, I finally arrive to Myles being quizzed by Eric about business – arguably his favourite subject. He's much more comfortable talking about work than he is talking about himself. He hasn't got himself anything to eat. "Do you want me to get you some breakfast?"

"Coffee is fine."

"You've just cooked breakfast for a group of people you don't know, but you're not having any yourself?" He shrugs and I study his face. I really don't understand this man, he's full of contradictions. "Let me get you something... Please!" I put my hand on his arm and immediately feel some kind of spark. His face tells me he felt it too.

"Fine."

"Is there anything you don't like."

"I'm easy!" he says with a smirk. I head off to load up our plates and he's back to business talk.

The very obedient Labrador, Max, is sitting patiently next to the food table. I call over to his owner. "Carley, can I give Max a sausage?"

"Yeah, but make sure he knows it's a treat," she calls back.

"Maximus the Great," I say to the dog. "I'm just gonna take his breakfast over to Smarty Pants over there, and then I'll be back to give you a treat." I drop both our breakfasts off at the table and make my way back.

"Where are you going?" Myles asks.

"Chatting to a friend!"

I kneel down on the floor and give Max a big scratch behind the ear. "So Maximus, your mum says this has to be a treat. No pinching food or begging, okay?" I show him the sausage. "Have we got a deal?" I lift my hand up for him to give me his paw, which he does. "Good boy!" I break the sausage in half and blow it to make sure it's not too hot. He takes it and lies on the floor, savouring every last chew while I head back to my seat.

"You'd rather have breakfast with the dog then?"

"Sometimes it's nicer talking to animals. There's no false truths with them. Well, domestic animals anyway."

"Interesting!" He says but doesn't follow it up.

We sit in silence eating our breakfast. It feels like he's assessing everything I say, but then asks no questions in return.

He stands and goes to tidy away our plates, but a hand touches his shoulder, placing him back into his seat.

"Let us do the cleaning up." Tom says. "You've made us all breakfast. You sit and enjoy another coffee."

It's clear that Myles is a doer and not a sitter. I don't even think the word *relax* is in his vocabulary.

"Tell me Myles, what do you do in your spare time?" I ask him.

"I don't know what you mean."

"You know, the time between work and sleep. It's called spare time."

"There isn't really any time between work and sleep. I'm always working in some form or another."

"That's just not healthy." He shrugs at my suggestion. "What about your friends and family. Do you get to spend time with them?"

"Well, I see my family, but as it's a family business, all we talk about is the company. Me and Seb, my brother, used to go climbing together, but we've not done that in a while." His eyes lose focus as he stares off into the distance. Then, with a shake of his head, he pulls himself out of it and changes the subject. "I wonder if the road has opened yet?"

"Dunno. At least it stopped raining last night."

"I wonder if Fi has officially cancelled the conference yet? I suppose so with half a day and an evening already gone."

"Fi? So you are on pet name terms with the organiser?" He looks sheepish, so I know full well there's a story there.

"*Fiona* is an old friend."

"What kind of *old friend*?" I put the word in quotation marks.

"Not that kind!" I still feel a pang of jealousy, but I try to shove it deep down. I shouldn't really be bothered, but he's always shooing away men from around my desk, with a curt *leave*, or a growl of some description. It works both ways.

My thoughts are interrupted by Jeff rushing into the restaurant to tell everyone the road is now open. Cara scurries off to check which staff members can get in.

"I suppose that means we should pack up and head off."

"I'll check and see what's happening with the conference and then we can drop in to see them."

"To see Fi?"

"May as well." I roll my eyes, then head to the room to pack my things back into my overnight bag.

It's taken half an hour to get my things ready to leave. About five minutes to pack my bag and the rest contemplating why I felt so out of sorts, thinking of Myles with a woman. He's my boss. I really don't care about him. Well that was until he started to properly talk to me, and I got a little snapshot into his life, even if it is a work heavy existence.

I walk down the large staircase and find him waiting at reception talking to Cara. I hear their conversation about the staff coming in and that Cara will finally be able to go home. The phone rings and Cara excuses herself to answer it just as I reach the reception desk.

"Ready?" he asks me.

"Yep."

"We'll just wait for Cara's cover to get here and then we'll head off. Drop into see Fiona and then we can head home." Our attention is drawn away with the sound of Cara's raised voice on the phone.

"I'm not sure why I have to pay for my own room when I couldn't leave. And I was working!" she says to whoever is on the other end.

Myles looks at me and I shrug. He gets Cara's attention and mouths *who is that? Boss* is the only word we get back. Myles gestures for her to give him the phone and he rounds the reception desk.

"Hello? This is Myles Beckett, is there a problem?" He rolls his eyes as he listens to the person on the other end. "Well it is my business as I stayed here last night and witnessed, first hand, the dedication of your staff members. They had no option but to stay here and look after your guests. Rather than demand they pay for their rooms, you should be giving them a bonus, or even a promotion." He listens some more and answers again. I love the authority he has. He's amiable but puts people in their place. "In that case, I will pay for their rooms and any other costs. But I will be telling anyone who will listen about your treatment of your staff and I will be encouraging them to seek employment elsewhere. Who? The CEO of the Institute of Hospitality... Yes, a personal friend." He shakes his head in disgust. "Good to hear!" and with that he slams the phone down. "Prick!"

"What did he say?" Cara asks. "Am I gonna have to look for a new job?"

"No, but I suggest you do. You won't be paying for anything." He hands her a business card. "And if you have any more trouble, just give me a call."

Another woman walks through the hotel and Cara gives her a wave and turns back to us.

"Thanks for everything." I open my arms for a hug and she steps inside and reciprocates. Myles holds out his hand for a firm handshake.

"We best get going." With that he picks up both our bags and heads out of the door. I already said my goodbyes to the other guests and I wonder for a moment how he navigated that small talk.

Not a word is said on the drive to the other hotel. It's less than five minutes away but even so, it's as if he has run out of words. I really don't have the energy to be the only one making an effort.

We walk in through the hotel foyer. It's worlds apart from where we have been staying. It's sleek, clean, business-like and sterile, with only corporate character. As we walk in a beautiful blonde-haired woman walks towards us. She's tall and slim, wearing a designer suit and stilettos and carrying a folder. She is probably the exact opposite of the way I look right now in my jeans and baggy jumper. She beams a wide, toothy smile towards us.

"Myles, how wonderful to see you." She leans into him, placing her super manicured hands on his shoulder and lingers a kiss on his cheek.

He smiles back. "Fi! Good to see you." This woman does not look friendly. She looks like she's ready to consume him. "This is Megan, my PA," he says, gesturing to me. Fiona looks me up and down and her smile slips for a second. I hold my hand out expecting her to shake it, but instead she slips her arm around Myles' elbow and angles him away from me.

"Come into my office, I have something for you." I bet she has!

"I'll just go wait in the car," I say in a clipped tone.

"You come too," he says to me. But I shake my head and as his smile drops, her smile takes on a sinister turn. "Wait here, I'll just be a minute." I roll my eyes.

"Grab yourself a coffee," Fiona says to me, pointing through the door to a bar area in the opposite direction.

I saunter in and find a place at the bar and hop onto a barstool. The barman turns to see me and smiles. Then sees my unamused face and his features drop.

"You look like someone that doesn't want to be here. Join the club," he laughs.

"You hit the nail on the head there. My boss has just buggered off and left me here."

"Oh. You want a drink? Coffee, tea, tequila?"

"Bit early for me, but a tea would be great."

"Coming right up."

It doesn't take long for him to come back with a tray containing everything you could need to make a cup of tea. He sets it down in front of me, then leans his elbows on the bar and leans forward to start a conversation.

"If I was left to my own devises by my boss, I would be happy."

"I'm just a bit annoyed with the double standards."

"In what way?"

"He goes all Alpha when men hang around my desk, but that woman just looked me up and down and froze me out."

"Is it the same thing? Why should you be upset he's with another woman if he's your boss?"

"I didn't say I was being rational."

"Do you like him?" Now that got me thinking. Do I like him? I like him more here than I do at work. "When you're at work, is he just concerned about your work rather than your welfare?"

"Maybe, but I should be concerned for him. She's a predator!"

"Who?"

"*Fiona!*" I can't resist using a mocking whiney voice for her name.

"Ah, now that becomes a bit clearer."

"Oh god!" He knows something I don't.

"Why don't you test the theory."

"What do you mean?"

"Well, when he comes back, I can do exactly what Fiona did to him, and we can see how he reacts."

"Are you coming on to me?" I slant my eyes at him.

"No. But I can pretend to!"

"I don't know what it will achieve."

"It may give you a clearer picture of what's going on?"

"I don't know what would be the better outcome? Him kicking off or him totally not giving a shit. Let me drink my tea and have a think."

"Okay. How long did they say they'd be?"

"Well, he said a minute. She said enough time for a cuppa!"

"Hmm."

"I know, right? Predator!"

He laughs. "Just for curiosity's sake, how did he describe her?"

"An old friend!"

"Then they've slept together."

"You don't know that."

"I speak MAN! I know that for sure."

"Maybe I should take your number and you can be my translator because I have no idea." I look at him. He seems harmless, but then again, I'm not a great judge of character.

"I know Fiona, and if she's out for him again, he must have been something special."

"Do not tell me that. I already had a sex dream about him. And WHY am I even telling you this?"

"That's your subconscious telling you something, isn't it?"

"My subconscious is not telling me anything, other than stay well away from men, especially good-looking ones."

"Does that mean I'm classed with the *not good-looking* ones?" I pull a quizzical face at him, a not very attractive one at that. "Because you haven't stayed away from me."

"Now even I know that's MAN for *give me a compliment, please say I'm attractive*."

"I'm waiting!" Now this guy, Noel, his badge says, is fun. I could get used to this banter.

"Okay Noel. You are very good looking with your cute little button nose!"

"No man wants to hear themselves described as cute!"

"That's all you're getting," I say, putting my hand up as a stop signal. I drop my hand and take a sip of my tea.

He looks up towards the entrance. "It's decision time. To flirt or not to flirt?"

"Erm, I don't know... Flirt!" He leans forward and whispers in my ear.

"This should get a reaction, but also seems innocent. Now do a little giggle." I do as I am told. He touches my cheek then leans in to whisper again. "Give me your phone, I'll put in my number and ring myself. I'll send you a debrief once you leave. You can block me after that if you feel the need." I nod and hand him my phone. I hear his phone ring in his pocket and he hands mine back. Coming close again he says. "When they speak, jump and act as if you weren't expecting them and look as though I told you something really dirty."

I am still processing what Noel said when Myles speaks. "What's going on here?" I really do jump out of my skin at Myles' accusatory voice.

"Erm, nothing," I say, putting my phone away.

"Time to go." His voice is sterner than it has been.

"Lovely to meet you, Noel." I say fluttering my eyelashes and looking doe-eyed at him.

"Call me!" he shouts as we leave.

"She won't!" Myles is mad.

I look back over my shoulder towards Noel and give him a cheeky smile. Myles practically frog marches me out of the building, like I'm a naughty child.

· ♥ · ♥ · ♥ · ♥ · ♥ ·

The first half hour of our journey home is in deadly silence. Myles is quietly fuming and pretending to concentrate on the road, but I can see it in his face. His mind is going a million miles an hour. My phone buzzes and I pull it out of my pocket and smile.

Noel

> Well, well, well. His face was like thunder when he came through that door. Does that answer your question?

Me

> Hee hee. I'm currently getting the silent treatment

"Who's that?" It's the first thing he's said since we got in the car.

"Beth. Wanting to know when I'm getting home.

"Oh."

"Can we stop at the services for food. I don't think I can be bothered cooking when I get home. And there's nothing in my fridge."

"Does it have to be the services?"

"No, but I want a dirty burger."

"How dirty?"

"Absolutely filthy!"

"I know just the place." And he's back with me, the Myles from the weekend, the fixer, the helper is here again. Thank god!

Chapter Seventeen

All in all the weekend went well. After our stop off at an American style diner off the motorway, Myles dropped me home. I had a lovely bath and got everything ready for work this morning. I was dragged back to reality when Mr *Designer Suit* Beckett appeared at work, and not Myles who I'd laughed with at the diner the night before. I could tell by the way he walked down the corridor towards me. He came in later than me, which was unusual in itself, and then proceeded to barely acknowledge my existence.

I texted Noel to tell him. In fact, I've texted Noel a lot since I got back. If we lived closer I'm sure he would have asked me out on a date by now. I also sent Dionne a message asking whether our running lunch date was still on. She messaged back a one word answer of, *course.*

Myles may have shut me out again, but he still has his office door slightly open. Every now and again I get a glimpse of him, all broody and gorgeous. And if he senses me thinking about him, he strides out of his office and hands me a post-it note. "Can you book a room for this meeting?"

"Yes sir!" His eyes narrow at me. "How many for?"

"I've emailed you the details."

"So why did you need to come out and tell me? You could have just shouted *read your emails* from your desk."

"You complain when I don't speak to you, then you complain when I do." Can he read my mind? He huffs back into his office, this time closing his door fully. Okay then!

Opening my inbox, I see his email and check out the conference room calendar for availability, book it and reply with a short. *Done!* An inaudible comment comes from inside the office.

I think that's my cue to go for lunch. I pick up my bag and contemplate whether I should just shout through the door like a teenager, but I decide to be the better person and I knock on his door. I hear a grumble inside and open the door, but only about three inches and speak through the hole. "I'm going to lunch, be back in a bit." I close the door before he can answer.

Dionne is in the foyer waiting for me. Today her hair is in buns on each side of her head, looking not unlike Mickey Mouse ears. She is in a black, long-sleeved dress that buttons up the front, with lace up boots. "A bit understated for you today, Dionne."

"Yeah, well I'm trying to keep under the radar."

"Maybe dressing more like yourself will keep you there."

"I was hoping to blend in."

"But why?"

"I dunno, I have a feeling that something is going down."

"Like what?"

"Not sure, but I found some anomalies in some of the accounts." Her voice has turned into a whisper. "When I questioned it, people were being cagey, or just plain stupid. I can't quite work that one out."

"It could be either to be fair, I've met your team."

"I'm gonna keep digging, don't say anything."

"I won't." We queue up in the lunch line for our usual paninis and find a seat out of the way.

"How was your weekend with Mr Hot CEO?"

"It was actually really nice." I explained what had happened with the cancelled conference and she listened intently. "But now we're back, he's being all Frankenstein with me."

"I don't get what you mean. Green and that?"

"You know. One minute he's nice, the next minute he changes personality to mean."

"You mean Jekyll and Hyde."

"Whatever." I'm not very good with analogies.

"But being a Jekyll and Hyde, he must have been nice at some point, but I don't quite see that happening. I will need evidence."

"I thought you might." I take out my phone and open my photo gallery, find the photo and face the phone towards her.

"Okay, that proves he doesn't always wear a suit."

"One moment." I swipe onto the next photo, the one of Myles smiling at the camera.

"Wow! He looks hotter when he's smiling. I didn't think that was even possible."

"I know, right? But now he's back to grumpy."

"Maybe it's this place. It brings out the worst in me too."

"Well he has no choice about that."

"Indeed he doesn't. Especially as he never wanted to be in charge in the first place. He actually studied law."

"I never knew that."

"Anyway, never mind him, look what I'm on." She shows me her phone with some kind of dating app. "It's called Love Pi."

"I don't get it."

"Pi the symbol. You know, as in mathematical... never mind, it's a dating app for people with higher than average IQs."

"Oh, right."

"I thought we could go out clubbing and try and meet up with a few of these *dates*."

"I don't think I'm their ideal audience."

"But you can be my wing woman."

"Well yeah, I'm up for that, but I can't do this weekend. I have the kids."

She looks at me with a strange expression. "Have I woken up in an alternative universe?"

"Ha, no. I'm babysitting Beth's kids on Friday night."

"So what about afterwards?"

"No can do, they're sleeping over at mine, so Beth and Steve can go out and come back and have noisy sex."

"Do kids stop you having noisy sex? That seems a bit unfair."

"The stories I've heard from Beth are absolutely hilarious."

"Can you do the week after?"

"Probably. Sean might be coming down but that'll be Saturday."

"Is Sean single?"

"Yeah but you'll not get anywhere with him. He has switched off the love button inside him. He won't entertain it ever happening to him. Something happened, I'm not sure what because it's one of our unwritten rules. We don't ask, we don't judge!"

"Hmm."

"So next Friday, we'll do your dating thing. But you'll have to tell them to bring a friend, I'm not being a raspberry!"

"A what now? Ah you mean gooseberry!"

"Whatever, raspberry? Gooseberry? Same thing!"

We finish off our lunch with a bit of office gossip and then head back to our respective desks. But I'm dreading the rest of the day with moody suit man!

Chapter Eighteen

Myles

This week I've been all over the place. I feel like I never really have a good week anymore. I can't concentrate on anything and I've gone to a new moody low. The weekend ended up being one of my best for a while, it was a fun. I was really stressed about the conference and not being able to get to it, but my mood took a massive upturn being in Megan's company.

The way she took charge and showed such compassion made me think even more about her. But then on our way home the dynamics changed. She started acting all weird and I caught her flirting with that bartender. When I saw him leaning into her and whispering in her ear, I just saw red.

She even gave him her phone number. He could have been any kind psychopath. I'm not sure why she would put herself in danger like that. The only saving grace is the distance between them. We were still away from home, so at least that's a non-starter, but when I thought he was messaging her, I lost my mind all over again. My hands still haven't recovered from the grip I had on the steering wheel. Once I realised he didn't stand a chance I relaxed a bit. But I have no right to act like that. She's my PA, not my girlfriend.

It would be all kinds of wrong to date my PA, even without the thought of history repeating itself at work. But whenever I'm with her she makes me feel different, more myself. And to be fair, I don't know whether she thinks of me in the same way. It's like a roller coaster with her. When I'm not with her the doubt filters into my brain, which starts working overtime. Then when I'm with her I pull back from her. But pulling back makes me feel like shit all over again.

Her reaction to my roller coaster of moods is to act all sassy and answer back, which I hate and love in equal measures. I decide to get an alternative opinion, so I pick my phone up and dial.

"What's happened?"

"What do you mean what's happened? Nothing!"

"Well, I only usually get an unsolicited call if something bad has happened."

"No you don't." This is Sebastian, my younger brother, being all over dramatic again. "I just wanted to ask your advice on something."

"This is a joke right? You never ask my advice. And even when I give it, you immediately dismiss it."

"Well, I'm asking now."

"What's the subject?"

I blow out a breath, I don't even know where to start. "Women!"

"Ha ha ha! Finally!" He continues to laugh. I'm not sure what's so funny. He always seems to have a woman hanging off him.

"Forget it!"

He stops suddenly. "No wait! Tell me."

"Not if you're gonna mock me."

"I promise I won't. Is it women in general or one specific woman?"

"It's nothing, it doesn't matter."

"So it is one woman in particular!"

"Bye Seb!" I hang up before he can answer. Asking him was a bad idea. He'll either just constantly mock me or give me some really shitty advice. I fling my phone on my desk and get back to work.

· ♥ · ♥ · ♥ · ♥ · ♥ ·

I'm elbows deep in a report when there's a little knock on my door. The door is opened slightly and an amazing pair of green eyes stares through. She opens it wider and waves a boxed sandwich at me. "I thought your current sunshine mood may be due to low blood sugar. I haven't seen you eat all day."

"You think I'm moody because I'm hungry?"

"Hangry, yes. Plus, I would rather that be the reason than you do actually hate me."

"I don't hate you."

"Tell your face that. And your tone, come to think of it."

"Sorry!" I answer and she shrugs, steps in and places the carton on my desk before turning to leave. "I've got things on my mind." I explain but she doesn't ask any questions, she just leaves me to my moodiness. She leaves the door slightly open as she leaves and I wonder if she knows I like to keep my eye on her. Or is she keeping an eye on me?

"Hello Mr Beckett." I hear her say, and my eyebrows knit together. It becomes very clear when I hear the answer.

"Well hello there, the gorgeous Megster. How the hell are you?" Sebastian's dulcet tones come through the door. A rush of panic hits me and I'm out of my seat in a shot.

"Sebastian. Lovely of you to drop by." I put my arm round him, manoeuvre him into my office and slam the door behind us.

"Why are you acting all weird." But the look on his face suddenly changes and a wicked grin appears. "Oh I get it. That woman you were talking about is Megan!"

"Keep your voice down." I think for a minute. My office isn't exactly soundproof, so I have to think fast. I open the door and stick my head out. "Erm Megan. Can you go down to security and look through the visitor sign ins for the last two weeks for a Trevor Watson."

"Or I could just email security to check?"

"I need you to do it in person. I don't want anyone else to know." She gives me a stony, unimpressed look. "You're the only one I trust," I add. She gives me a sarcastic smile, she can see right through me, and pushes her chair away. She rounds her desk, not taking her eyes off me. Once she has turned and headed down the corridor, I pull myself back in and shut the door.

"That little display there told me everything," Seb starts.

"I don't know what you mean."

"Spill, before she comes back and I go out there and ask her out myself."

"You wouldn't!"

"Wouldn't I?" He's right. Sebastian has always been seen as the playboy brother to my sensible brother title.

"Okay." I take a deep breath and try to order everything in my head. "I don't actually know where to start."

"Start with the fact that she's gorgeous."

"That's not even at the top of the list of her attributes. She doesn't care about status, money and all that pretentious crap. She's a helper and a lover of everything. Yes, she is attractive, VERY, but she doesn't even realise it. All the men in this building gawk at her and she never notices. She sees the good in most people." A thought crossed my mind. "Except Fawcett actually," I think I'll park that thought and revisit it later. "But most of all she makes me think about myself differently, especially away from this place.

"She calls me out when I'm being a knob and she sees me as Myles and not a Beckett."

"Wow that's a lot! So what are you gonna do?"

"That's the point. I have absolutely no idea. One minute I think I need to stay so far away from her, mainly to make sure we don't have another Beck scandal, and then another part of me wants to hold onto her and never let her go."

"You're not our Dad, Myles."

"I know that, but the outside world doesn't. They'll see that we are cut from the same cloth."

"And you have no idea if she feels the same way?"

"Absolutely none. I thought we had a moment when we were away, but that could have just been one-sided."

He thinks for a minute. "You need to work out if she feels the same. Preferably away from here. If she doesn't, this whole dilemma becomes irrelevant."

"But how?"

"I don't know. If it was me I would stage a situation where you had to bump into her."

"Like what? We're always together, but here."

"We could find out where she goes drinking and *bump* into her."

"What so I casually ask her where she hangs out?"

"You don't have to be obvious about it." He pulls a face that tells me I'm being a bit stupid.

I'm so out of my comfort zone with this, it could be situated on the moon. My dating life has been non-existent since I got this job. I have attended gala style nights and award dos, all with dates chosen by my mother. All from the pool of wannabe millionaire wives, all as boring as the next. Some of them I couldn't even stand enough for a one-time fuck, let alone a relationship.

There's a knock on my door and we both look towards it, our conversation stopped in its tracks. "Yes!"

Megan pushes the door open and stands, cross-armed, in the doorway. "There has been no person of that name visiting the site within the past two weeks." Her voice sounds robotic. She drops her arms and continues in her normal voice. "If you wanted me out of the way, you could have just told me to get lost for a bit." She turns and walks out, closing the door behind her.

"As if you didn't just make the whole situation about a million times worse. Now she hates you." Sebastian isn't wrong on that count. "Think about what I said. Give me a call if you find an in." With that he stands and makes his way to the door.

As he leaves, he says, "Goodbye Megan, you vision of loveliness."

"I hope you've talked him off the ledge," she says, with a giggle.

"I am here you know!" I shout through the open door.

"And don't we all know it!" The sass level is getting higher, but I do at least deserve it this time.

My brain has gone into overdrive thinking about ways I could see Megan out of the office, without directly asking her out, but I come up with a blank.

Chapter Nineteen

Megan

The working week has dragged on and on. Myles has been yoyo-ing between moody, grumpy boss and trying to wheedle personal information out of me. I'd quite happily have a normal conversation with him about my private life, but it seems forced or something. This all started happening after his brother visited the office.

The two of them are like chalk and cheese, complete opposites. Whilst Myles is moody and straight laced, Sebastian is the flirty, outgoing, fun brother. He's also really attractive, but in a completely different way. There's no spark there for me. He's lacking something that his brother has, but I can't quite put my finger on what.

I'm back home, out of my work clothes and into comfy lounge wear. My hair is tied up and I'm wearing slippers with bunny ears that Beth bought me last Christmas. My living room is beginning to resemble a blanket fort with rugs, cushions and blankets all over the place. There are two make shift beds on the floor for my two guests.

Beth is due any minute to drop off Poppy and Jonah. It's the first time they have spent the night with me. There was no way I would have been allowed to have them stay over with me while I was seeing Darren, and I wouldn't have wanted them to experience that kind of toxic environment.

I have bookmarked a load of kids' films on pretty much all of the streaming channels and I have frozen pizza and popping corn ready to be cooked fresh. I bought Poppy's favourite, and the only breakfast cereal she'll eat and some cookie dough to make fresh cookies, if they get fed up of the film.

I've been around Beth's kids since they were both born, but they change so quickly. Every week they are into something new, I just can't keep up. I have missed out on so much of their lives over the past two years, not being able to just pop over when I wanted. It's one of the biggest things I regret about staying with Darren for so long.

The doorbell rings. I know it's going to be them, but I check the video on my phone, just in case. Sean has drummed it into me to always check, especially when he's not here. I see Beth on my screen, and the tops of two heads bobbing up and down.

I open the door in a rush and the two kids pile in. Poppy grabs me round the legs and squeezes tight.

"If you don't let go, how is Megan gonna make you any popcorn?" Beth says to Poppy. She lets me go and we all head into the living room. Jonah jumps on his makeshift bed, looking round and saying things like *cool* and *awesome*.

"Thanks Megs, I really appreciate you having them overnight."

"Don't thank me until you get them back in one piece," I laugh.

"Jonah can't have raw tomatoes because he's allergic."

"Yes, I know."

"But he can have tomato ketchup," she continues, in mummy mode.

"This I also know."

"Yeah, sorry. Just ring me if you need anything or are not sure."

"Nope, we'll be fine. Just go and spend time with your husband. I'm surprised his mother hasn't found out and invited herself along."

"Just don't even say that. It's not funny, we've already had to lie to her."

I take her shoulders, turn her round and push her towards the door. "Shout bye to mummy, kids!"

There's a unison of byes. Beth is standing at the door with her arms outstretched waiting for them to run up and hug her but they've both completely blanked her. Jonah is scrolling through the list of films and Poppy is rearranging the cushion on the sofa. I shrug, push her out of the door and close it in her face.

"Right kids, what's first? Pizza?"

"Auntie Megan, I don't like mushrooms, or peppery or sweetcorn on my pizza." She pulls a face like she just stepped on a slug. Bless her she means pepperoni.

"I know sweetheart, I got you a margarita pizza. I have some ham you can put on top because you sometimes don't like the ham that they come with. For you Jonah-Balona I got mighty meaty because you love it packed with meatiness." Jonah fist pumps the air. "For me I have Pepperoni and I'll add extra mushrooms. Do you want to help Popster? I know you like to be in charge." She nods, jumps off the sofa and follows me into the kitchen.

· ♥ · ♥ · ♥ · ♥ · ♥ ·

The pizzas have been demolished and we are currently sitting watching some kids' film that I'd never heard of. Jonah was very disgruntled about the choice, but he hasn't taken his eyes off the screen. My phone rings and I look at the screen. It's Myles, at 6pm on a Friday evening. I bet he's still at work.

"Hi."

"Hi Megan. I need some help with some files I can't find, can you come back in?" The kids, who I haven't heard a peep out of for the past 40 minutes, are suddenly interested in me.

"Who's on the phone Auntie Megan, is it Uncle Sean? Can I speak to him?" Jonah pipes up.

"Myles I can't, I have company." I put my phone against my chest to answer Jonah. "No it's my boss."

"Oh, I'm sorry to interrupt." I'm unsure whether he sounds disappointed or annoyed.

"Auntie Megan..." I don't even think Poppy has anything to say, she just wants to be in on the action.

"Myles, can you give me a sec?" I put my hand over the phone again. "Kids! Is that Mummy and Daddy pulling up outside?" They both go stiff as I look out of the window. "If you sit still and be very quiet I'll tell them to go home. Unless you want to go back?" They both sit up straight, Poppy puts a finger on her lips. I move from the sofa and go outside to take the call, standing on my step.

"Sorry about that," I say, talking to Myles again.

"What's going on there?" He sounds intrigued.

"I'm babysitting."

"Ah!"

"So these files? I can't come in, but you can come over and we could look when the kids are settled. Unless you're allergic to children."

"Not that I know of," he answers, as if he's thinking about it.

"Well, I'm here all night. It's up to you. But I have to go before Jonah pulls the place apart." I hang up before he can answer. If he comes, fine. If he doesn't, well, that's also fine.

We don't even have time to find the next film, although it does take ages for the two of them to decide, before the doorbell rings and I check my phone. It's Myles on the doorstep, so I get up to answer it.

"Hey."

"Hey. I brought supplies, but to be fair I have no idea what kids like," he says with a smile.

"You didn't need to do that. Come on in." He's looking as gorgeous as ever. He obviously came straight from work, but he's lost the jacket and rolled up his sleeves. He has his laptop bag over his shoulder and is carrying two takeaway cups, precariously balanced in the cardboard holder, in one hand and a brown paper takeaway bag in the other.

I walk him through to the kitchen, where he places the goodies on the worktop. Jonah and Poppy run in to see what's going on.

I do the introductions. "Guys, this is Myles. Myles, this is Jonah and Poppy."

Myles stretches out his hand to shake theirs and is met with quizzical looks and he quickly pulls his hand back. "Hi. I brought some things over, but I'm not sure what you like so I might have this completely wrong."

"Mum doesn't let us drink coffee, it's for adults!" Jonah states looking at the takeaway cups. "We're just kids." His sass is off the scale.

"Oh no, I thought you," he says pointing to Jonah, "were at least 20, and you," pointing to Poppy, "were 17." She giggles, which is unusual for Poppy when faced with a stranger.

"No, I'm nearly 7," says Jonah, folding his arms in front of him with a look of distrust.

"Good job I got hot chocolate then." Jonah's eyes are as big as saucers. "And a variety of doughnuts." Poppy licks her lips, and they both start to bounce on the spot. And that's before the sugar high they're inevitably going to get.

"I'm allergic to tomatoes," Jonah states, making a vomiting action.

"I can guarantee these don't have tomato on."

"Are you Auntie Megan's boyfriend?" Jonah continues.

I jump in, "No, he's my boss." Myles' expression changes as if he's disappointed at the statement.

"So you tell her what to do?"

"Kind of." He answers.

"Well, good, cos mum says that Auntie Megan's boyfriends are pond life. She said it like it was bad, but I know she likes frogs." He gives a shrug.

"Thanks Jonah," I say through gritted teeth. "Maybe save Myles the commentary on my life?"

"I don't know what that means." Jonah looks at me deadpan.

"Stop telling him stuff," I explain.

"What? Like the time you got your bum stuck at the top of our slide? Or the time you were nearly sick on the bouncy castle at Poppy's birthday?"

"Enough, Jonah!" I put my hand up and he shrugs again before looking into the bag of doughnuts.

"Well this is enlightening." Myles smirks.

"How about both of you take one of those and go and find that film?" I turn to Myles. "I'll split this hot chocolate between them and just pray they don't vomit."

Again, they run and land on the sofa, bouncing up and down and squealing. Oh god it's gonna be a long and embarrassing evening.

I turn towards Myles who has a cheeky grin planted on his face. "Forget you heard any of that!"

"Not at chance. We'll revisit it later."

"Shall we get these two settled and then look for the files?"

"Sounds like a plan," he says.

"You wanna split the rest of this hot chocolate? Actually, have you eaten?" I know he doesn't make time for food. He's often eating at his desk, that's if he remembers at all.

"Kat brought something in for me, but hot chocolate sounds good." Kat? I don't even want to think about who that is. I get four cups out of the cupboard, a miss-match of presents and promo mugs, and distribute the hot chocolate between them. I take the kids' two mugs over, and Myles follows with ours.

"You two sit on the floor with these." The kids jump off the sofa and position themselves with their little carpet picnic, while Myles gets comfortable on the sofa.

"Can we watch Jaws?" Jonah directs his question to Myles.

"Yes, sure," he answers.

"Absolutely not. Taking away the fact that you are far too young, it'll give you nightmares for a month, and your mother will kill me."

"Stranger Things?"

"Again no. And how do you even know about them?" Jonah shrugs again. I think that's the only gesture he ever does. "What about Yes Day? That has loads of chaos for you Jonah and is vaguely age appropriate." I press play, giving them no option.

The kids are loving the film. It's all about saying yes to anything the children ask to do in the space of one day and the chaos that causes. "Can we have a Yes Day Auntie Megan?" Jonah asks.

"You virtually always have a Yes Day when I'm with you."

"Can I go into Uncle Sean's room?"

"Nope. He gets cross when you touch his stuff."

"Can I go outside and look at Myles' car?"

"Nope. It's dark, cold and too late."

"Not much of a Yes Day, this then." He huffs and sits a little too close to Myles.

"How about we look at it through the window?" says Myles, "and you can go and have a look and sit in it another day?" Jonah jumps up and heads to the window, followed by Myles, while Poppy snuggles into me.

"You're my best friend, Auntie Megan."

"Ah Pops, you're my best friend too. I'm only mates with your mum to see you!" Poor Poppy doesn't make friends easily. She's very shy, unlike Jonah. "Right you two, come back and finish this film."

"Aww," groans Jonah.

"Or I'll tell Uncle Ben you've been naughty." His eyes widen.

"How many Aunties and Uncles do these kids have?" Myles says quietly and sits next to me, a little closer than before.

"Well, we're not technically related but we are such close friends its virtually family. Jonah idolises the men in the group. You'd think he didn't have a great father figure in his life, but his dad is the nicest person and lives with them, so I'm not sure what the fascination is. I think as a group, a lot of us don't have close relationships with actual family.

"Emma's kids, for example, don't see their dad. Mainly because he's a prick, but Ben has really stepped up and taken on her teenage boys. It's really lovely to see. He's taken on all the kids really. He's gone from bachelor life to attached, two step-sons, four nieces and nephews and now found out he has a girl of his own. It's just funny what constitutes family. It's not necessarily blood."

"I know what you mean. I'm not very close to my parents. I actually think I resent them a little bit. We had money growing up and had all kinds of stuff bought for us, activities paid for, which were amazing. But I think, looking back, I really just wanted time with them. I suppose the thing that did come out of it was that me and Sebastian are close, although neither of us wants to admit it."

The kids have settled down and are watching the film again and laughing proper belly laughs that just warm my heart. I gesture to Myles to go in the kitchen. That way we can look for the files.

He places the laptop on the work surface and logs in.

"The files from the finance department on the sustainability project had just vanished. I looked to see if they had been accidentally dragged into another folder, but I couldn't find them anywhere."

He clicks into the folder, and I point a finger to the files, sitting in the correct folder. "I promise you. They weren't there before." The confused look on his face.

"Are you losing the plot Mr Beckett?" I tease.

"Now it looks like an excuse to come over, and it really wasn't."

"Easy mistake." I shrug, his face is a mix of embarrassment and anger. "I believe you," I laugh.

"It's not funny. They really weren't there two hours ago."

"Can you look at the history or properties?"

"I know someone who can." He takes his phone out and dials. "Seb! Stop talking I have company... Yes! Later. I need your help. If I needed to know if and when a file or folder had been moved or altered and by whom, how would I go about it? Right can I send you the info to look at? Great!" He hangs up. "It's good having a brother who knows his way around IT and also has access to everything."

"Could you not get our IT department to do it?"

"On a Friday night? Plus, I want to keep this under wraps. I have a strange feeling about all this."

"Auntie Megan, the film's finished. Can we do some cooking?" Poppy shouts from the sofa.

"It's getting a bit late, Pops."

"Pleeeeaaaasssssseeeee!"

"I can do it with them if you like," Myles suggests.

"Really? I do have some cookie dough ready to go for this exact eventuality."

"Well leave it with me then. Go and chill on the sofa for a bit."

"Are you sure you can cope with these two?"

"I run a multibillion-pound company, how hard could it be?" Fool!

"If you're sure? I need to text Beth back before she turns up here in a fluster."

Myles rounds the kids up and they start chatting in the kitchen. Poppy knows where everything is better than me, so they should be fine. I pull my phone out of my pocket to see that Beth has messaged several times, so I message back.

Me

> Chill yourself, they are both alive and well

Beth

> I'm not actually worried about them. I'm just hoping you haven't lost your mind and they haven't wrecked your house

Me

> No all's fine AND I have help.

Beth

> ???

Me

> Myles came over

Beth

> Did he now?

Me

> Don't be weird about it. He needed a work thing looking at

Beth

> Course he did

Me

> Shit, I should have asked if it was okay to have him round the kids

Beth

> It's okay. Jonathan already did some kind of check on him

Me

> Sneaky

Beth

> I bet Jonah is loving it

> **Me:** He's all over him, new besties
>
> **Beth:** Ben will be gutted
>
> **Me:** Right, you go back to being with your husband!
>
> **Beth:** *heart*

I focus back on the chaos in the kitchen and it's all very civilised. Myles has them under his spell. He is covered in flour and so are they, but there's a calm about it all. They are looking up at him, taking in every command, every word, every action. I have never seen these two working so well together. I pick up my phone again and snap a sneaky photo and send it to Beth, with the words *child whisperer* underneath.

· ♥ · ♥ · ♥ · ♥ · ♥ ·

I lift my head off the cushion to see the television is flicking through the streaming channels screen saver and the room is deadly quiet. Poppy is in her makeshift bed on the floor, fast asleep. Myles is asleep next to me on the sofa, with Jonah draped across him, eyes flickering in his dream state. Either we were all completely exhausted or that last film was really boring.

Once the cookies were out of the oven, everyone was back to the living room with milk and cookies and another film. It's been a really lovely evening. Myles has been back to Myles again rather than Mr *Designer Suit* Beckett and he has chatted openly with us all. He's answered the million questions thrown at him by Jonah and he's even got Poppy onside. There's been no mention of what had him all moody last week.

I pull myself up off the sofa and gently wake up Myles. We lift Jonah into his bed on the floor. Myles stretches his arms out. "I can't believe I fell asleep. I usually have trouble sleeping, I must have been exhausted."

"Kids can do that. Plus you work, like, 100 hours a week. I'm surprised you get chance to sleep at all." He just laughs and looks at his watch.

He frowns. "I need to get going." He looks round the downstairs of my house, it does look like a bomb has hit. "But I'll come back in the morning and help you clean up."

"There's no need, really. They'll be up at the crack of dawn, so I'll have plenty of time to sort it out."

He grabs his laptop bag and heads to the front door. He turns and looks at me. There's an awkward moment between us, the air crackles with electricity. He is posed like he's either going to say something or lean down and kiss me. He shakes his head as if to let go of the thoughts in his head, which gives me an unexpected sense of disappointment.

"I really have had a great evening," he says like it has surprised him.

"Me too!"

He turns and heads out of the door, and his car beeps. I stand and watch him, but he waves me inside and I close and lock the front door. Myles Beckett is a very complicated creature indeed.

Chapter Twenty

The kids have been up since 6am and had one breakfast. According to Beth, they could eat up to four breakfasts a day, so it's going to be a long morning. I've started the clean-up but haven't got very far. As soon as I clean one surface, there's a child on it pouring milk, juice or cereal onto it. How does Beth's house ever get cleaned?

The doorbell rings and I look at my phone, its 7.30am and, true to his word, Myles is here.

I open the door. "Morning."

"Morning, did everyone sleep well?"

"Yes but we were up at 6." I frown.

"That's my usual wake-up time."

"Are you like the undead?"

"Maybe. Are you gonna let me in?"

"I thought you shouldn't invite the undead in."

"That's vampires. And it's bright sunshine so I can't possibly be one. Anyway, I brought breakfast!" He lifts up a paper bag and I open the door further for him to come in. He looks all casual but sophisticated. He's wearing black jeans and a designer jumper. He smells amazing, that mix of man and cologne. "Where do you want me to start?"

"How about a coffee first?"

"Sounds good. I didn't bring coffee, *because the kids are too young*," he says, raising his voice so Jonah can hear. "I also spied you had a super coffee machine."

"Yes, that's Sean's. I barely know how to use it to be honest. It's just too complicated."

"So, is Sean your brother?"

"No, he's my best friend. But I suppose I look at him as a brother."

"He's not here though?"

"He only stays here when he's down on business. He lives here as a way of helping me out." He looks at me quizzically. "That's a story for another time. But basically, I couldn't afford the rent without him when I needed a place to stay."

"You earn a good wage at Beck though?"

"I know, but I didn't then, and I was left with virtually nothing once I'd paid the rent. I'm back on my feet now, but Sean being here is just convenient for both of us." I'm not sure how much more I want to tell him. If I go into it anymore, I will have to tell him about Darren, and I want that time of my life to stay buried and not taint this time, especially time with him. I don't want him to look at me as a victim and treat me with kid gloves.

"I'll make the coffee. My machine is like yours."

"Okay. Did Sebastian get chance to look into those files?"

"I doubt it. He was out when I called last night, and this morning he'll be nursing a hangover."

We take our freshly made coffees and sit on the sofa. The kids are watching a weird looking programme and Jonah is also watching a very shouty YouTube video on his tablet.

"Do you have these two all day?"

"No, I think Beth is picking them up later on this morning."

"What are your plans after that?"

"Pretty much snoozing on the sofa without a care in the world. You?"

"I've got this family thing." He doesn't seem too happy about the thought. "I wish I was snoozing on your sofa." His eyes widen as he realises what he just inferred, and we drink our coffee in silence.

At 9.30 there's a ring on the doorbell. I look at my phone to see Beth, come to collect the kids. I open the door and her face is all scrunched up. She points, "Whose is the car?"

"Myles."

"He stayed over?" Her eyebrows shoot up.

"No! He came back this morning to help tidy up. Plus Jonah wanted a go in his car."

"Bet Ben is relegated now then."

"Probably! Come inside."

She comes in through the front door and stands statue-still as she looks on at the scene. "Oh my god!" The three of them are sitting cross legged on the floor playing a board game. "Who are these kids and where have you left my devil children?"

They don't even look up from their game, Poppy is giggling and Jonah has a face I don't think I have ever seen before. It's pure concentration. "See? Child whisperer!" I say under my breath.

"Should I go and come back tomorrow?"

"God no! I need some sleep."

"Ah... rough night?"

"Just late night and early morning. They both slept well."

Beth moves closer. "Hey guys, should we pack up and go home?" The three of them look up from the game as if they had only just noticed. Myles smiles and the kids pull sad faces.

"Aw, no mum..." Jonah groans.

"Sorry, we have to go to Granny's house."

"Aww, which one?" he asks.

"Granny Ivy."

"Well that's not as bad as it could be!"

"Jonah!"

"Well I'm going to have to head off now too, I've got a family thing." Myles directs this towards the children as if he knows him leaving will make things easier.

"Ah well, I will come then."

"Cheers Jonah, you didn't want to stay with me then?" I ask sarcastically, and he just shrugs again.

"Gather your stuff kids." I help them gather their belongings and we head to the door. Jonah gives Myles a fist bump and Poppy hugs him round his legs, which is weird in itself. Beth mouths *child whisperer* to me while Myles' attention is elsewhere.

I close the door and there is an awkward atmosphere between us. Myles stands with his hands in his pockets looking at the ground, and I'm just staring at him.

He looks up at me, eventually. "I best get going. Get there before Seb so I can lord it over him all day."

"Well, thanks for coming back and helping out. You've really made an impression on the kids. I've never seen Poppy take to someone so quickly."

"I really enjoyed getting to know them. They have good taste, which is obvious because they love you." He hardens his expression as if he's said something he shouldn't have.

"I think that may have been a compliment there?"

He laughs, "I think there might have been." He gives me a little smile and makes his way to the door. The house feels empty as he leaves. He gets in his car and all I can do is stand and watch as he drives off.

Chapter Twenty-One

I feel like I have worked a full week in the past three days, I'm absolutely exhausted. Partly because of not getting enough sleep at the weekend, plus the number of meetings and projects I have had to set up for, sit through and type up minutes for. The only saving grace has been my lunches with Dionne.

Myles has been a less moody-boss this week, but not as friendly as over the weekend. I can understand that we need to have a bit more professionalism and this seems like a happy medium. The only problem is, I'm still having the sex dreams. I'll wake up in the middle of the night, pulse racing and dripping in sweat. That's the other reason I'm so tired.

I pack up my things and knock on Myles' door. "I'm heading home now, if that's okay? I'm no use to anyone."

He gives me a cheeky little smile. "No worries, I think I'm going to head home myself."

"That's not like you. I thought you had a bed made up in here." He laughs. I give him a little finger wave and leave, closing the door behind me. Picking up my coat and bag I walk down the corridor towards the lift, trying not to make any eye contact with any of the other people on the floor so I can get out of the building without delay.

The lift pings to say it has reached the ground floor and the doors open. I step out and give Fran, the security guy, a little wave while totally blanking Cruella. As I beep through the staff barriers the hairs on the back of my neck stand up and a prickling sensation runs down my spine. It's then I see him, propping himself up next to the door, his face contorted.

There's no way of getting out without walking straight past him. But even as my mind races, thinking of ways to escape unnoticed, his eyes land on mine and narrow at me. He pushes himself off the wall and comes towards me.

Getting too close for comfort, I see his blood shot eyes and the grimace. He leans in at the same time as grabbing me by the elbow. I stop in my tracks. If I leave the building no one will know what is happening.

"Well, well, Megan," he spits out. "Landed on your feet here didn't you! We need to talk."

"I don't have anything to say to you Darren."

"Well I have plenty to say to you. You and your meddling friends have ruined my life. My girl has left me, my friends won't speak to me, I have been barred from my local. And to top it all off, I've been pulled in by the police because of you. Again!" His grip gets tighter and tighter around my arm as he tries to pull me out of the door.

"Stop it. You're hurting me."

"You're coming with me. And you can clear up everything with the cops."

"Oh no she isn't!" A familiar voice from behind stops Darren in his tracks.

Chapter Twenty-Two

Myles

I've had enough of this week already. Work has been full on, especially having to endure Saturday with my family. I would have loved to have spent Saturday afternoon cuddled on the sofa with Megan. Not that she invited me or that it could actually happen, but it was a nice thought. Instead, I had to sit around the dinner table listening to my father lecture me about business and brag about his golf achievements. And watch my mother act as if he wasn't a cheating arsehole.

The only good part was spending time with Sebastian, who had figured out what happened with the files and who had been manipulating them. The only thing unclear is why?

After Megan left for the day, I decided I was going to have a rare night off and packed my laptop bag up and left my office. I just missed Megan leaving in the lift and was hoping to catch up. When I walked through the foyer I couldn't quite decipher what was going on by the door. But then I heard Megan's frightened voice and sped up.

The man was only a few inches taller than her, weasely looking, with hatred in his eyes. I saw his hand wrapped round her arm, pulling her towards the door and I just snapped.

"Stop it you're hurting me," Megan's voice, frightened.

"You're coming with me. And you can clear up everything with the cops." He spat out his words with such venom.

"Oh no she isn't!" I pull him away from her and motion Megan to move away. Grabbing him by the front of his shirt I slam him against the wall. "What the fuck do you think you are doing?"

"What's it got to do with you?"

"It's got everything to do with me. This is my office."

"Well... I have some unfinished business with *her*." His face is contorted.

Finally, our security guy comes to help out.

"Is everything okay Mr Beckett?"

"Clearly not! He is just leaving before I call the police." With my hands still fisting his shirt, I throw him towards the door. "Escort him off the premises!"

I watch them leave then turn to see Megan shaking uncontrollably. I walk towards her and envelop her in a hug. She starts to sob. The security guy walks back in and I glare at him without letting go of Megan.

"What the fuck happened?"

"I don't know. I didn't even know he was in the building. Martina sent me on a wild goose chase up to floor three."

"You!" I point at the receptionist and her face doesn't change from the motionlessness of too much Botox. "Did you know he was here?"

"Yes. He said he was her boyfriend." Her voice is monotone.

"Well, he clearly isn't."

"I didn't know that."

"But why didn't you know? Any why did you send Fran upstairs, knowing we had a visitor in reception? A visitor you knew nothing about." She doesn't answer. Nor does she move or make any appearance of remorse. "Report to HR in the morning. This is completely unacceptable." This woman is unbelievable. I'll send a message to HR, I do not want to see her again.

I push Megan out an arm's length to check her over. She's still shaking and I angle her in front of me and guide her to the lift. There is no way I'm letting her leave while he could be out there. How do I even handle this situation? A rush of something I haven't felt before washes over me. I just need to protect her, to look after her. The lift doors close, encasing us in a silver box, and I wrap my arms around her again, holding her against my chest, hoping the rhythm of my heart will calm her down.

Luckily there's no-one about on the fifth floor, which saves some awkward conversations, at least with anyone else. Guiding her into my office, I kick the door shut and manoeuvre her to the sofas at the furthest end.

Sitting down she looks like a tiny, scared animal, still shaking and curled up. Opening the cabinet, I pull out two cut crystal glasses.

"Whiskey?" I show her the bottle and she shakes her head, pulling a disgusted face. "Not your drink?" I root around the cupboard and locate the bottle I'm after. "Ah ha! If any situation ever deserved the finest Ukrainian vodka, this is it." She gives me a weak smile. I take that as a yes.

I stand and poor the clear liquid in equal measures into the glasses and take them over to the sofa. Not wanting to have any distance between us I sit on the coffee table opposite her and hand her the glass. She cradles it with two hands and gives it a sniff.

I take a large drink and feel the liquid warm my insides on the way down.

"Wow, that's strong. And not like the usual stuff. Smoother, I think. Have a drink, it may calm your nerves."

She lifts the glass to her lips and, as if in slow motion, she tips the glass. Seeing the effect it has on her makes me smile and she gives a little shudder.

"That's something else." The first words she's spoken since downstairs.

"Do you want to tell me what that was all about?"

"No, not really!"

"I'd like to know, so I can help." She shrugs. "At least tell me his name."

Putting her glass on the table next to me, she blows out a breath. Knitting her fingers together on her lap she looks resigned to the fact that she'll have to tell someone. "His name is Darren and he is my ex. I was hoping I wasn't going to have to tell anyone here." She sighs and takes another deep breath, readying herself to tell her tale. "I thought everything was a bit too quiet, too normal. I thought I'd finally fully escaped."

"Is he the reason you were left with nothing?"

"Yeah. He was controlling, took all my money, treated me like rubbish. Then when I decided I'd had enough, he flipped and hit me. I moved out, moved on. But he's now blaming me for people finding out and not wanting anything to do with him. He said something about the police. I'm wondering if something else has happened. You see, Sean took my phone from me so Darren wouldn't be able to contact me. But I found out he gave it to the police a few weeks ago."

"Do you know what was on the phone? Had he been sending messages?"

"I don't know, but it must have been bad if Jonathan escalated it at work." I give her a quizzical look. "He's my friend Lizzie's husband. He's in the police and he helped me out last time."

"So what are you gonna do now? I'll make sure you get home okay."

"I better call them to come over and talk about what happened."

"Shall we take a look at the CCTV, see if he's still hanging around?" I get up and pull her up from the chair. We make our way to my desk. I sit on my chair while Megan leans up against the desk. She's so close we're almost touching. I bring the CCTV up and the screen is divided into four black and white squares, each with a different live feed of inside and outside the office.

"I didn't know you could access these!" Her tone is surprised.

"Perks of being the boss." I smirk. "Can you see him? You'll be able to recognise him better than me."

She leans closer and squints slightly at the monitor. "I don't know." I instinctively put my hand on the back of her leg to reassure her. She stiffens and looks down at me, something crosses her face that I don't quite recognise, but then her body seems to relax again. "Myles, can I ask you something?"

"Sure."

"When I first started, why did you hate me?"

"I didn't hate you!"

"Okay, why didn't you want me working here?"

Oh god, how on earth am I going to answer that? I suppose she deserves some honesty tonight. "I thought you were too much of a temptation."

"For who?"

"For every man in this building. But mainly for me."

"Why am I a temptation?" Her innocence is incredible. Because she really doesn't understand how amazing she is.

"Because every time I look at you, I imagine all kinds of things."

"Like what?" The air crackles with the electricity between us and she looks down at me with glistening eyes.

"Like things I shouldn't tell my PA!"

"Tell me." Her voice is now a low whisper.

"Like... I think about kissing you. All the time, to the point of distraction."

"And?"

"Like I think about lifting you onto my desk," I whisper back.

"Do it!" She surprises me with her answer and I couldn't be happier.

Without another thought, I stand, put my hands on her hips and lift her onto the desk. She gives out a little squeal as if she wasn't expecting it.

"What else?"

"I think about how your skin would feel on my lips, about how you would taste."

"Then taste me!"

"I..." My brain does some kind of glitch and I hesitate not knowing what to do for the best? Though now I'm incapable of rational thought.

"You've thought about it, and so have I. Do it!" She urges me to continue.

I part her legs and step between them, putting my hand around her throat as I kiss up the side of her neck and onto her pillowy lips. Goosebumps scatter over her skin and she shivers, but she doesn't feel cold. She feels warm and inviting. As my tongue sweeps over her lips, the taste of vanilla and liquor fills my senses. She parts her lips, inviting me in. I'm on autopilot now. My dick is in control and it's now admitting that it's wanted her since the day I laid eyes on her. I push forward and deepen the kiss. I just can't stop myself, my tongue crashes into her mouth.

She pulls away. "What else have you imagined Myles?".

"I've imagined pushing this skirt up and licking you all the way up."

"Oh yes." Her breathy voice shows the affect I'm having on her. I push the silky pleated skirt up her legs until it can go no further and fall back into my chair so I can see her. I push her legs wider apart and her breath is so quick she's panting.

Delicately kissing up the inside of one of her slender, toned legs, I stop halfway up. I turn my attention to the other and again stop just short, earning myself a disappointed moan. I gaze at her pink lace knickers and push my thumb onto the spot I know she'll like. Her head tips back and I'm rewarded by a warm, damp sensation.

"These need to come off," I say, hooking my fingers under the elastic. She lifts slightly so I can pull them over her bum and down her legs, pocketing them for later. I push her legs back open to see her glistening pink pussy, waiting for me.

"Absolutely perfect!" As I move forward, I pull her closer to the edge of the desk, and with one long motion, I lick right the way up her folds. Another moan escapes her lips and she's now watching me, as I continue my assault of her needy body.

It doesn't take long for her body to tell me she is close to an orgasm, her swollen clit begging to be sucked. I take it into my mouth, and, after a few sucks, let go. "You taste amazing!" With that her body goes ridged and I give another long lick of her pussy. She groans out my name, her body shaking. I continue devouring her until her body stills.

I kiss back up her leg and bring my body up to press against hers. My hand makes a trail under her tight jumper, skimming the underneath of her breast as my mouth is back on hers. This is like a dream come true.

I hear movement outside the door and I freeze on the spot, my brain engaging. Realising where I am, what is happening, I pull back, scooping Megan off the table and onto her feet. Her skirt falls back into place as she teeters, not quite knowing what is happening.

There's a knock on the door and I step back from her as the door opens.

"Hello, Mr Myles." Kateryna says weighing up the scene.

"We're just a bit busy right now." My voice not sounding like my own as I readjust my trousers.

"No problems. I come back in half hour." She says, turning to leave. "I have favourite biscuits to go with tea for later." She closes the door and I blow out a breath.

"Well, that was close," Megan exclaims.

I regain some brain power as the blood starts to flow back up there. What the fuck am I doing? I swore I wouldn't become him. But here I am with my PA, on my desk. This can't be happening, what was I thinking?

I try to avoid eye contact. "We better get you back home!"

"Right." She looks at me for a time. "I'll text Lizzie to meet me at home. Are you coming?"

"No, I have something to do. I'll make sure you're dropped off safely."

"Right!" Her tone is impassive. I've really fucked up here and I don't know what to think.

Picking up her stuff she leaves the room without another look. I follow her, just a few steps behind.

· ♥ · ♥ · ♥ · ♥ · ♥ ·

"Mr Myles, I have tea!" Kateryna opens the door with her elbow, two cups of tea held in one hand, and a plate of biscuits in the other. She pushes through into the room. "You look like shit! What happened? Something to do with before?"

I'm back at my desk, elbows on the table, head in my hands. "Oh god, I've massively fucked up!"

"How?" She places the tea and biscuits down and pulls a chair opposite my desk. It's a familiar situation. While Kateryna is a cleaner here, she has also been a great support and confidant to me. The number of times we have sat here, going through everything that's been going on.

I've tried to give her a more professional, permanent job with me but she's having none of it. She's still in a state of limbo and wants to return to the Ukraine as soon as possible. "I see you cracked open the good stuff." She points to the opened bottle of vodka, a present from her, of course.

"There was an incident after work. We came back up here and got close. Basically, I was thinking with my dick and not my head and I've well and truly fucked it up."

"But you like her?"

"Of course I like her. But I can't like her. She's my PA."

"Okay... but why you so bothered?"

"Because of him, my father! He's just tainted it for everyone."

"Can't be that bad."

"I walked in on him myself, getting sucked off by a girl from HR, of all people. But it wasn't just the once. It was many, many times. The number of staff we went through, and the many times we had to pay women off, was ridiculous. We ended up being black listed by temp agencies and everyone in the industry knew about the company's reputation. It was humiliating."

"What about wife?"

"My mother did nothing. She just kept up the appearance of the dutiful wife. She still does. It's sickening. And he walks away from the business, just like that, and I have to pick up the pieces."

"You must hate him for that." She points her finger at me, prodding me in the arm. "But you not your father Myles!"

How many times have I heard that? But when will I actually believe it? "You want relationship with her?"

"How can I?"

"Forget Beckett. Forget being you. If ideal world, would you want relationship?" She's getting really animated, the way she always does when she's getting a little bit angry with me.

"Yes of course. But I am Beckett!" The words wash over me and I rub my hands over my face.

"Shush," she says sternly. "Tell me what you like."

"About her? Everything!" I smile thinking about her, my eyes light up as I think how perfect she is.

"Like?"

I sit up straight. "Like she doesn't care who I am. If I'm rude to her she gives me hell. She doesn't realise quite how beautiful she is. And beautiful is an understatement."

"More. How do you feel with her?"

I think about the warmth I feel when she's around. "She makes me feel more like me, not a CEO, not a Beckett. Just Myles. I want to spend every moment with her. I want to protect her from harm."

"So why no relationship?" She folders her arms across her chest, giving me a pointed look.

"Because I am a Beckett. Apart from the fact that, as her superior its unethical to be in a relationship with her, I'd want to protect her from my world, from being a Beckett. And that's even before I think about the fact that she's way too good for me."

"That ridiculous!" I pull a face. "People in work place always dating. Yes, her being in direct line of command is probably no good, but being under someone else command would be fine. Just tell the HR."

"But I'm direct command for everyone, I'm CEO."

"And that mean you never date?" She looks at me sternly.

"No one here!"

She rolls her eyes. "You never anywhere else!"

"Drink your tea and stop telling the truth!" I say and she shows me a little glimmer of a smile.

Chapter Twenty-Three

Megan

My mind is a blur over what has happened over the past few hours, a proper rollercoaster. Why did I even imagine that I could just walk away from Darren? I knew that speaking with his friends would make things a million times worse. As for going to the police, this is why I didn't want to press charges in the first place.

Then there's Myles coming in like some kind of savour, calming me down. I really didn't want anyone at Beck to know about my past trauma. In my circle of friends, it feels like it defines who I am. I'll always be the girl who was manipulated by some bloke. I'll always be the victim. *Poor Megan!*

I don't want to be that Megan!

But then Myles made me feel alive, attractive and desired. The flashbacks that have been going through my head have brought with them all the feelings. The way he touched me, kissed me. The way he devoured me until I was a shaking mess. But I wanted more.

Then as if a switch had been flicked, he shut down.

If we hadn't been interrupted, would it have gone further or would he have pulled back then anyway? I get that his office desk was maybe not the best place to be intimate, given our roles, but still.

Another thing that occurs to me is the relationship between him and the cleaner, Kateryna. I've never seen her before but there seemed to be a familiarity between them, like close friends.

An alert on my phone indicates someone at my door. Now more than ever I need to check who is there. A wave of anxiety prickles up my spine. What would I do if Darren turned up here? It's been my safe place, a place untainted by him. Would I ever feel safe again?

I check the camera and it's Lizzie and Jonathan, so I go to answer the door.

"Hey!"

"Hey lovely, everything okay?"

"Not really. You both better come in."

"I have a feeling I know what this could be about." Jonathan says as I flop on the sofa and they take the other end of the L-shaped chair.

"Erm, well… Darren came to my work today."

"Oh my god!" Lizzie says. Jonathan's expression has hardened and he shakes his head. "I think I better put the kettle on!"

As Lizzie heads to the kitchen, Jonathan leans closer. "This may be partly my fault."

"I know you have my old phone."

"Do you know what was on it?"

"I don't think I really want to! Do I?"

"No, I'd rather you didn't see it." He takes a breath and gets ready to explain. He looks like he's blaming himself. "Sean kept hold of your phone. We thought it would be better to keep it, so Darren didn't try to communicate with you another way. If you had blocked him, he'd just keep changing his number to get round it.

"Sean kept an eye on it. It was the usual nastiness, until it wasn't, and then he passed it to me. I needed to do a few checks before I passed it further up. I honestly didn't know they had pulled him in until Lizzie called. It was out of order not letting any of us know."

"How did he know where I worked? He was waiting for me in reception. He tried to drag me out, blaming me for ruining his life. I'm so glad Myles was coming out behind me or I hate to think what might have happened." I feel a wet sensation on my chest as silent tears start to roll down my face, the enormity of it all sinking in.

"I have no idea how he knew. Megan, I think we need to apply for a non-molestation order and call Sean." Before I can even argue the fact that Sean is too busy to babysit me, his phone is out of his pocket and he's dialling. I sit with the tears still pouring down my face, listening to his side of the conversation. "Yes! No, at work... I'm here now. Bye!"

"That was short!"

He smiles. "We talk a lot, and I'm sorry to say we anticipated this happening. He's on his way."

"He can't come all the way here to babysit me!"

"This was always the plan."

"It was never my plan."

"I know. I'm sorry." Lizzie brings in cups of tea and places them in front of us on the coffee table.

"Did you know about this Lizzie?"

"I know as much as you, honestly. When you sent me that message, I rang Jon straight away. It was only then I knew the extent of it all."

"Maybe you should take tomorrow off, so we can work through what we do next. I'll request the CCTV from Beck and we'll have more than enough evidence to get you an order," Jonathan explains.

I can't even comprehend what that all means and thinking about what he may have done and sent to my old phone, to warrant the blossoming friendship between Sean and Jonathan. Sean obviously knew why he was calling. I hate to have pulled Sean away from his life yet again to sort out my mess. I don't want him to regret us starting this friendship, because it's clear to me that it's very much one sided.

I feel exhaustion wash over me and next thing I know I'm being dropped in my bed, surrounded by the familiar smell of my best friend.

Chapter Twenty-Four

It feels like my head is full of stuffing right now. Sitting at my desk I can't concentrate on anything. I walked through the building earlier and felt like everyone was looking at me. They probably weren't, but it just felt like eyes were following me all over.

Myles has been avoiding eye contact – I didn't expect anything else, really. *Mr Designer Suit Beckett* was back in full force, not quite grumpy, but avoiding me like he's embarrassed about what happened.

I wouldn't be surprised if he started getting grumpy and bossy soon though, because I have been particularly rubbish at my job today, along with the backlog from me being off yesterday. I would rather have been at work to be honest, because it was a tough day.

Sean took me to the police station, where we met Jonathan and went through everything that had happened. Mixed emotions floored me, and I just couldn't process what was happening let alone the consequences.

Darren shouldn't get away with what he's done. No-one else should have to suffer like I did. But I don't really want him to be charged because that just means I am still connected to him in some way, for longer. I just want to move on, but to be safe at the same time. Is that too much to ask?

I lift my head and see the welcome sight of Dionne making her way down the corridor. I called her on Thursday morning before she got into work, updating her on the situation, which also included my history with Darren. I may or may not have shed a few tears.

You know when you meet people who just get you straight away – your people? Dionne is my people. She knew just what to say to make me feel safe and comfortable, no judging, no pity, no bullshit.

"Well hello my beauty. How are you today?" She sits on the corner of my desk – her usual position.

"Shitty. You?"

"Same old! Word is, Cruella got sacked."

"Oh god, is everyone blaming me?"

"Hell no! Why would they? No one liked her, and she did it to herself. Seems like she even admitted in one way or another that she was getting back at you for taking her job. But they fired her for gross misconduct."

"Maybe we'll get someone who actually smiles on reception now."

"You never know. Anyway, back to more important things. My dating app has been blowing up and I've arranged to meet some of them in that new club in town tonight. And you're coming with me!"

"I'm not sure, after everything that's happened. Sean is like my shadow. I doubt he'd be happy about me going out."

"He's not your dad. And it would do you the world of good."

"Maybe. I haven't really been out in ages."

"It's a date then." Just as the words came out of her mouth, the door next to us opened.

"What's a date?" Myles' brows are knitted together, but it's the first time he's looked at me and his eyes have a pained look.

"Hello Mr Beckett. How are you on this fine morning?" Dionne says in her sarcastic but sweet tone.

He narrows his eyes at her. I hadn't explained the full details to Dionne, of what went down on Wednesday night. I didn't want to admit to anyone, how hurt and rejected it made me feel. It's not often that a man makes you feel amazing, gives you an orgasm with his tongue and then makes you feel all kind of shitty by not acknowledging that it had even happened.

"Date?" he says again still with a cross expression.

Dionne turns to me and says, not quite under her breath, "He's very nosy, isn't he?" Then turns to him and exclaims, "Megan and I are going out tonight, on dates!" His eyes widen and there's a flash of something that he immediately tried to quell. "We're going to that new club in town... what's it called? Horizon or Sunset or something." Why is she giving him so much information? I would rather have this all under the radar right now.

"We'll see," I say, dismissing the suggestion.

"No, you should go, enjoy yourself," he says, not realising that he has hit yet another blow to my self-esteem.

"Well, I will then." I say with a bitter edge. "Maybe he'll be my prince charming!" Myles grunts at the suggestion and heads back into his office, closing his door again, but not before ordering Dionne back down to the fourth floor.

Chapter Twenty-Five

I stand in front of the mirror, running my hands down my clothes. It's a strange experience, after all the years of being told what I could or couldn't wear, I'm finding it difficult to make that decision. I've gone for a sexy, classy look in all black. My strapless corset top has beading through the shear fabric of the front panel and it shows a little bit more chest than I'd like, but it'll have to do. My trousers are fitted at the top but flow down my legs and my hair is up in a high ponytail. The outfit is completed with matching silver sequin stilettos and clutch bag. I look good if I do say so myself, but I'm also stalling.

Dionne has been sending photos of her outfit choices but I'll only find out what she's gone with once we meet up. I haven't mentioned my night out to Sean. I just don't want that confrontation, but I have to do it sooner or later. I take a deep breath and head downstairs.

"Hey babe, what's the plan for tonight then? I made some pasta and left you a bowl on the side, should still be hot." Sean has heard me make my way downstairs but hasn't got his head out of the fridge yet to see me.

"Erm, well."

He obviously hears something in my voice and pays attention and he lifts his head up suddenly to meet my eyes. It takes a few moments for him to sort his thoughts out and speak. "Wow. You look amazing. What's the occasion?" His eyebrows knit together.

"I'm going to a club with Dionne."

"Absolutely not!"

I roll my eyes. "You can't dictate to me Sean, you're not my dad! And even he couldn't."

"But it's not safe for you."

"I am sick of living my life in fear of one person. Why is it me who has to change my behaviour because of the actions of someone else? I never asked for this!"

He rubs a hand over his face. "I get that. But I want to keep you out of harm's way."

"How about instead of me having to change my behaviour and you having to keep an eye on me, you keep an eye on him?" The fire brimming up.

"What do you mean?"

"You watch everything I do so he doesn't come near. I can't go places because he might be there. Why don't you watch him? Make sure he doesn't go near me and not the other way around?"

"Like, keep surveillance on him?" His brain is moving into action.

"If it means I get one free night out with a friend, without having to constantly look over my shoulder, then yes."

"Hmm."

"I'm not waiting for your permission Sean, I'm going whatever. If you want to keep me safe, if it will make *you* feel better, watch him!" I'm getting angry now. I'm just sick of changing my life to fit round him.

"Can you at least give me a little time to sort things out?"

"You've got half an hour and then I have to meet Dionne."

"Give me an hour and I'll drop the two of you off myself."

"FINE!" I say, virtually stamping my foot.

"Fine." The corner of his lip pulls up to a cheeky smile.

He takes is phone out and dials "I need a favour..." I hear him say as he walks from the room and up to the privacy of his bedroom. I go into the kitchen and pick up the bowl he has left me. I eat my food standing up. I get a tea towel out of the drawer and tuck it into my top to be on the safe side.

I don't even know why I thought it would be a good idea to go on a date. Just now has made me realise that Sean has totally spoilt me for any boyfriend. He knows me inside out. He cooks for me, checks in on me, buys me little presents, keeps me safe. The only thing lacking, and would never happen, is the sex. Maybe I should make a pact with him that if we're both single when I'm 40, that we have a marriage of convenience.

I hear him coming down the stairs and put the thought out of my head. "Right, missy. All sorted. Me and Jon will keep an eye on him, so you can go out and enjoy yourself."

"Thank you!" I put my bowl down and step towards him, putting my arms around him for a hug.

"Whatever, loser!" he says with a smirk and pushes me away like I'm the annoying little sister. "Get your shit together and let's go! Are we getting Dionne?"

"If you don't mind. I'll send her a message."

· ♥ · ♥ · ♥ · ♥ · ♥ ·

As I stand on the pavement outside the club, Sean rolls down his window. "Have a good time. Not too good mind... will you need picking up?"

"I don't want you to have to wait up for me."

"I'll be awake anyway, keeping an eye on dickhead. Just message when you want to leave."

"Okay, thanks."

"BE GOOD!" he says, and I roll my eyes and wave him away.

Dionne stands next to me as we look up at the club. "You look amazing by the way," she says as she looks at me.

Her hair is tamed at the front with a metal hairband, she's wearing a silky black top with spaghetti straps, purple shorts, paired with Dionne-style patterned tights and lace up combat-style boots.

"You too babe, your dateS," I emphasise the 's, "will be blown away."

"I know, right!"

I turn her round to look at her full on. "While it's just me and you, I have something I want to ask you."

"Sounds intriguing." She looks at me quizzically.

"After everything that's happened, I was thinking about going to a self-defence class."

"Sounds like a good idea."

"But I'm too chicken to go by myself. Will you come with me?"

"I'm not sure it's my kind of thing. I'm a lover not a fighter."

"Me either, but I need to be able to protect myself. I don't want to rely on a *knight in shining armour* to come and save me. I want to save myself." She pulls a face that means she's weighing things up. "Plus there will be a fit, barely dressed, buff instructor. Possibly."

"Okay, you've persuaded me. Sign me up."

"Great, I can't wait to kick some ass," I laugh.

She hooks her arm in mine and we make our way to the front of the queue where two big men stand, head to toe in black, ID badges on their sleeves, looking unamused. Dionne gives the woman with the clipboard our names, who ticks us off a list, then one of them moves out of the way to let us through. His passive face never changes.

The thud of the music hits us as soon as we set foot inside the building. It echoes through my body as we head up the stairs to the main bar area. The place is pretty packed and the air is filled with the heat of everybody and the smell of alcohol and perfume. We manoeuvre our way through the throngs of bodies and find ourselves at the bar.

"What are we drinking?" I ask.

"Cocktails may be a bad idea if we are meeting random men. Wine and beer are too much liquid, we'd permanently be in the queue for the toilets... Vodka and..."

"Cranberry?"

"Sounds like a plan. Doubles?"

"Is there any other measurement?"

"Nope! Just checking we were on the same wavelength!"

"Show me who we're meeting."

Dionne pulls out her phone and navigates to her dating app. "Firstly there's Jeremy, 38, he's 6 foot, so really he's 5 foot 10, computer programmer, so hacker, who likes Star Wars, so lives with his parents and goes to Comicon."

"It doesn't say that there," I say, pointing to his profile.

"I'm reading between the lines."

"Okay. Next..."

"Next is Anthony, 33, 6 foot 2 inches, so 6 foot, likes Xbox and sports, meaning he likes playing FIFA, likes food, notice not cooking, so that will mean ordering in a take-away whilst playing on his Xbox. Sounds like a dream." She rolls her eyes.

"Okay, next!"

"Toby, 35, 6 foot 4 inches, is a forensic Accountant who likes hiking, travel and dangerous sports."

"You didn't read between the lines on that one," I say, trying to weigh her reaction.

"No, I think I quite like him. But he's probably a spy, or a gangster or something." She shrugs.

"Their photos all look quite normal."

"You've never used a dating app, have you?"

"Nope!" How does she know?

"The photo doesn't usually match IRL."

"Huh!" Now I'm confused.

"In real life."

"Ah. Where do we meet?"

"There are some booths on the second floor. I said to meet us there and for them to bring a friend. If they have them other than IG – In Game!"

At last we get to the front of the bar queue. The barman is pretty hot and clothed in a black shirt, unbuttoned most of the way down, with rippling abs. We order the drinks and have a bit of a look around. If these blokes are no good, I might chat up a barman instead.

The place is modern and decorated in chrome with neon lights and signs everywhere. There's a dance floor that's lit up, like it's some kind of old school computer game, with neon squares. We move around the groups of people, sipping on our drinks, until we find a neon sign saying *Level Up* and head for the staircase.

The second floor is a lot more subdued. There are a lot fewer people and those who are here are sitting around tables or in booths. Dionne points to a booth, the music too loud to communicate any other way, so we make our way to the empty seats and sit down.

The booth buffers the music sound so we can actually have a conversation, which is lucky, as Dionne wants to get to know these men. We sit chatting for a little while and I tell Dionne about the conversation with Sean earlier. About how he forbade me from coming out and my fears that I'll never find a boyfriend that matches up. She updates me on the accounts she's looking into at work and what she might do next.

In my peripheral vision I see someone standing outside the booth, waiting to be acknowledged. He's older with thick rimmed glasses and a faded looking t-shirt. We both turn and look up to him at the same time.

"Hi! I'm looking for Dionne." Oh god no, this cannot be one of her dates. He looks nothing like any of the photos."

"That's me," she answers.

"Hi I'm Jeremy." He holds out his hand for Dionne to shake. She does not take it, she just stares back at him.

"You are not the same man as in your profile picture."

"Erm, well I am. It was just taken a long time ago." He looks sheepish about his lie.

"Jeremy! I don't mean to be unkind, but this is not going to happen. You are nothing like your profile describes. Do you live with your parents by any chance?"

"Well yes, but..."

"And do you go to Comicon, dressed as a stormtrooper."

"Erm no... as a Jedi Knight, usually Obi-Wan." He looks rather pleased with himself.

"For fuck's sake Jeremy. I bet you are more like 40 than 38 too?"

"41!"

"And I asked you to bring a friend."

"Erm."

"Do you have any friends Jeremy?"

"Not many, no!"

"Right!" She says, standing up to face him. I think she's going to give him some kind of lecture and send him on his way. But she moves out of the booth and points to the seat. "Sit yourself down there. You are going to make some new friends tonight."

"Really?" I think he was assuming he was getting dismissed too.

"Really. And don't lie on your dating profile again. You'll get someone more suited if you're honest. Someone to be your Princess Leia."

"Thanks. Shall I get everyone a drink before I sit down?"

"That would be lovely, Jeremy. Vodka and cranberry," I say.

"Same," Dionne says. Jeremy wanders off to the bar as we exchange looks.

A few minutes later he wanders back and puts the drinks on the table. Dionne moves to let him in. Out of the corner of my eye I think I see someone familiar, but in a flash, they're gone, and I struggle to search for them again.

"What's up?" Dionne asks.

"I thought I saw someone."

"Not Darren?"

"No he's under surveillance tonight. It looked like Seb." She gives me a questioning look. "Sebastian Beckett, Myles' brother? But I doubt he'd be in here."

"Why not? All the cool kids come here!" She points to Jeremy and he laughs. I shrug and pull my attention back to the three of us. It must have been someone who looks like Seb.

"Just seems odd."

"So Jeremy, can I call you Jez?" Dionne turns her attention to our newly found friend.

"Yes."

"Jedi Jez?" He makes a face. "Too much? Okay, well Jez, tell us a bit about yourself, the truth this time." She continues.

Jeremy tells us about his family life and his hobbies, and his job as a finance officer at one of the local authorities. He is a lovely bloke and he seems really happy to be out on a night out with us. Dionne takes some selfies of us all and gets Jeremy's details and social media, so she can tag him into photos.

I look at my phone for the first time since we got to the club. Sean has sent me a message and I immediately go cold before opening it. My brain is starting to run through a few different situations. But when I open the image, it's of him and Jonathan in the car with take away drinks, smiling. The captions says, *On our stake out.*

Sean

> Things under control here. Having a good time?

I quickly type back.

Me

> All going great!

Bless them both. I'm so lucky to have friends like these guys.

"Everything okay?" Dionne looks at me, concerned.

"They're on a stake out." I turn my phone to show her and Jeremy the photo.

"Ah, bless them!"

"Isn't your next date meant to be here by now?" I ask Dionne.

"There was a next date?" Jeremy asks.

"Of course Jez. You always need to double up so when one is a no show, you haven't wasted time making yourself look amazing!" She looks at her phone. "And proving my point, Anthony has bailed."

"Never mind, there's still Toby," I say.

"I thought you said double up, not triple up." We both shrug and take a sip of our drinks.

"Covering all bases!"

From the corner of my eye I see the familiar figure again, at the bar. I was not mistaken. It is Seb Beckett. I wonder what he's doing here.

"Di, it was Seb. I'm going over to say hi."

I get out of the booth and head over to the bar, tapping him on the shoulder. He turns and smiles.

"What a surprise to see you here Megan," he says, putting his arms around me for a hug. He doesn't seem surprised at all.

"Hiya Seb, good to see you. Are you here on your own?"

"Out with friends."

"Ah, yes me too." I point over to Dionne and Jeremy.

"Nice. I'll get these and come over to say hi."

I turn and walk back to the table. It seems a bit of a coincidence that Myles overheard me and Dionne at work, and now Seb is here. He speaks to the barman, points to our table and turns back.

I sit down, trying to scan the room to see if anyone else might be here too, but there's no one I recognise. Seb comes over, hands full of glasses. He's bought a round and places the drinks on the table before taking a seat next to Dionne.

"Do you know everyone Seb?"

"I think I should know you," he gestures to Dionne. "I'm Sebastian Beckett."

"Dionne."

"You work at Beck, don't you?"

"Yes, in finance."

"And you," he looks at Jeremy, "I do not know."

"Jeremy, this is Seb, our boss's brother and general trickster." I say.

"Now that's unfair." He genuinely looks sad.

"Okay, general Romeo and playboy trickster." He frowns again at the description, I love having the little banter we always do when I see him, it's a side I don't see from Myles.

"That's a bit unfair too, let's go back to trickster."

"Romeo trickster it is then!" He frowns again.

"So, no Myles then?" I question him, but he evades the question.

"Can't I go anywhere without him?"

"Just asking. Chill."

"So, Dionne. Tell me about yourself."

"Why?" She looks at him like his usual charms have absolutely no effect on her.

"What about you Jeremy?" He turns, realising he won't get very far with Dionne.

"Well, I live with my parents, I like Star Wars and anything…"

Seb holds his hand up to stop him. "Never mind!" He shakes his head and I feel a little protective over Jeremy.

"You're acting strange Seb, *You Okay Hun?*" As I say this, Dionne spits out the mouthful of drink she just took. I pass her a tissue but she's still laughing.

A tall blond man walks over and stands at our table. Everyone peers up to him. He's well-built and particularly good looking.

He looks around the table, wondering if he's in the right place. He looks at my friend. "Dionne?"

"Toby?" He smiles, reassured he has the right place and holds his hand out to shake her hers.

"What's going on here then?" asks Seb, looking puzzled.

"Toby is my date," Dionne says, indicating for Seb to move out of the way, so she can get past. But he doesn't move an inch.

"Is he now?" He's still not moving, just looking Toby up and down.

"Sebastian!" I chastise. "You're being weird. Move, please." I speak with an air of authority. He holds his hands up in surrender and moves out of the booth, enough to let Dionne out, but not Toby in, then regains his place.

Toby gestures to a high table nearby, Dionne picks up her drink and they stand at the table, to talk. Seb's eyes never leave them. He seems quite affected by Dionne and I wonder what he's thinking. I'm hoping he's not going to do anything stupid and ruin her night, but I wouldn't put it past him.

Chapter Twenty-Six

Myles

This is not really my scene, the place is full of overly sweaty people, the bass is too loud and what's with all this neon? But when I heard the girls making plans for this evening, I was straight on the phone to Seb, to get plans in motions.

I look over to the booth they are sitting in. Megan keeps looking over to the bar, she's obviously seen Sebastian and is looking to see if I'm around. It seems a bit obvious that they mention being here and we just so happen to turn up, especially when Megan knows I don't go out much.

She gets up and makes her way over to Seb and I see their interaction, but she heads back to her friends quite quickly. She looks amazing. Her hair is up off her neck and I imagine kissing it all the way down. She has a strapless top that pushes her full chest up into delicious spheres. And those trousers are fitted in all the right places, making her arse look squeezably magnificent.

There's three of them sitting together, unlikely pairings. Surely the bloke can't be one of their dates? He sticks out like a sore thumb. He's not dressed for this kind of atmosphere and he looks twenty years their senior. He's got *geek* written all over him.

We decided I'd keep out of their way until Seb had well and truly inserted himself into their group, then me joining them wouldn't seem so unusual. But now I'm here, I'm starting to have doubts. What if she doesn't want anything to do with me after the other night? I completely shut down on her and it's my biggest regret. My feelings for her were overpowered by the feelings of doing the wrong thing at work, living up to people's expectation, and also the thought of becoming my father.

My attention is drawn back to the booth. Who the bloody hell is this now? They are joined by someone else. A tall, blonde man, who looks like he works out. In fact he looks like a brick shit house. He moves away from the group with Dionne. I'm going to have to make myself known before some other muppet comes along. The bloke sitting with them must be Megan's date. Well I'm happy to split that little couple up.

I make my way over and slide into the seat next to Megan. It takes her a few moments to register that I'm here and she turns to me.

"Hi," I say, smiling down at her, getting an amazing view of her cleavage.

But she looks to Seb. "I thought you said he wasn't here!"

"I didn't say he wasn't here. I said, I could go places without him."

"Clearly not!" She turns back to me. "What are you doing here?"

"I heard this club was something special…"

"Bollocks!" She cuts me off. "You came here because we said we were coming."

"Okay, you got me!" I hold my hands up. "I just wanted to spend some time with you."

"You could have spent time with me the other night, but instead you decided to be a dick about it." She folds her arms across her chest with a look of annoyance, but instead of the effect she's after, she's framed her tits very nicely indeed.

"I know and I'm sorry." I give her a little smile, willing her to forgive me.

"I think we need to go to the bar," Seb says to the bloke next to Megan.

"I'm fine. I still have a drink." Jeremy holds his drink up to Seb.

"It wasn't a suggestion Jez, let's go!" He gets the message and they leave us to it.

"You planned this whole thing then? To get me on my own."

"Kind of." Okay now it's starting to sound bad.

"And to achieve what?" She seems mad, I may have to backtrack a little.

"To tell you that I really like you."

"You could have done that the other night too."

I take a breath and try to think. "I wanted to tell you away from the office." I'm just going to have to make my move.

I cup my hand around her face and lean in. She doesn't pull away, which is a good sign. I gently brush her lips with mine and whisper, "I want to kiss you away from the office." And I kiss her harder and she opens her mouth a little. My other hand finds her waist and the small slither of exposed flesh on her back. I rub my thumb over it sending, goose bumps all over her skin. "I want to touch you away from the office." She sighs and I swallow it down with another kiss. Moving closer to her neck I drop a gentle, barely touching kiss. "I want to lick you away from the office." I lick the spot just behind her ear. I can feel her pulse rise where I'm touching so I move up and whisper in her ear. "I want to fuck you away from the office."

She pulls back a bit as she takes in what I have suggested, and we look into each other's eyes. She squirms in her seat and I take the opportunity to pull her face forward to mine and our lips meet, mouths open and tongues touch. I pull her closer, totally consumed by her, the need is making my brain backfire. I've been rock hard since I sat next to her. She makes me lose control every time I'm near.

She pushes me back and breaks our contact, still panting, lust in her eyes. "What are you saying?"

"Come home with me... now!"

"I can't leave Dionne."

"She has enough people here for her. I'll get Seb to look after her."

"Yeah. Seb looking after her is exactly what I'm worried about."

"He'd never put her in danger."

"I need to speak to her first. I'm not sure this is a good idea."

"Sure." I get up out of the booth to let her out and she heads over to Dionne. They make their way out to the ladies together.

"What's going on?" Seb has made his way back over, leaving Jeremy to talk to the blonde beefcake.

"Not a lot. She's not sure it's a good idea," I explain, with a stony expression.

"Your Beckett charms didn't work on her then." I fake smile at him. He's trying to get one up on me, but I saw him getting blown out by Dionne.

"We'll have to see. She's having a conference with Dionne about it as we speak."

"She might need a bit more convincing. But it's obvious she likes you."

"But likes me enough to get over what a dick I've been?" He shrugs and the girls are back at the table, arm in arm.

Megan looks down at me and says, full of confidence and sass, "I'm not ready to go home yet. We are going for a dance." And with that statement they turn and head for the stairs.

Jeremy joins us back at the booth and I decide to go and stand at the balcony to keep an eye on them. I see them, hands joined, snaking their way through the crowd of people. They find a spot right in the middle of the neon dance floor. I can't take my eyes off her as she moves her body to the rhythm of the music, throwing her head back and laughing. Everything about this woman has me captivated.

I feel someone stand next to me. Thinking it's Seb I turn to say something, but it's the blonde guy, and he's watching them too. He turns to me. "Hi. Toby!"

"Myles!" He stretches out his hand and I take it in a quick shake and just as quickly, we move our attention away again.

We watch the girls on the dance floor and it just makes me want her even more. Both of us stand up straight, on high alert at the scene that's starting to unfold on the dancefloor. There are a couple of guys putting their hands all over the girls. I look at Toby and he se sets off to rescue them.

"Give it a minute. They'll not be happy if we go in all guns blazing. Unless it gets really bad, we can't step in."

"Right. But we can go and dance though, can't we?" He gives me a cheeky grin.

"Can we?" I reply, "I'm not much of a dancer."

"Better to be close though." Toby offers.

"Fair point, come on," I say, making my way towards the stairs, I can't lose this chance with Megan.

We make our way through the hordes of people. The place seems to get busier minute by minute. I spot the girls and point them out to Toby. They seem to have got the situation under control, moving out of the men's way every so often, so we stay back. I wouldn't call it dancing but we are moving to the beat, one of us has our eyes on the girls at all times.

We've been there about three song changes when it eventually happens. One guy moves himself in front of Megan. He bends down, grabs her round the thighs and lifts her off her feet. She pushes his shoulders to get him off, but he doesn't budge. Without a second thought I'm behind her. One arm round her waist, the other pushing him off.

"Get the fuck off her." It comes out as a growl.

"Fuck off man. Get your own." I see red. But before I can react, Toby is behind him and he's crumpled to the floor. I'm not sure what he did, but I'm impressed.

I put Megan back on her feet and she turns to face me.

"You okay babe?" She doesn't speak but raises her arms and wraps them round my neck, pulling me down so she can plant a kiss on my lips. Well I'm not going to argue with that. I reach round her and envelop her, pushing her mouth open with my tongue, to deepen our kiss.

She pulls away. "I think I'm ready to go home now," she says, looking up at me with big eyes. I don't need to be asked twice. I grab her hand and pull her out of the crowd towards the exit.

Chapter Twenty-Seven

Megan

I feel like my head is in a spin. I'm standing outside a modern-looking building waiting for Myles to pay for the taxi. I don't even know how we got here. I was pulled through the club and into a taxi before I knew where I was. I had to message both Dionne and Sean, telling them where I had gone. The rest of the journey I was being devoured by the beautiful man beside me.

"You okay? Not having second thoughts? Because you absolutely can, you know. I'll just call another cab to take you home," he says, walking up beside me.

"I'm not the one who usually changes their mind." Which is totally true. It's usually Myles flip flopping between yes and no.

He laughs and pulls me towards the building. Buzzing himself in the door and we enter a spacious and modern hallway. It's pristine. No bits of bikes, rubbish or scuffed walls that you'd find in bog standard communal spaces. No, this is next level.

We head over to the lift and he presses the button. Immediately the door opens, no waiting, no having it stuck on the top floor. And no funny smell. We step in and as the door closes Myles has me in his arms again. He smells amazing. He tastes amazing. But before I can register how great the kiss is, or how weak my legs have gone, the doors are opening again and we're heading out and towards a front door.

He unlocks the door and we step into a hallway that has two doors. He opens the first and ushers me in. My mouth drops open at the sight before me. The place is huge for a start, you could fit the ground floor of my house in this space, three times over. The place is warm and inviting, it smells of pine and linen and the lighting has a soft glow.

To the left is an L shaped sofa, like mine except bigger and squishier. Straight in front are some steps leading up, with a glass and steel banister. I never even considered his flat would be on two floors, I didn't even know that was possible.

To the right is a modern, sleek-looking kitchen with an island in the middle housing the sink and a funny looking hose for a tap. Unlike mine, there's nothing cluttering the worktops. It seems everything must have a place, but that place is obviously hidden away. Where's the fridge and the cooker? He said he had a fancy coffee machine but it's nowhere to be seen.

I'm snapped out of my thoughts when I feel Myles' hand on my lower back. "Do you want a drink?" He navigates me into the kitchen and I lean on the island as he looks through the concealed fridge. If I had needed to find it I wouldn't have known where to look, everything is hidden.

"No, I don't think so."

"Have a drink of water. Your body will thank me for it tomorrow." He opens another cupboard to get out a glass and pours me a drink. He hands it straight to me, knowing that I won't drink it if I put it down.

I drink half and put the glass on the island as he moves closer, pushing his body against mine. He bends down to plant another kiss on my lips. My whole body is vibrating at his closeness. His arms close around me, as he once again finds that slither of exposed skin and the contact feels electric. His hands move down my body and over my bum, squeezing gently, then moving further in one movement he lifts me to sit on the worktop.

Our faces are now at the same level and he deepens the kiss further, pushing my legs open for him to stand in between.

Every bit of him is rock hard. He moves his hips which rubs his erection over my core and I'm wondering if he can feel how wet I am through our clothes. He releases my lips and I pant as he trails kisses down my neck and chest. My body is on fire, heat rising from my toes all the way up my body.

I want to touch him. I push him back and our eyes connect, the eerie grey almost gone with the size of his dilated pupils. I start to undo the top button and trail my fingers down his chest with each button I open. Once the last one is done, I push the shirt over his shoulders, revealing his bare chest, taut and sculptured. He has a speckling of dark hair that peters out and follows a faint line that disappears into his trousers.

I start my own trail as my lips gently touch the skin on his neck, just under his ear. Myles takes a sharp intake of breath and his skin is covered in goose bumps. It's good to know I affect him as much as he affects me. I raise my head to meet his and he starts another frenzied kiss. His hands, which have been scooting up and down my back, are now heading over my rear again. He pulls me forward and tilts my hips. I have no doubt that if I was wearing a dress, he would be almost inside me.

As if reading my mind, which is a funny habit he has, he breaks away and says, "Upstairs?" At this point I don't know my own mind, let alone be able to form a coherent sentence, so I just nod. He wraps my legs around his waist, scoops me off the worktop and, with big strides, takes us both upstairs.

He kicks open the door to another huge room and lowers me onto a massive bed. He joins me, my legs still wrapped tight around his waist. Placing his arms either side of my head he looks at me. "Is here okay?"

I nod but add, "I do need to use the bathroom though." He pushes himself up and off the bed, grabbing my hand and pulling me up. Turning me around, he gestures to a door and I make my way to it.

I actually do need to go to the bathroom, but I also needed a few moments to breathe, to contemplate what is happening and make sure I'm making the decision with my head and not my vagina!

I walk back into the bedroom. He is lying on the bed, arms behind his head. "You okay? We don't have to do this if you don't want to."

"I do want to. I just needed a minute for my brain to engage."

I stand at the side of the bed as he moves to the edge. He's sitting with his legs off the bed. He pulls me between his thighs again. "As long as you're sure." I nod. "Then we better get you naked!"

Undoing the button and zip of my trousers he lowers them down to the floor and takes my hand as I step out of them. He smiles as he comes face to face with my black lace thong. He turns me quickly to undo my corset, taking it from my body and launching it across the room. He turns me back just as quickly.

"So beautiful!" he says, almost to himself, as he presses his lips to my stomach. "Now these need to go." He hooks his fingers into the sides of my underwear and pulls them slowly down my legs. As I step out of them he lifts one of my feet onto the bed, opening me up. He moves his mouth slowly up my thigh with alternate kisses, licks and nibbles.

As he gets to the top, without warning, his tongue connects and licks all the way up the length of my hot, wet folds. I feel like I'll pass out with arousal. He moans as he pulls away. "You taste amazing!" I never knew I could get turned on so much by words, but that's twice it's had the desired effect. "Give me more, I want more. I want to feel you come on my tongue and then I want to push deep inside and feel you pulsate around my cock!"

I'm done. This man can have me anyway he wants, as long as he keeps talking to me like that. Right now I would do absolutely anything he asked. He licks again and pulls me closer to his mouth as he makes circles around my throbbing nerves. I can hear myself moaning in between panting breaths. But it seems so disconnected, like I'm having some kind of out-of-body experience. I feel the arousal starting at the bottom of my spine, working its heat through my body as he continues to eat me. And then, like a flash of fireworks exploding in my stomach, I go stiff. The assault on my senses continues and he never breaks pace, until I feel my body fall and he pulls away to catch me, his strong arms wrapped around my body as I am straddled across his lap.

"I really enjoyed that, did you?" I don't think he really needed to ask, my body told him everything. He doesn't need to wait for the answer and he kisses me on the mouth. I taste myself on his lips and I open my mouth to let him in. I can feel him harden even more and I realise he still has trousers on.

"You've still got clothes on!"

"I can rectify that." He lifts me off him and onto the bed. Standing, he takes down his trousers and boxers in one swift movement. I'm not exactly inexperienced when it comes to men, but Myles is definitely the biggest I've seen. My eyes widen as I'm not sure how he will fit. "Don't worry, I won't hurt you."

I move up the bed to put my head on the pillow and he crawls over me, kissing up my body as he goes. Oh my god, this man is something else. He stretches out to reach the bedside drawer and picks out a condom. He rips the packet with his mouth and pulls back to put it on.

Lowering himself again, he pulls my legs round his hips and pushes inside me. I feel my body shiver and a gasp leaves my mouth. He holds still. "Babe. You need to relax, you need to let me in." Easier said than done.

He leans forwards and kisses me, knowing this is the way to talk to my body. He must feel my body open up so he pushes all the way, and I'm filled with him, surrounded by him, my brain misfires and our eyes meet. He starts moving and my body takes over, and it's all a haze of moans, panting and a feeling of ecstasy.

"Oh god Megan, you feel so good wrapped around me. I'm not sure I'm gonna last much longer with you squeezing my cock so hard." His words push me over the edge and my body explodes. My legs shake and I call his name. I'm all done. My brain has checked out. With a growl he moves at a supercharged rate and his eyes roll to the back of his head. He stills and shakes, whispering my name as he comes with an explosion.

I think I'm in shock. I have never had an experience like that before. I have definitely never had two orgasms like that, and definitely not one from penetration. Size really does matter and so does knowing a woman's body. I really don't want to think about how much experience he has with other women, but I know you only get that good from practice.

He's lying on his back, panting, sweat glistening on our skin. I turn myself onto my front, next to him, my body still shaking and limp. "Give me a few minutes to be able to feel the rest of my body and then we'll go and clean up."

"I think I'll need more than a few minutes," I say, and he starts to laugh. It's infectious. He smiles down at me and brushes his thumb over my cheek.

· ♥ · ♥ · ♥ · ♥ · ♥ ·

I slowly come around from my sleep and stretch out, feeling the twinge of muscles I don't usually use. I lean over to wake Myles, but the rest of the bed is empty and cold. I lift my head up in confusion and see a note on the bedsheets.

Megs,
Had to go into the office. Make yourself at home.
Myles x

When he says *make yourself at home*, does that mean go and snoop round his flat? I'm pretty sure it does. I pull myself out of bed and head for the bathroom. I know for a fact that the shower is amazing because he made me come twice in that shower last night, which gives another meaning to the words *steamy sex*. I make a mental reminder to have a really long shower after breakfast.

We went in the shower to clean up, but only ended up getting messy, both in the shower and when we got out. By the end of our mammoth sex session, he had me on all fours, begging for more. It was by far the hottest experience I have ever had.

I barely noticed any of the details of this place last night. My head was full of lust and vodka. I grab Myles' shirt from last night, which is draped over the back of an arm chair, and have a quick look upstairs.

His bedroom is very masculine. The walls have dark grey, linen-textured wallpaper, the headboard is grey and the bedding is a different shade of grey. In fact, looking around, the only thing that isn't grey is the wood flooring.

He has an en suite the size of my full bathroom, with that amazing shower, and next to that a walk-in closet, which obviously I'm going to look through.

If you can imagine a picture-perfect closet, with everything in the correct place and special compartments for things like ties and watches, Myles' closet is exactly that. Unlike mine. Maybe because there isn't room for a closet, just a wardrobe with clothes thrown on the chair in the corner. The nickname of *Mr Designer Suit Beckett* is even more apt as I snoop in the closet. There are suits of all labels filling one whole wardrobe space.

I have a real urge to move things about and see whether he notices, to unravel the perfect picture. I take one of his carefully rolled up ties, unwind it and shove it back in the drawer with a giggle.

Moving on I wander into the hallway and stick my head round the remaining doors. A bathroom with an amazing-looking deep bath, I file that nugget of information in my brain for later. A spare bedroom done in light greens with green fern printed sheets. The final room is an office with a desk and a bookshelf. I wonder why he has this when he clearly stays at work all hours. Wouldn't it be nicer to work from home?

I make my way down the stairs and realise I haven't seen my phone for a while. Or my shoes, for that matter. My clutch bag is on the pristine worktop, the only thing that's on show, and I check it to find my phone. I spot my shoes next to the sofa.

I fish my phone out of the bag but the battery has died. Where would I find a charger? I can't even ask Myles because I'd need my phone to do that! The coffee table has a gap down the middle, so I figure out it must open in some way. After a few failed attempts I can't for the life of me find how, so I give up rather quickly. Walking round the living area I spot a charging port, the kind you place your phone on to charge when you're not using it. I place my phone down and wait for the charging symbol to light up.

I definitely need coffee this morning, but where is this coffee machine? If it's like the one at mine, I'll not be able to figure it out anyway. I'm in the kitchen staring at the cupboards with no indication of where everything might be, so I just randomly open them all up.

I think you can tell a lot about people from their kitchen cupboards. Myles' are all neat and tidy, everything has a place. My cupboards have things stuffed in them because I don't know where else to put them, or I need to tidy up quickly when people pop round.

I have given up on the idea of coffee and open the fridge to find some fruit juice, that'll have to do. I take my drink and sit on the sofa to check on my phone. Luckily the charger is super-fast and I have enough battery to check it.

It turns on and notifications spring up immediately. Many from Dionne, a few from Sean and Beth, but surprisingly none from Myles. I dial him to ask a completely made-up question, because I just want to hear his voice. The phone goes straight to answer machine, which is odd because he never turns it off.

I distract myself by checking Dionne's 182 – maybe an exaggeration – messages and decide to call her because it will take way less time.

"Oh My God!"

"Hello to you too Dionne."

"Hiya Babe. You'll never guess what happened to me last night."

"Go on!" I'm interested now.

"Well... I went home with Toby."

"Okay!" Is that it?

"But Seb came too."

"What?!" That can't be right.

"You heard right."

"So... you had a cosy night in watching a film or something?"

"No! I had a rampant night of sex with not one, but two absolute gods!"

"At the same time?" I didn't think Seb would be one to share.

"Yep!"

"Oh my god! And how did you leave it?"

"Well, we all fell asleep together and this morning Seb dropped me back home."

"And are you gonna see either or both of them again?"

"I don't know. I hadn't really thought that far. But I have to say, I have never had so many orgasms in my life. In fact, I think I had more last night than I have in total."

"Wow!"

"Sorry Babe, I didn't ask. How was last night, where are you now?"

"I'm still at his flat.... Alone! He got called into the office and he left me to sleep."

"On a Saturday! How was last night? How did you leave it?"

"It really was amazing, but we've not had chance to talk about it because he had gone by the time I woke up."

"So, what's your plan?"

"Dunno. Get a shower, see if and when he comes home, I suspect. I've tried to call him but his phone is off."

"That's odd. He never turns off his phone."

I feel the heat of panic rising up my neck and boiling my face. "I know, right? Should I worry?"

"Nah, I'm sure it'll be fine." I bloody hope so.

"I'm gonna take a shower and see what's happening after that."

"Okay. Keep me posted!"

"Will do. See ya!" I hang up and reply to some of the other messages before I head for a shower.

· ♥ · ♥ · ♥ · ♥ · ♥ ·

It's nearly lunch time and still no word from Myles. I tried him again earlier, but his phone is still going straight to answer machine and it's starting to really piss me off now. I mean, a quick message is all it takes. I'm showered and back in my own clothes. I didn't want to do the walk of shame, so I raided the closet for a hoodie. It swamps me, but it's better than a corset top in the middle of the day. I try to call Myles for the final time, because literally it's three strikes and you're out! But again, it goes straight to answer machine. Should I call his desk phone? Without thinking I dial that too and it's engaged.

I order an Uber and leave the flat. It's amazing what a difference 12 hours can make. Last night I was so happy. Orgasmic, for want of a better word, and now I feel deflated and betrayed. I keep questioning whether something might have happened, or has he just gone cold again? I thought this time would be different, but who am I kidding? He has form, and why I couldn't engage my brain and realise that last night, I have no idea.

The Uber drops me home and I push through the front door. I am met with the smell of coffee and warm bread. Maybe I should just stick with Sean, he makes the best fake boyfriend.

"Hey chick." He greets me with a smile. But when I don't reciprocate, his face falls. "What's happened?"

"Nothing, I'm fine. But I am starving."

"Tell me!" He knows me too well.

"No, it's fine."

"Megs!"

"Fine." I sit on the sofa next to him and take a deep breath. "So! You know I went back to Myles' flat?" He nods so I continue. "Well, we had a good time, great actually. And when I woke up, he'd gone. Left a message saying he'd been called into the office."

"It happens."

"But he never came back, and his phone keeps going straight to answer machine."

"Oh no!"

"That's bad, isn't it?"

"I'd say so. I mean, something may have happened." He pulls a face. "But also, He might have lost track of time, or been on calls constantly. Or... I'm so sorry Megs." He gives me the knowing look, of a man that has ghosted someone before too.

"What do I do? I'm not gonna be that girl who keeps checking her phone, waiting for him to call."

"Okay then. Turn it off. Leave it here and we'll go out for the day."

"Why can't the men I date be more like you?"

"Cos I'm one in a million." He gives me his winning smile. You'd never think he doesn't give love the time of day, the way he's going on.

"I'll go get changed."

"Turn your phone off."

I turn off my phone and throw it at him, so he can be gatekeeper.

Chapter Twenty-Eight

I've kept myself busy all weekend. Well, in all honesty, Sean kept me busy. My phone has been more off than on, and I'm just trying not to let the anxiety of seeing Myles today embed itself completely in my head. And you guessed it, he never called or left a message.

I decided to go all bombshell in my sexy but professional outfit with my hair up in a tight bun on my head. I'm trying to portray a confident *Fuck You!* persona, but inside I'm actually crying and humiliated.

I push through the revolving doors and I'm so glad that Cruella isn't on reception desk anymore. I tap the entry plate with my card and go to walk through but the gate doesn't open. I try it again and it flashes red. You cannot be serious. Has he fired me as well, just to top off my humiliation? Again, red! I make my way over to reception.

"Hey Finn, my card isn't working."

"Hey Megan! Let me just check the system." He looks at his screen and looks back at me with a puzzled expression. "It says to keep you at reception and call Ms Hughes." He picks up his phone and dials. "Hi. I have Megan Scott at reception... Okay then." He puts the phone down. "She's coming down." Finn gives me a clipped smile and I feel totally humiliated.

Oh my god, what is actually happening? I start biting my fingernails, I can't even remember the last time I did that. I see the lift opening and the tall, elegant figure of Imogen Hughes comes towards us, her heels click-clacking on the marble floor. I think I'm going to be sick.

She sees me and gives a cheek-cracking smile, opening her arms out to greet me. "Megan! How exciting! I'm so pleased I get to have you with me."

"With you?" I'm confused.

"Yes. I have been begging Myles to have you for ages. It was beneath you working for Mr Grumpy on the fifth floor."

"So, I've been moved?"

"He didn't tell you? Maybe I was meant to tell you, but I got a bit over excited when he gave it the go ahead."

"Who is his PA now then?" Please don't say they brought back Cruella... I swear I would walk out right now.

"Eric. He was originally gonna be stepping in for Millie's maternity, but we did a switcheroo." Millie is Imogen's PA, who, it seems, has been pregnant and the size of a house since forever.

"Is this job only temporary then? Maternity cover?"

"Definitely not. I want you on my team until they cart me out of the place, and then I still expect you to be carrying the lot of them afterwards. Millie has indicated that she would be dropping her hours when she gets back anyway. It's just been perfect timing."

"Hasn't it just." Oh yeah, just perfect, the angry boils up my body. I'm not sure which way round this has happened. Did he move me, then sleep with me, or did he sleep with me then decide to move me? Either way, it's a dick move.

"Let's get you settled in and then you can fetch your things from the fifth floor." She puts her arm around my shoulders and manoeuvres me to the lift. She's fizzing with excitement and I'm fizzing with anger. I'll never forgive him for this.

I'll give Imogen her dues, the Marketing Department is A LOT more energetic and exciting than the fifth floor. It's so much more relaxed and the energy is off the scale. The space is even less formal, and they have an area specifically for people to throw balls at each other to brainstorm. Totally mental!

I went up to the fifth floor to pick up my things, but Myles was in a meeting. I left a message with Eric to tell Myles to go fuck himself. I doubt he'll pass it on. The phone rings on my desk and I answer it. "Hello Imogen Hughes' office, Megan speaking."

"Megan!" It's him, absolute cheek of him. "It's Myles."

"Yes!"

"I'm sorry you found out about the job like that."

"You slept with me, then you demoted me. I don't think it matters how the news was passed on."

"That's not how..."

I cut him off, "Myles, I will never forgive you for this." I hang up before he can say another word.

It's nearly time for lunch, so I go for Dionne because I haven't had chance to update her yet. We're now on the same floor, just a different wing, so I walk along and come up behind her.

"What you doing?" I ask, still unnoticed. She jumps a few inches out of her chair. "Obviously doing something a bit suss!"

"Shhh!" She turns, putting her finger on her lips. Then she gives me a funny look, probably because I never usually pick her up from her desk. "Why are you gracing the fourth floor?"

"I live here now."

"Eh?!"

"Come on, I'll fill you in over lunch." I practically drag her out of her seat and march towards the lift.

We sit down in a secluded part of the office restaurant, so I can tell her without anyone listening in. "I came in this morning and I've been demoted!"

"No way!"

"Yep. Only knew about it as I was stopped at the barriers this morning."

"He didn't tell you? No hand over, no nothing?"

"Not a thing. I'm fuming!"

"Wow! That's a proper dick move!"

"Even more reason to take up martial arts classes."

"Hang on, you said self-defence." She looks a bit concerned now.

"I know but now I really want to hurt someone. Have you heard from your two men?"

"In bits and pieces. Nothing of any substance."

"Well, that's men all over. I know it's only Monday, but do you fancy a quieter night out on Friday, I'm gonna call a girls' night at my local pub."

"Do I get to meet your friends?" She starts bouncing like a five-year-old who has just been told he's going to see Santa.

"Yes. I'll message them now."

Me

> SOS. Need a therapy session on Friday, Dog and Swan. I'm bringing my friend Dionne

Lizzie

> Oh god, what's happened now?

Emma

> Ben's in Edinburgh so its good timing for me

Beth

> Hell yes!

"We're on! Come round to mine, it's not far from the pub."

"Good plan."

We chat a bit more, I fill her in on my friends a little bit and eat our lunch. Though nothing really sits well in my stomach, I'm too full of rage to enjoy my food.

Dionne looks at her watch. "Better get back to business." Our lunch break is over way too fast, and we both head up to the fourth floor.

Chapter Twenty-Nine

Myles

Well, this week has been an absolute shit show. Whatever could go wrong, went wrong, starting on Saturday. I wanted nothing more than to have a lazy day in bed with Megan, but Seb called me with some more information about the strange goings on with the sustainability project. She looked so peaceful when I left, I kissed her on the forehead. But everything after that was a bit of a whirlwind of phone calls and heated debates. When it was past lunchtime and my phone had died, I realised I had neglected Megan. I'd left her in my flat and hadn't told her where anything was or when I might be back.

I got some power back in my phone and turned it on to find three missed calls and several messages from her. I called and it went straight to answer machine and before I had time to message my phone rang again. I didn't leave the office until after it got dark. I really fucked things up.

As a consequence of that, and the stuff that was unfolding in the company, I couldn't let her know about the change of job. I did leave it in the hands of Imogen, but I think our wires were crossed. Megan is particularly upset. She thinks I have demoted her because we had sex, and knowing that's what she thinks and now doesn't want anything to do with me has sent me spiralling.

My new PA isn't a patch on Megan. I knew he wouldn't be, but needs must. It's another evening in the office for me, trying to catch up on everything, when I haven't got the motivation. There's a knock on my door and it opens.

"Hello Mr Myles, I have cake." Thank goodness for Kateryna, if it wasn't for her, I probably wouldn't eat or speak to another human in person. "What wrong?" Her face falls. Is it that obvious how shitty I feel?

"Everything!"

"Things not go to plan over weekend?"

"You could say that. I spent some time with Megan."

"You don't have feelings?"

"I do very much have feelings, but I've messed it up. I took your advice though."

"You told her your feelings?"

"Well no, but I moved her jobs, so she wouldn't be directly under me, so to speak. But she didn't take it well."

"You told her first?"

"Erm... no."

"You idiot man!" She throws her arms up in the air. "I said to tell her feelings. Tell her you loved her!"

"Well..." She's now walking round my office waving her hands about and ranting in Ukrainian.

"You no listen Myles. What she say?"

"She thinks I demoted her because we had sex. And she hasn't been demoted. She's still on the same wage."

"You took her from top," she puts her hand at eye level, "to middle." She lowers her hand, indicating the drop. "It demotion!"

I pull my hand over my face, I really didn't see it like that. "Can you help me?"

"I can't even look at you!" She storms out. Great! That's two women I've pissed off. I turn back to look at my screen, at the spreadsheets I've been pouring over all day and got nowhere.

After ten minutes of getting nowhere, Kateryna walks back in. She doesn't knock, she just places a cup of tea and a piece of cake on my desk before walking out, shaking her head.

· ♥ · ♥ · ♥ · ♥ · ♥ ·

It's the end of the week and I've got myself into a bit of a bad habit. Every day at about 8.55am I sit watching the CCTV on my computer screen to check that she gets into work okay. And every day, at 5pm without fail, I check the CCTV to watch her leave. It's pathetic. Although it makes me feel a little better knowing we're in the same building, the pain in my chest hasn't left and I'm even grumpier than usual. Eric is regretting his new position, I can tell. He winces whenever I open my office door.

I tried several ways to get Megan up to the fifth floor, but she always sends someone else. I've tried to get Dionne's attention when she comes up, but she just shakes her head. I actually miss quirky Dionne too. The fifth floor isn't as vibrant and happy without the two of them.

The working week is coming to a close, but I doubt I'll leave the office before 9pm. I go to bring up the CCTV to watch for her and my desk phone rings.

"Hello Mr Beckett, it's Finn on security. You asked us to inform you if someone came in for Megan at work again."

"Shit! I'm on my way!" I grab my phone and all but run down the corridor. This can't keep happening to her. I decide to take the stairs because the lift will be packed and take forever at this time of the evening.

I skid out of the stairwell and into the foyer at the same time Megan is approached by a really tall man. It's not Darren, but you can't be too careful.

"Megan!" I say as I get closer. The man is smiling at her and squeezes her shoulder. She jumps at my voice and turns to look at me with a shocked look on her face.

"Myles, what are you doing?" I make a move to pull her away from him without even realising what I'm doing. I stop dead at her words.

"Who is this?" I sound accusatory and I have no right. The man looks me up and down and puts his arms around Megan's shoulders, confidently.

"I'm the boyfriend!" He smirks at me. Megan looks up at him with a surprised look on her face. Perhaps it has taken this moment to show her his intentions. Megan looks back at me with a curt smile, he turns her and they walk out of the building together.

A hundred thoughts fog my mind. Did what happened push her towards someone else? Have I been one of many? Have I lost her forever? I thought I'd have some time to win her back. I realise what I've lost and I feel like I've been winded. Like someone has kicked me in the chest. I turn and walk slowly back to the lift. Alone, I head back upstairs to wallow in self-pity.

Chapter Thirty

Megan

We open the door to the pub and the familiar aroma of beer, sweat and something I'd rather not identify wafts over us.

"What even is this place?" Dionne says. I'm not sure if she's in awe or absolutely horrified.

"This, my dear, is The Dog and Swan!" I open my arms out as a big reveal. "And that bunch of reprobates are my friends." I point over to our usual place on the sofa. I guide her through the groups of people, the place is busy tonight again. I look over to the bar and give Mitch a wave. I catch his eye as he's serving someone, and he waves back with a big smile on his face. "And that's my favourite barman, Mitch!"

We get to my friends and they beam up at us both. Beth stands up first. "You must be Dionne. Welcome to the madhouse. I'm Beth."

"Hi Beth, are you the one with Jonah and Poppy?"

"That's me. Oh god, what did they do?"

"No, nothing. Megan just said about babysitting."

"Hiya, I'm Emma."

"Lizzie!" Always to the point. "I got you the same drink as Megan. If you're not keen, I'll go get you something else."

"Thanks. Lovely to meet you all."

We sit down and the chat starts back up. There's a lot to catch up on.

"Then I get a call from the headteacher asking us to go in and talk about Jonah." Beth continues with the story she started before we came in. "So, we go in and she says she's quite concerned about some of the language Jonah is using at school. Naturally, I thought he might have dropped the F bomb in class, but no! He told his class teacher to stop asking him questions because he was having an existential crisis. Well... you can imagine. I just burst out laughing. It was hilarious. But the headteacher was not laughing. She said the teacher got upset because she had to google what it meant."

"I can see how that would upset some teachers, especially primary teachers," Lizzie laughs. She knows all too well working in a secondary school full of hormonal kids. "It's not Jonah's fault he has a higher IQ than her!"

"Well exactly, and I said as much to the headteacher, but it didn't go down well. Not along with him telling his teaching assistant to *chill her boots*, and telling the dinner lady she should really pick another profession."

"Eeee, what a character!" Emma laughs.

"That's my boy!" I say, proud as punch of this kid.

"And then there's the mother-in-law telling us we should start saving up now for him to go to Oxford University. Can you imagine Jonah somewhere like that?"

"You should have heard what he was telling my boss when I was babysitting. Told him about the time I got stuck on the slide. Oh my god, I was so embarrassed."

"Can we just go back a step or two," says Emma. "Your boss helped you babysit?"

"Kind of. But there's a whole other story to go along with that. Dionne can fill you in while I go to the bar." I get up and Dionne starts telling them what's been going. To be fair, I'm sick of telling the tale, it brings back all the feelings.

Putting the drinks on the table, I hear Dionne finish off the story. "No, not a word."

"That's awful. Have you spoken to HR?" Emma says, looking towards me.

"No. What's the point? I'd rather not draw attention to it. I just feel so stupid."

"In Myles' defence, I'm not sure, in his head, it was meant to happen like that. I saw the way he looked at you in that club. And Seb said something about finally getting his act together," Dionne explains.

"Wait, what?"

"It came back to me the other day, and I forgot about it again until now."

"Has he tried to talk to you about it?" Beth looks concerned.

"He rang and I shut him down. And then he's been trying to get me on errands upstairs, which is just a ploy, so I send someone else."

"But he is all kinds of gorgeous." Beth has hearts in her eyes again.

"True!"

"But you think everyone is gorgeous." Emma says.

"And all the men that I have commented on, have been. Ben being a good example."

"Do you remember when we met Ben and his friends and instead of saying hello, you blurted out that he was gorgeous?" I remind Beth and she goes a funny shade of pink.

"I was just saying what was on my mind. Emma will vouch for his gorgeousness."

"I will indeed." Dionne pulls a face not understanding, so Emma shows her a picture on her phone.

"Wow!"

"Yes, wow!"

"And he's your husband?" Dionne asks.

"Noooo! I suppose he's my toyboy!"

"Anyway, back to Megan. If things had gone smoother, would you have wanted a relationship with him?" Lizzie's back on track.

"I really, really like Myles. But I don't like the person he becomes when he puts on that suit. He shuts down and stops communicating."

"The not communicating is totally a man thing. Jonathan does it all the time. I think that's why we split up."

"Oh! And to add another layer of shitshow to the mix. Sean picked me up from work tonight. Myles came rushing over out of nowhere and started with all the questions."

"It shows he cares at least."

"Well, Sean only went and said he was my boyfriend. So not only does he now think I'm a crazy woman, he also thinks I'm easy for picking up someone else so quickly. Or even being with him while I had someone else."

"Doesn't he know about Sean?" Emma asks, knowing how close we are.

"He knows about Sean, but he's never met him. And Sean only introduced himself as my boyfriend because he knew that. He thought it was hilarious."

"Men!"

"And how is it with you and Jonathan now?" You never quite know what their relationship status is.

"Same. We get on, we have great sex, but we also like our own space."

"Now, do you both like your own space or is it just you?" Beth laughs.

"I don't know. He hasn't said, which kind of proves the point. He's currently still going on like a dick about Sienna's boyfriend. Who, might I add, he has terrified with his overbearing dadness."

"Keeping with the overbearing masculinity. What happened with Ben and Charlotte's new boyfriend?" I ask, before turning to Dionne to explain. "Ben found out he's a dad, all's good. The baby mama gets a boyfriend, and he goes all alpha male."

"Ah well. They are having a right bromance now. They're talking about taking lads' trip together and everything. Honestly, it's ridiculous. But I suppose it makes for happy families. I think Ben will be heartbroken if Charlotte breaks up with this guy."

"I think Dionne is feeling all left out, not being able to join in with this gossip," I say with a smirk. "Tell them who you went home with last Friday!"

Dionne looks all sheepish. "You're not gonna get all judgy with me, are you?"

"Of course not. We've all done crazy shit, makes life more interesting," says Lizzie, the one you would think would be the most judgemental, but is actually super cool about everything. I suppose she's heard a lot of crazy shit in her job.

"Well, I had a date, well three, but that's a different story. I went home with him... and someone else tagged along." She's still looking sheepish.

"A threesome? Mint!"

"Another woman?" Beth asks, brows knitted together.

"No!"

"Even better. I'm kind of jealous," Lizzie says.

"But where did everything go?" Beth pulls a face like she's trying to work it out.

"Beth, lovely... just google it when you get home. But not on the kids' tablet." Lizzie says with a grin.

"Was it good?" The girls are hanging on for every detail.

"Oh god, yes! I have to say, it was the best sex of my life."

"Wow! That's a very big statement to make!"

"I know. And I usually find the better sex comes when you know someone a bit better, rather than a one night stand. Until now, that is."

"And are you gonna go there again?"

"I think it was a more of a *right time, right place* kind of experience. And the other guy makes things a bit complicated."

"Why so?" asks Lizzie.

"Erm... well he's Myles' brother. Bit close to home on both the personal and work side of things."

"Tricky!" says Beth sounding a lot like Jonah. They all look pensive, probably trying to work out what they would do and how everything could work out.

I love that Dionne fits in so well with my friends. It could seem like an unkind move dropping her in it like that. But I know my friends are nothing but supportive and this way makes Dionne instantly one of us. I decide I'll add her to group chat once I get home, now she has officially been adopted.

"Whose round is it?" I break the silence and Beth gets up and heads to the bar, while the rest of us chatter on about everything and nothing. I love my nights out here, it feels like home.

Chapter Thirty-One

It's no normal Wednesday night. For a start we are wearing gym gear, which in itself is unheard of. We push the heavy double doors open, and walk into a large hall that smells of old books, fresh tea and old people. We are at the local community centre to start our self-defence class.

"Are you sure we have the right place?" Dionne asks.

As I look around the room, crash mats on the floor, there are four other people. Two older women – and when I say older I'm talking in their 80s covered in Lycra – a short man wearing an oversized hoodie and joggers – when I say oversized, think about when you got handed down clothes and they were way too big, but your mum always said you'd grow into them, and you thought *only if I was a 6 foot body builder called Jeff* – and a young woman who is looking around nervously.

"I'm pretty sure." I look around and a man's voice speaks from behind as someone enters the room after us.

"Hey Ladies. Are you here for the self-defence class?" We both turn to look at him. He's an average height and just looks like a normal bloke in his late forties. I expected he'd look something like The Rock and I'm now wondering if we have come to the right place.

"Yes, I messaged. I'm Megan and this is Dionne."

"Ah yes, welcome to the class." He makes his way to the front and turns to face everyone.

"Okay everyone, just to make sure we are all in the correct place." Dionne looks at me, eyebrows raised. "I'm Martin and this is self-defence for beginners. It's a six-session course, same time and place every week. If you feel confident and want to get a bit further, I do an advanced session that follows on after this one."

There's mumbling around the room but no one leaves.

"I always find it best for everyone to get to know each other a bit more before we start. We're gonna be working closely with each other, so I want you to all feel comfortable. We'll go round the room, if each person can tell us your name and your reasons for coming. I'll start... My name is Martin and I'm a black belt in karate. My reason for coming is that I want to empower people to be able to get themselves out of tricky situations."

He points to the two old women next. "Hi! My name is Betty and this is my friend Veronica. We have come because we wanted to get out a bit more and you can never be too careful nowadays." Veronica does a little wave and we all wave back. All eyes move over to the undersized man.

"Hi, I'm John and I'm here because I seem to be the one who always gets targeted in a group." Martin nods and we all look at the young woman next to him who is fidgeting with her jumper sleeves.

"Erm yes... I'm... I'm Verity." She pauses as if weighing up what to say next. "Erm I'm here because I was attacked."

"I'm so sorry to hear that," Martin says. "I hope this class can give you a little bit of confidence in protecting yourself going forward." She nods sheepishly, and everyone turns to us.

"Hi I'm Megan. I'm here because my abusive ex tried to grab me and someone else had to rescue me."

"Well hopefully this class will teach you how to rescue yourself," Martin says.

"That's the plan."

"Hi, I'm Dionne and I'm with her." She points to me.

"Excellent. Well, it is lovely to meet you all. First things first, let's warm up a bit. We are gonna be moving about and maybe activating muscles we haven't used in a while."

We all follow along and he swings his arms about and stretches this way and that.

"Okay. Before we do any moves there are a few things we can do before we need them. The first thing is to avoid putting yourself in an unsafe situation." He looks around the room because I'm pretty sure all the women have rolled their eyes. "I know you are gonna say that every situation is potentially unsafe, and we shouldn't have to change our behaviour. I completely agree with you, but the world is the way it is, and bad people exist, so we need to do what we can to lower that potential risk.

"Secondly, the initial defence mode is flight. Get yourself out of the situation the quickest and easiest way you can and then run until you are safe.

"Thirdly, there won't be any MMA-style flinging people about. Well, not until advanced class. We will be aiming to hit vital points on the attacker's body to render them incapable of continuing an attack.

"Fourthly, I will teach you that if those things have not worked and you are being held by your attacker, how to get away."

"There's one other thing I would like to say. If you are ever attacked, even if you aren't hurt or didn't see who it was, please report it to the police. I know that its often not handled well enough, but if its recorded officially, an issue can be identified and hopefully dealt with. We don't want attacks just brushed under the carpet. The more it's reported, the more they have to take action."

There is a noise at the back of the room as someone comes in late. We all turn to see a young man, probably in his late teens or early twenties, in sportswear. He doesn't look like someone who would need these classes.

"I have roped in Will, my son, to help us out with the demonstrations. But he is, as always, fashionably late." Will mouths sorry to everyone as he walks to the front of the room but takes a too-long look over at Verity. "Right, pair-up people." We all move about and the class starts with excited chatter.

· ♥ · ♥ · ♥ · ♥ · ♥ ·

As we approach the end, I admit to myself that I have enjoyed every bit of this class. It's been fun and we've all had a little giggle at our attempts at manoeuvring our partners about. Our octogenarian friends walk over to us and Betty, who seems to be the spokesperson, speaks. "We were thinking of popping over the road for a quick drink, if you fancy joining us?"

"Why not! Verity, John, do you fancy a quick drink?" John nods but Verity looks unsure.

Betty looks at Verity. "The more we get to know each other, the more comfortable we'll feel throwing each other about." Her words seem to have the desired effect as Verity nods in compliance.

We make our way out of the room, all buzzing and chatting. I look back to see Will pick up his things and head out after us. "Will!" I shout. "Do you not have to stay for the next class?"

"No, they don't need me."

"Why don't you join us, if you haven't got any other plans?"

"Erm..." He looks at Verity and she gives a cute little smile. I think I see Will's cheeks blush. "Okay then, why not?" I think we might have a budding romance starting here. Let's just wait and see.

Chapter Thirty-Two

Myles

I'm not sure how much more I can take. My head is clogged with thoughts of things I have no control over. On top of my already packed work schedule, this thing with the sustainability project is taking up a lot of my headspace. I say *thing* because I really don't know what's happening. Everywhere I look I come up blank. And then I get a nugget of information and it throws another spanner in the works because I don't want to believe what it's saying.

Then there's Megan! I am pining for her like a love-sick puppy. I check where she is at any point in the day. I make sure she is in work, I make sure she leaves work, I make sure she's having a lunch break. I've given up on trying to get her attention because she won't even engage with me. Especially now she has someone else in the picture.

I'm finding it uncomfortable being in the flat. I know it's not a rational thought, but it just reminds me how much I fucked up. How she could have been spending time with me there, but she isn't. In some ways I wish we hadn't slept together, because then I wouldn't have moved her away from me, and at least I could have her in my life in one form, as my PA. I mean, what would be better, going on in the same way on an eternal loop of boss and PA, or to have had that amazing time with her, where she made me feel something, feel alive, loved, and then for it to have been taken from me? I just don't have the answer.

It's mid-week, I think. The days are just merging together. Every evening I get a lecture from Kateryna about staying too late, working too hard, not eating enough. At least I didn't burn my bridges there, I know her nagging at me just shows she cares.

It's 8.55am and I've had the CCTV on my screen for the past ten minutes, waiting for a glimpse of her, but nothing. Megan is a creature of habit, so I do get a bit edgy when I don't see her, but she always gets in round about the same time. My desk phone rings and I answer but I'm not actually paying much attention.

When I put the phone down I realise she's 20 minutes late. Maybe I just missed her. Maybe she came in early. I pick my desk phone up again and call reception.

"It's Myles, can you run me a report on who we currently have in the building, as a matter of urgency and email it to me?"

"No problem Mr Beckett, I'll do it straight away." It's the new receptionist, and after everything that's been going on I've completely forgotten her name, or in fact what she looks like. My email pings and I have the report. I open it and sort the list alphabetically. Nothing! I search again. Nothing! I feel perspiration form on my top lip and a wave of sickness and panic floods my body.

Think rationally! I pull up the HR schedules for annual leave and sick days, still nothing. I take two long, deep breaths in a vain effort to calm myself and pick up the phone. It's answered in three rings. "Imogen?"

"No, its Rob. Imogen's in a meeting. Can I take a message?"

"Erm... no it's fine. Is Megan there?"

"No, I'm not sure where she is actually."

"Is she sick or on leave? Has she rung in?"

"Not that I know of."

"Right, thanks!" I slam the phone down, grab my phone and keys and rush out of the office. A million things chase through my head. Did she have an accident? Has Darren got to her again? Didn't she get a restraining order on him? Should I ring the police, the hospitals? First things first I head over to her house.

I don't even remember the journey as I screech to a halt outside her house and run to the door. My brain is only just registering that this may look a little bit deranged of me. I bang on the door, not waiting long enough for an answer, I bang again.

There's movement inside and the door is opened in a rush.

"Where's the fire?" Megan says and I breathe properly for the first time since leaving my office. I bend over, hands on my knees and try to calm myself down as relief washes over me. "What are you doing here?"

I finally look up at her. "Can I come in?"

She rolls her eyes and opens the door wide to let me in. I smell her perfume as I get close and it throws up emotions that I've been pushing down for the past week or so.

"What do you want Myles?"

"I came to make sure you were okay."

"So, now you've seen! Why wouldn't I be okay?"

"You didn't turn up for work and I started to panic."

"How do you even know I wasn't in work?" She narrows her eyes at me. "I'm not sure I want to know."

"I checked the CCTV."

"You were watching me on CCTV? Do you know how messed up that is, spying on me! Don't you think I've had enough of that kind of thing already?"

"I didn't mean any harm. But then I rang down to your office and they didn't know where you were."

Megan shakes her head. "Imogen knows where I am, I had an appointment. Not that it's any of your business."

"I was so worried."

"Why?" She folds her arms across her chest. "I think I'm missing something here."

"Megan!"

"What, Myles? Spit it out!"

"I... Megan... I'm in love with you."

She looks at me for what seems like forever. "And what do you want me to do with that information, Myles?"

"Well... I want you to think about being able to love me back."

She takes a deep breath. "Myles, I don't trust you! I can't love someone I don't trust."

"I can explain about the other week."

"But can you explain why you did something that had a massive effect on my life, without consulting me? I can't have another person like that in my life. And don't even get me started on the flip flopping between Myles and Moody Beckett." She's fizzing with annoyance.

"I want to explain, prove it to you, but I seem to be too late anyway." She gives me a quizzical look. "Your boyfriend!"

"Ah, well that was Sean. He was just being a dick because you had hurt my feelings." Another wave of relief.

"How can I fix this? What do you need?"

"It's not for me to tell you what to do, it's for you to know." She shakes her head. "I want to be someone's everything. I want to be a main character in a love story, not just someone who comes in to help the storyline." My brain is going 100 miles an hour. What does that mean? I need an instruction manual rather than a film-worthy quote.

She blows out a breath again, she's not waiting any longer for me to jump into action. "Do better Myles!" and she points to the door. "Now go!"

I turn on my heels. I'm going to need help with this one. As I drive back to the office I make the necessary calls.

· ♥ · ♥ · ♥ · ♥ · ♥ ·

It's not usual for me to leave the office in the middle of the day other than to attend a meeting, so sitting in the local coffee shop is a new experience. In fact, I never even knew this place existed. It's a quaint little place down a side street and the insides looks like an old sweet shop. There are rows of big glass jars on shelves behind the counter, pictures of jars of sweets adorning the walls and the display cabinet is antique wood and glass. Megan, with her sweet tooth, would love this place. I wonder if she's thought of bringing Jonah and Poppy?

The door opens and I look up to catch the eye of my friend. I wave and indicate that I've already ordered.

"Hey!" She sits next to me looking at the tea I've already ordered. Such a role reversal.

"Well this is different. Not like office!" Kateryna looks round at the surroundings. I don't think she recognises me outside of work.

"No, I needed to get away. And also I needed to see you at a decent time of the day."

"What's wrong?"

"I need help."

"You always need help, but never take advice."

"That's not entirely true."

"Okay. You take advice, just do opposite."

"Fair point." I look over to the door where Seb has just come in. I wave him over. "Kat, have you met my brother, Seb?"

"I don't think I've had the pleasure," Seb says, shaking her hand, "although you do look quite familiar. Do you work at Beck?"

"Yes and no!" She doesn't elaborate.

"I'm looking for some advice from my two favourite people."

"Not quite favourite," Seb hits back.

"That's why I need advice."

I explain what happened at Megan's house and how I feel about her.

"And what did she say to that?" Seb asks.

"She said, and I quote, what do you want me to do with that information?"

"Harsh."

"Not harsh enough," Kateryna bites back.

"Where do I go now?"

"Go big or go home!" Seb smirks.

"Absolutely not!" Kateryna looks at me. "You're brother idiot man too!"

"You need a grand gesture."

"NO! NO! NO! You need to communicate with her. That what got you in the mess first time." Kateryna is doing her rapid hand gestures to show how annoyed she is with Seb's advice.

"How so?" Questions Seb. "Because he didn't run around after her?"

"Because he didn't tell her what was happening."

"We were really busy," Seb explains.

"Whether you were or no, she feels she's an afterthought. Not worthy a thought. And as for moving her, I have no more words for you!"

"Talk to her? What else?" I ask.

"What about the usual? Fancy dinner, take her to a show?"

"You have no clue about woman." Kateryna fold her arms across her chest and glares at Seb.

"I'll have you know I am very good with women!"

"Do you have a girlfriend?"

"Well… no!"

"This why!" She smirks. These two are something else. I'm definitely questioning my own judgement bringing these two together.

"Can we stop bickering and get back to a plan?"

"Make a list of things that you could do. Each one ask, would Megan like this? If yes great, if no..." She pulls a sad face.

"And if that doesn't work?"

"You need to ask her what she wants and figure out if you want that too. And when you do, find a way to make it happen." Seb surprises us both.

"Finally!" Kateryna throws her hands up in the air.

"I don't know what I want, other than I don't want this. I don't want to feel like I do right now. Like I'm spiralling out of control and the one person that can calm me and make me feel anything, doesn't want to know."

I rub a hand over my face. Seb and Kateryna look at each other, concern on their faces.

Chapter Thirty-Three

Megan

This is the third morning I have come into the office and been met with a take away coffee with a sticky note underneath that today says *Cappuccino with Amaretto syrup because you like it sweet! Mx.* I know he's been speaking to Dionne about me because she can't keep a secret to save her life.

At least he isn't giving up. I'm still mad that he moved me without any communication, although I do really love where I am now. The team is full of energy and life, and I'm not just doing PA stuff. I also get asked my opinion, which is a really weird thing for me. I have people at my desk all the time for one reason or another.

I'm just about to leave my desk when my phone rings and I roll my eyes. It's like people have a sixth sense about me leaving or something. "Hello, Imogen Hughes' desk, Megan speaking."

"Megan, can you swing by reception on your way to lunch please, I have something for you." The new receptionist, Annabel, started a few days ago.

"No problem, I'm just on my way."

I pick up Dionne on the way to grab lunch and swing by reception, Annabel is holding out a brown paper bag.

"What is this?"

"Lunch I presume."

"But who from?" She shrugs, but the corners of her mouth tilt up into a smile. I look inside the bag and find a little sticky note. I pull it out for a better look.

Megan,
I made your favourite sandwich, enjoy.
Mx

"Hmm…" Dionne says looking down at the note. "How does he know your favourite sandwich?"

"I don't know." I inspect the bag further and it's an egg mayonnaise sandwich, very roughly made and not so delicately cut into a heart shape. "Ah. We talked about it with the kids. I said mine was an egg mayo sandwich, but it had to have the crusts cut off."

"Interesting!" she says, as we walk into the restaurant.

We sit out of earshot of anyone else – our go-to seat of choice. Everyone just ignores us. I tell her what happened when Myles rushed over to mine and how he professed his love for me.

"And how does that make you feel?"

"I don't know. I told him that I didn't trust him, and I don't. There's always going to be a time that he's too busy, forgets the time or whatever. I just don't want to be someone's second thought, I want to be their only thought.

"I want someone who knows me, who knows what I want and what I need. I need a partner not a father. I want support not control. I need someone to think about me. I don't need things, I need a someone to be *my person*. Is that too much to ask? Did I watch too much Disney as a kid?"

"It's absolutely not too much to ask. And by the looks of that sandwich, he really is trying."

"Yes... but he still hasn't explained himself, or apologised."

"You haven't exactly let him though, have you?"

"Okay, fair point. If he offers to explain, I'll let him." I quickly change the subject. "What's new with you anyway?"

"Not much. I'm still chatting to both Toby and Seb."

"Okay, and how's that going?"

"Really well. A bit too well."

"How so?"

"Because I like them both. And at some point, I'll need to choose."

"Not yet you won't. Just keep reminding them you are seeing both of them, and then there won't be any bad feelings between you all."

"It's not as if they don't know about each other, they've been in the same bed."

"Don't remind me. I will see Seb in a completely different light from now on. Have you worked out your little accounting anomaly yet?"

"Well no, and it's not so little now I have looked further."

"You really need to go and see Myles, sooner rather than later."

"Yeah, I think I'll find a quiet time later today."

"Come on then, best get back to work. Still on for fight club tonight?"

"Hell yeah." We stand up and make our way back to the fourth floor and back to our desks. When I sit down, I find a note on my desk.

I hope you enjoyed your lunch
Mx

He really is trying. I move the note and find an invitation of sorts.

Ms Scott,
Please give me the pleasure of cooking dinner for you, tomorrow evening at my residence 7pm.
I will be serving batonnet de poisson, avec frites chaudes et haricot
Myles Beckett x

Ah god, sounds a bit fancy, but maybe this is a good time for him to explain what happened. I did promise Dionne I'd let him. My phone rings and I just know its him.

"Did you enjoy your lunch?" his voice washes over me like a warm blanket and I realise I'm not quite as mad at him as I was.

"Yes, thanks you. Someone made me my favourite but in the shape of a heart. Looked like Jonah had made it."

"I'm glad you liked it, I asked his advice! Did you get my invitation?"

"I did!"

"And?"

"And... "

"Have I overstepped already?"

"No, it's just... what's the occasion?"

"I thought we needed to talk about what happened and by way of an apology, I thought I'd cook rather than go out for a fancy meal that we'd still feel hungry afterwards." I think he's getting the point. He knows I'm a home bird and I like the simple stuff. But as for the food, the jury is out.

"Far enough. I'll see you there then."

"Great!" he says, and I hang up before I change my mind. Let's see what happens, this meal could really be make or break.

Chapter Thirty-Four

Myles

I'm sitting at my desk in my office. Seb is sitting relaxing, as he most often does, when there's a knock on my door. Dionne pops her head round. "Can I have a private word?"

"Yes sure!" She pushes the door further and walks in, coming to an abrupt halt when she sees Seb. His stance matches hers. They look between each other for a bit, while I try to weigh up what's going on.

"Can Seb stay or is it personal kind of private?"

"No, it's business and it's probably best if he does stay."

"Okay, why don't you sit on over there." I point to where Seb is sitting. "Can I get you a drink?"

"No, I'm fine, thanks." Seb looks like a deer caught in the headlights and I'm not quite sure why. God, I hope she's not trying to bring some kind of sexual harassment case against him. I just don't need that kind of shit, with everything else going on.

"What can we do for you?"

"Well, I've seen some anomalies in the account schedules for one of the projects." I look to Seb and he gives me a knowing look, but Dionne has intercepted the silent communication between the two of us. "But that's obviously not news to you two."

"Which project?" Seb is direct and straight to the point.

"The sustainability one. Project Tree."

"What kind of anomalies?"

"Well there's a few things. It seems to be way over projected budget for no apparent reason. The invoices data seems to be massively inflated and the figures just keep bouncing about."

"Bouncing about?"

"You would anticipate expenditure to increase month on month. I feel like the figures from the previous months have changed but I can't prove it because previous reports seem to keep going AWOL, or when I go back into an account it's not how I remember. But I have no concrete evidence and I know for a fact that if I mention it anywhere else, they'll mark it down as it being *the time of the month* or some other kind of bullshit!"

"Oh god!" Seb shakes his head.

"We've seen some things too. A few weeks ago one the folders for the project went missing, but appeared again within a few hours. I got Seb to look into who had been working on it."

"And who was it?" She asks.

"It was you, Dionne!" Seb says bluntly.

"Me! You can't think this is me, surely?" She looks between the two of us, panic on her face.

"We were maybe 95 percent sure it wasn't you, until just now."

"And now we are 100 percent sure it isn't," says Seb.

"What now? Is someone trying to set me up?"

"It looks that way." She gets up and starts pacing, her brain going 100 miles an hour.

"Look, we know it's not you, we just need to find out who it is."

"The thing is, we might need to prove it's not you first. I have a log of when things have been moved about so we can go through that, get you an alibi," Seb suggests.

"But it needs to be done covertly. Just have a quick look through the log now and see if any days stand out, then go off site to get the evidence sorted," I say.

"Won't it seem a bit odd, going off site?"

"I can take you out on a date! I'll pick you up after work, but you'll have to make it look real. Giggle and look up at me with puppy dog eyes." She narrows her eyes at Seb's suggestion.

"Firstly, I have never giggled and looked at a man with puppy dog eyes, and secondly, I have self-defence class tonight, so it will have to be tomorrow."

"Self-defence?"

"Yeah, me and Megan are doing it. Thought it would be a good idea after Darren grabbed her. She said she didn't want to rely on a man coming to her rescue." That hits me hard in the chest. The fact that she'd need to do that to keep herself safe, and the fact she didn't want me to save her again.

"Whatever, sit down and look through these," Seb says.

Dionne scans the documents with the times and dates. "Have you checked that I was tapped into the building with security?"

"Yes, first thing we did."

"There!" She points at an entry on the screen. "Saturday 18th."

"What about it?"

"Well, I was at a club with both of you!"

"But this was early hours of the morning from a remote IP address."

She rolls her eyes and looks to address Seb. "I couldn't have done it because I was in bed with you!"

"What?" This is news to me. Seb and I usually share everything and now he looks a bit sheepish.

"I don't have evidence of the fact as such, but I do have a bite mark about here." She points at her hip.

"I thought you were with that Toby bloke?"

"We were!" They both say in unison.

"Okay, I don't want to know any more. We need other examples though."

"I better get back. They'll be wondering where I am, and I don't want to raise suspicion."

She makes her way to the door, gives us both a quick, sarcastic wave and closes the door behind her. I really hope Seb's antics don't land us in more bother. I wait a few moments until I think she is far enough away to not hear our next conversation.

"Fucking hell Sebastian!"

"What? It's not like that I promise you. I really like her. It hit me like a fucking brick wall at the club and I knew I couldn't just let her go home with him, so I went too."

"For fuck's sake!" I shake my head.

"At least she won't forget about me in a hurry." He grins at me.

"You are unbelievable, you know that right?"

"At least I didn't demote her after I got my dick wet!"

I'm never going to shake off that bad decision when even my own brother keeps reminding me!

Chapter Thirty-Five

Megan

I get myself ready, physically and emotionally, for dinner with Myles. I know we need to talk about what happened and what we do going forward. But in all honesty, I don't know what I think of the situation. I'm really apprehensive about what he has to say.

I like Myles, a lot, but I can't get over the fact he's a man of power, which he can use to manipulate my life. I have had too much of that already to want to dive into a new, controlling relationship. I want to be me. I don't need fancy things, I don't need to go to fancy restaurants and clubs and I don't want a hand up the corporate ladder. I'm a people person not a business entity.

I look at how far I have come, taking the example from my self-defence class. This time last year I wouldn't have been able to do that kind of thing. Darren wouldn't have allowed it and

I wouldn't have had the confidence to stand up for myself and fling another person onto a crash mat, even if that person is my friend.

I would never have been allowed to make new friends like Dionne before or have people around me that could challenge my reality. My head is so messed up right now. Is it fair to tar Myles with the same brush as Darren? Am I still just really messed up over what happened with him, that I'm not ready for anything with anyone else? Or will I ever be?

God, I just wish someone would tell me what to do. But then again, that was bad for me too. I need to start making my own decisions and work out what I want from my life, from a relationship. Why does it have to be so hard? Whenever I'm away from Myles I see him as the big bad wolf, but as soon as I see him being his real self, I melt and think about the possibilities.

Standing on the pavement outside Myles' flat I take a deep breath. His place is really beautiful, warm and cosy, but yet it holds some bad memories that I'm not sure I will be able to overcome. I suppose only time will tell.

I press the intercom and hear his voice.

"Come up." The door buzzes and I push through before taking the lift to his floor. I step out and his door is already open, but he's not there. I can hear soft music and the clatter of kitchen utensils. I step into the hall and poke my head round the corner, standing just inside the door. I can see him getting things ready and I wait for him to notice I'm here.

It gives me enough time to take him all in. His short hair that's just long enough to get my fingers through, his tight, toned body that, even through his now casual clothes, is very evident, his soft lips that I long to be on mine, and his eyes, an eerie, piercing grey as he looks up and meets mine. A smile curls on his lips.

"Hi." I say fiddling with my sleeves.

"Hi. Come in. Do you want a drink?"

"Erm, yes." He comes over and I'm feeling really nervous for some reason. Wrapping his arms around me and I melt into him. He smells amazing as usual, and a feeling of calm falls over me as if things are going to work out just fine, one way or another.

He releases me, looks down and gives a quick kiss on my lips that takes me by surprise. "I didn't know what you'd want, so I got a few different options."

"Okay. I think something non-alcoholic," I say, looking at the multitude of different bottles laid out on the kitchen island. I follow him to the kitchen and he hands me a tumbler of clear, fizzy liquid. I take a sip and I'm hit with the unexpected taste of lime.

He takes in my reaction for a moment. He seems like he's on high alert, like if he makes a wrong move and I'm going to do a runner. "That okay?"

"Yummy, thanks. How did you know I like lime?"

"Well, it was an educated guess. It was the mojito lip balm, lime cola, those sour sweets you always have, that candle you had on your desk, those key lime pie pots you always get from the bakery, just down from the office. Although the vodka and cranberry at the nightclub threw me a bit."

"Am I that predictable?"

"No, you just have things that you like, which is nice. Like that pen with the feathery thing on the end and the way you make lists because you like ticking things off, so you add stuff you've already done, just so you have more ticks."

"Okay then!" My eyebrows are in my hairline as I contemplate all the things he's committed to memory.

"I like your little quirks."

"What's was for dinner again?" I change the subject, not really wanting to dwell on how much he's been thinking.

"Here, sit down and I'll serve it up." He points to the dining table on the edge of the kitchen. It's round and seats four and the chairs are curved to fit snugly. It has a clean, white table cloth and the place settings are made to look like a restaurant, with a tall candle sitting in a silver candlestick holder, in the centre. All very fancy! If we were having dinner at mine, it would be a tray on your lap, sitting in front of the TV.

He brings over a plate which is covered in a silver cloche thing, like those you see on films when they serve room service in hotels. Oh god, I don't like fancy food. I never quite know what I'm eating, the sauces are usually an afterthought of a drizzle on the edge of the plate, and I never know which knife and fork to use.

"Today, madame, will be having batonnet de poisson, avec frites chaudes."

"Oh!" He lifts off the cover and I stare at my plate before looking up at him. "It's fish fingers and chips!"

"Yes it is! I wasn't sure whether you would have baked beans or peas with it. So you have the choice, or both."

"Never both!" I keep looking between the plate of food and him. He really has been paying attention. "I can't believe you made me this. How did you know?"

"Could have been the way you always make a face when people mention *fancy* food and restaurants." He puts the word fancy in air quotes. "And the fact your face lights up when you mention fish fingers."

"I'm just a simple girl."

"You're far from it! What is it to be? Beans or peas?"

"Beans, I think." He passes over a pot of beans and sits down with his own plate.

"I think we need to talk through what happened!" My shoulders tense up around my ears. I know this needs to be addressed, but I'm nervous. It's him that needs to answer to what happened, but I think the nerves are because I so want him to explain it in a way I can accept.

"Go on."

"I left you here by yourself on that Saturday morning, when all I wanted to do was to stay wrapped up in you. I really wanted a rerun of the night before to be honest." His mouth lifts at the side and I have a mini flash back of us in the shower. I shove it to the back of my mind. I think he's having the same flash back. "But I have something going down at work and it was something I couldn't avoid. I didn't want to wake you up. You looked so peaceful and you needed the sleep. And then time just got away from me. I was constantly on the phone until my battery ran out."

"Can you understand how I felt though? You left me alone, in a flat I had never been in before, I didn't know where anything was, or when you'd be back. I mean look at the place." I point to the kitchen area. "Everything is hidden! At least if you were left at mine you'd know where the kettle is and could put on the TV!

But that isn't the point, you could have sent me a quick message. As far as I knew, you'd just abandoned me, I was forgotten."

"You were never forgotten, Megan."

"But I didn't know that."

"I tried to ring later on, but it just went to answer machine."

"Can you blame me? By that time it was too late. Communication Myles, that's the key. It doesn't have to be much. I understood you had things to do."

"I'm sorry!"

"But that isn't the really bad thing, is it? I could have got over that bit."

"I know. I should have communicated what I was thinking."

"Myles, you demoted me after we had sex!"

"Okay, I know it looks that way."

"It totally was that way!"

"I freaked out about what happened in my office. I couldn't control myself with you around. I didn't want to be THAT man!"

"But you ended up being THAT man!"

"Friday night was a test to me, a test of my feelings. Could we be something away from the office? And when I knew, at least on my side, we could be, I knew you couldn't be my PA. It had all kinds of lawsuits hanging over it.

"Imogen had been banging on at me for months about how you should be on her team. You were a better fit there and I was holding you back keeping you up on the fifth floor, out of the way. So I gave in and called her. We must have got our wires crossed. I thought she said she'd contact you."

"Whether she did or not, it should have been you. You should have told me all this, instead of making me feel like shit. I don't know whether I can get over that."

"I'm sorry. And it wasn't a demotion. You have the same wages and conditions."

"Myles. I went from the top job to somewhere in the middle, it was a demotion."

"That's what Kat said, I didn't see it like that. I'm sorry."

We don't continue the discussion, we both have a lot to think about, so we eat in silence.

Once we finish our meal, Myles takes the plates away and puts them in the dishwasher. I'm noticing the way he likes order and everything in its own little box, so I can kind of see why he had to take me out of one and put me in another. Doesn't mean I have to like it.

He sits back down. "So tell me about these self-defence classes."

"How did you know about those?"

"Dionne came up to see me on Wednesday."

"Oh, how did that go?" He looks at me before answering.

"You know what it was about?"

"Kind of, not the details. I told her to see you."

"Just out of curiosity, when did she first tell you about it."

"I dunno, a few weeks ago. But she wanted to get more evidence, dig a bit to make sure she hadn't seen something that wasn't there."

"Right, good to know. What's the deal with her and Seb?"

"He hasn't told you?"

"No. Should I be concerned?"

"No, but it's his information to give not mine."

"Okay, back to self-defence class."

"Oh right, yes. Well it's just a little class at my local community centre. There are only six of us. I just wanted to be able to hold my own if I got into a sticky situation. But also, to feel more confident about being places on my own."

"And how's it going?"

"Great, I do really feel better. I know, if I have to, I can take care of myself. And we have such a good laugh. Our little group is such a mix of characters and we go out for a drink afterwards. It makes flinging each other around a lot more comfortable."

"I'm so glad. Do you want desert?"

"Always, what is it?" He stands and leaves the table to take something out of the fridge and places it on the table. "Key lime pie?"

"From the same bakery you like."

"Oh my god!" He really has thought of everything, and I'm wondering if I really am such a creature of habit to always have the same thing and go the same place. I may need to shake that up a little.

"And I thought we could maybe watch a film afterwards?"

"Sounds like a plan."

He dishes me up a slice of pie and I tuck in straight away. As the flavours hit my mouth, I let out a groan and my eyes roll back. "Don't make noises like that, it does all kind of things to me." He squirms in his seat. I let out a little giggle and file away that little nugget for next time.

I polish off the whole piece of my pie in record time. If I could have licked the plate I think I would have, but I was trying to show a bit of decorum. I stand and take our plates over to the kitchen and Myles follows me. Loading them in the dishwasher, then turns back to me, leaning up against the island.

"Megan!" It's not a question, he just looks at me, threading his fingers round my neck and moves closer. He plants a gentle kiss on my lips and pulls back, looking for my reaction. I reach up and kiss him back and he swipes his tongue through my mouth. Tasting of the amazing pie and I yet again melt into him. The buzz of my phone in my pocket pulls me back to reality. I pull it out.

Along with a number of messages, my phone is ringing. Beth's face displayed on my screen. "Sorry, if I don't answer she'll keep ringing." He nods and I answer. "Beth what's up?"

"Megs I need your help, Jonah has fallen off the bed and I think he's broken his leg. Steve went out with work and I can't get hold of him. Can you come and look after Poppy?"

"Yeah of course. I'm over at Myles' so it might take me a bit longer than usual to get over."

"Oh I'm so sorry, I'll ask someone else. I don't want to ruin your night."

"Hang on." I put her on mute and look up at Myles. "Did you hear that? Jonah has a suspected broken leg."

"Yeah, I heard. What do you need?" He looks at me with a concerned face.

"To get to Beth's and look after Poppy."

"Right, I'll take you. Traffic should be okay this time of night, should only take 25 minutes or so."

"Thanks!" I take Beth off mute. "Beth? Myles says it should take about 25 minutes. We're setting off now." Beth lets out a big sob. "I'll ring you once we're in the car." I hang up and give Myles a quick thank you kiss.

There's a flurry of activity, picking up keys, phones and so on and we rush out of the flat. Before I can register anything we are in the car and driving to get to Beth's as quickly as we can.

I pull my phone out again to ring Beth back. It's the first major child incident that I can think of and she's in major panic mode. "Why don't you pair you phone to the car? That way, you can distract Beth and if you need, I can distract Jonah."

I pair the phone and ring Beth. She answers with a shaky voice. "Beth, we are on our way. Do you have everything you need so you can just jump in the car?"

"Erm no, I don't want to leave these two."

"Right, keep those two together, put your phone on speaker and give it to Poppy, then go and get sorted." I go into organiser mode.

"Right!" I can hear her fumbling with the phone. "Talk to Aunty Megan while I get some stuff."

"Hi Aunty Megan." Poppy's voice is really loud, as if she's holding the phone up close.

"Hiya Pops. I'm coming over to look after you while Mummy takes Jonah to get checked out."

"Okay."

"Is Jonah with you?"

"Yes."

"Can he hear us?"

"Yes."

"Can we talk to him?"

"Yes."

"Do you say anything else other than yes?" She gives us a little giggle.

"Jonah has been crying," she says, eventually.

"No I haven't." I can tell by his voice that he has.

"Hey Jonah, it's Myles. Have you been practising your sky-diving off the bed?"

"Hiya Myles, can we go in your car to the hospital?" His voice is a lot perkier now he knows Myles is here.

"I'm not sure I can fit a broken leg in my car, as well as you and your mum."

"It hasn't dropped off you know, it's still attached to my body." I can tell he's rolling his eyes. Poppy makes a fake vomiting noise.

"Talk me through what happened then." Jonah tells Myles the tale, including a very in-depth back story and exactly what was going through his mind. Myles asks relevant questions, and before we know it, we're pulling up outside Beth's. We jump out of the car.

I use my spare key and walk straight in the door, shouting to them to let them know we're here. Myles follows me through the door and we come face to face with a manic Beth. I grab her by the shoulders. "Beth you need to chill. It will be fine. I can sort Poppy out and you can take Jonah."

"Shall I carry him to the car?" Myles says from behind me and Beth nods. He takes the stairs two at a time and I follow him up.

Once they are all packed in Beth's car, we wave them off and head back inside. Poppy is sitting on the sofa. "I'm sure it's time for bed for you Popsicle."

"Well, I'm too awake now." She gives me those puppy dog eyes of hers and I roll mine.

"Fine!" She wriggles in her seat, all excited to be staying up.

Myles stands behind me. "Megan, I'm really sorry. Seb has been on. There's an emergency family meeting tomorrow, but I need to prepare for it." Myles looks over at Poppy and raises his voice for her to hear. "Is it okay if I leave you here where Poppy can look after you?" She giggles on the sofa again.

"Is this the thing with Dionne again?" He nods. "So it really is that big?"

"Yes, massive, or I wouldn't go."

"It's fine, just do what you need to do. Just stay in touch."

"I'm really sorry." He comes closer and wraps his arms around me, leaning in to kiss me. I forget where we are and open up to him, deepening the kiss.

"Eww," comes a little voice. "I thought you said he wasn't your boyfriend." With that, Myles heads out of the door and I sit myself down on the sofa next to Poppy. She gives me a look only a five-year-old can. She knows I'm not telling the truth.

Chapter Thirty-Six

Myles

Yet again the best laid plans have been thwarted by the shit that's going on in the office. My evening with Megan was ruined on Friday and I didn't get a chance to see her all weekend. But I did keep in touch, to keep her in to loop and let her know that I was thinking about her.

I'm now on catch up with the rest of my work because I have been dealing with the sustainability project. Seb called me on Friday to say that Daniel Fawcett, our chief finance officer, had been seen having dinner at a very exclusive restaurant with the CEO of one of the major plastics firms. A family meeting was called, so we could work out the significance.

My father, although he was an HR nightmare, knew a lot of people in the industry and did quite a bit of digging. He came up with some theories of what and why this is happening. Now we need to find evidence to substantiate these theories. As far as we know, Daniel is none the wiser we are on to him.

Seb and Dionne looked through the transaction data so she could put evidence together to prove it wasn't her. And thank god for their self-defence class. Not only am I pleased that Megan will be able to look after herself, but they only went and took a selfie of themselves, with the rest of the class, at the time one of those transactions occurred. Not only is there evidence, but also witnesses.

My desk phone rings and I pick it up. "Myles, it's me!" I can't get enough of hearing this woman's voice.

"Hey, everything okay?" There's a slight panic to her voice.

"Is Dionne with you?"

"No, why?"

"I can't find her. We go for lunch at one o'clock on the dot, but she's not at her desk. I've waited for her for ten minutes and I've checked the toilets and asked reception."

"Come to my office and we'll check CCTV."

"On my way."

She's up at my office in record time, and her face is not the usual sunny, smiley self. She's clearly concerned.

"Hey," I say as she walks up to my desk.

"I know you probably think that I'm overthinking this, but I have a really bad feeling."

"Well, let's go with that then. I've been checking people coming in and out and she's not left. I'm just looking at her floor from half an hour ago." I point at the screen. "You can clearly see her there." We watch as she answers the phone, gets up and leaves her desk. We follow her as she takes the lift. The way the cameras are positioned we know she gets in the lift, but not to which floor.

"Check the time stamp to the same time on each floor, starting with this one." She obviously has an inclination as to where Dionne was going now.

"Yep, there she is on the fifth floor." We watch as Dionne stops at Fawcett's office door. She looks at her phone and then puts it back in her pocket. She knocks and enters.

"What time was that?" I check the screen.

"12.55. That's fifteen minutes ago now."

"Fast forward. Check she doesn't leave."

"Nope. Let's go." We both rush out of the room and I turn to Eric, my PA. "If we're not back in five minutes, call security." His eyes widen and he nods.

We stand outside the CFO's door and I try the handle. It' locked. I give Megan a side eye. I put my head to the door to see if I can hear anything, but there's no sound.

"What now?" Megan mouths, and I shrug but my hand automatically raises and I knock on the door.

There's sound coming from the other side of the door, like something hitting the floor and some groaning. Then I hear her, really quietly at first, but it gets louder. It's Dionne shouting for help.

"Break the door down," Megan cries. I barge my shoulder into the door once and it doesn't move, so I try it again. This time the lock breaks and the door flies open.

The scene that awaits us is baffling. There are things from the desk all over the floor, and Dionne is holding a chair as a weapon, legs forward towards Fawcett, who is doubled over in pain, unable to speak or breathe.

"Thank god you're here," she says with a sigh, the relief washing all over her face and down her body.

"She bloody attacked me!" Fawcett finally manages.

"I thought you might pull something like this, so I had my phone on record the whole time." Dionne pulls the phone out of her pocket and presses play. Fawcett's voice takes on a sinister tone.

"I've seen you have been meddling. Well it won't do you any good, because although you might think you're smart, I have made sure the paper trail leads directly back to you..."

"You really are a piece of shit, Fawcett." I say.

He seems to get another wind of energy and makes a bolt for the door, pushing past Megan, but hits the brick wall of security that Eric called up. They grab hold of him.

"What do we do now?" Megan asks.

"We'll have to restrain him and keep him in the office. I'd like to ask him a few questions of my own before the police get here." The security guards bundle Fawcett back into the office and one of them puts his hands in restraints, before sitting him on the sofa at the far side of the office.

"We know what you did Daniel."

"What did I do?"

"You were working with Anthony Banks to try and make it look like the sustainability project was draining money, which in turn meant that everyone would turn back to using the plastics that Banks supplies. But why try to pin it on Dionne?"

"Why? Because she thinks she's something special."

Someone rushes into the room. "She is something special," Seb announces, going straight for Dionne and checking she's not hurt.

"Is she another one shagging the boss to advance her career?"

"What is that supposed to mean?" Dionne is angry that this is even a consideration, as am I.

"Well that's what happened when Marcus was in charge. If you shagged the boss, you got a better job."

"If that were the case, the fifth floor would be full of women. And it's not, unless you are saying that you shagged Marcus to get where you are." Megan crosses her arms across her chest and gives him an evil stare.

"Everyone has their position in this company based on merit. Well, apart from me, and obviously you by the looks of it," I say.

"Shut up, pretty boy."

"That all you got?" I laugh at him. "In fact, talking of merit, there's an opening for the position of Chief Financial Officer, Dionne, I think you should take over as interim CFO and apply for the job."

"Me?"

"Of course. You've shown how good you are, and you've shown the company such loyalty."

"I don't know what to say."

"Say, *Of course Mr Beckett, it would be my pleasure.*"

"Okay, I'll take the job."

"Well excellent, that clears up that then. One less thing to think about."

Eric pokes his head round the door. "The police are in reception."

"Could you go and get them Eric, bring them up here."

"No problem." Eric leaves us to it.

I turn to Seb. "I suggest you take the ladies into my office, while I have a little word with our man here." With that, they leave the room and I'm face to face with Fawcett. "I should have listened when people said there was something off about you!" He sneers up at me.

Chapter Thirty-Seven

Megan

Everyone has calmed down a bit now. We sat in Myles' office for a few hours with countless cups of tea and everyone coming and going. The police came to discuss the possibility of pressing criminal charges against Daniel Fawcett. Beck's board had to be called for an emergency meeting. What was funny was that when Seb came rushing in, the first thing he did was go and see Dionne. Tells you something that, doesn't it?

I've hardly seen Myles. He's been Mr Designer Suit Beckett again. I can see why he has to be like that, but it doesn't mean I like it. I insisted that Dionne stays over at mine tonight, just in case she needed to talk about anything. She's been anxious about the whole thing, over the past few days especially. I can tell in the way she's been holding herself, the lack of daft chat and messing about.

I'm just glad it's all over for her now. And what a turn up, the self-defence classes worked. Things haven't really changed for me and Myles and I still feel a little shut out by him, emotionally.

I decide to walk up to the fifth floor to see him as it's all been playing on my mind, the way he's been all wrapped up in work. I understand that's the nature of the job, and I wouldn't want him to change a job he loves because of me. But I just don't know how I will manage if we are a couple.

He needs someone that won't mind if he cancels dinner at the last minute. Someone who he can show off at corporate events and can laugh at the men's jokes and talk to the other partners about living with a CEO or whatever they talk about. But that's just not me. I want someone who is available both physically and emotionally.

I walk down the corridor and get to the PA's desk.

"Hi Eric, Is Mr Beckett available?" I'm not sure Eric knows the nature of our relationship. To be fair, I'm not sure I know the nature of our relationship.

"He's just about to go into another meeting, but I can check." He calls through and I hear his side of the conversation. "Ms Scott is here to see you, I said you were due in a meeting... Okay then." He looks up at me and puts the phone down. "He says go on in." Eric gives me a curt smile and I walk through the door.

"Hiya, sorry I have only got a few minutes." He sounds apologetic.

"It doesn't matter then." I've changed my mind. I turn to walk out. This was a bad idea but also proves my point.

"No stay, tell me what's up." He stands from his chair and comes round to the front of his desk.

I let out a big breath. "I realise you have a lot on, but I'm not sure I can see myself playing the part you want me to play."

"What do you mean?"

"This." I gesture around the room. "I know it may seem needy to you, but I haven't seen you all week and I don't like it."

His face drops. "I know, and I'm sorry."

"I understand this all comes with the territory, but I don't think I'm cut out for it... being runner up."

He looks down at the floor, leans back and props himself up against his desk. "This last month has been totally full on, I get it. Can you just have a think about what you want? Don't make any rash decisions. Maybe go and have a session with your friends at the pub and talk it through with them. I think Dionne could do with unwinding as well." And with that the phone rings. "I'm sorry, I have to go."

"Okay." The sadness sweeps over me as I turn, open the door and walk out. I walk back down the stairs, giving myself a bit more time to pull myself together. Tears are ready to fall and I think if anyone even speaks to me I'll have a breakdown. I don't know what I expected Myles to say, but I thought it might be a bit more than he did.

My phone beeps and I take it out to find the start of a conversation in our girls' group chat.

Dionne

> Right girls, we need a Dog and Swan meet tonight. Megan needs to talk things through

How does she know? I haven't spoken to her about what happened with Myles.

Beth

> What's happened?

Dionne

> Well apart from Megan needing help with making some life choices, I was just kidnapped at work

Emma

> Kidnapped?

Lizzie

> What?

Dionne

> Okay well maybe that was a bit dramatic, but I can fill you all in tonight

Emma

> I'm in!

Lizzie

> Me too

> Beth
> Hope you're okay Megs, I'm in!

> Dionne
> Megs?

> Me
> Okay I'm in, but I'm not great company.

> **Lizzie**
> You never are mate!

> Me
> Funny

Looks like we're all off out to the pub tonight then.

· ♥ · ♥ · ♥ · ♥ · ♥ ·

For once we all arrive at the same time to the Dog and Swan, and as we walk in, we see our usual seats are free, but there's a big, reserved notice on the table. Well this night sucks already, I just want to turn around and go back out, but instead I follow the rest of them to be bar.

"Ladies!" exclaims Mitch, as we wait to be served.

"What's going on there then?" Lizzie asks, gesturing towards the table.

"The table's reserved!"

"I didn't know you could reserve a table."

"You can't! Unless you are special guests of the landlord." He looks at us all individually and laughs. "It's reserved for you lot, and all your drinks have been paid for."

"By who?"

"I'm not at liberty to say!" He looks round us all again. "Okay you forced it out of me. It was a gentleman by the name of Myles." I take a sharp intake of breath. Why would he do that? I know he wanted me to talk things through, but is this to get my friends on side or is he just being a nice guy? I have such a warped sense of people right now.

"Excellent, keep them coming landlord!" Lizzie says.

We take our usual seats and Mitch brings over our drinks.

"Right before we get into why Myles bought our drinks and why Megan is sad, tell us why you nearly got kidnapped at work today," Emma says, looking at Dionne.

"Well, you couldn't write it. The short story is that I found some discrepancies with the accounting, it was our CFO and he was pinning it on me. He trapped me in his office and I did some of my new ninja moves from self-defence, and now I'm interim CFO."

"Ninja moves? You kicked him in the bollocks, which is actually the second rule of fight club." I say.

"Wow…. That's immense. I feel like I may need to process that and come back with more questions," Emma says.

"So Megan, what's going on?"

I start to tear up and take a deep breath to pull myself together. "I don't know, it's Myles."

"Did he explain the whole demotion thing?"

"Yes, and I get why he did what he did, he just didn't communicate it with me. I told him the whole reason we fell out was because he didn't tell me what was going on, I was left out of the loop. And that controlling my career was absolutely unacceptable."

"And what did he say to that?"

"He apologised. And he's been doing cute little things to show he cares, which is lovely. You know he invited me to his for dinner, made out if was some fancy food and he'd made me fish fingers and chips, which is my favourite. He'd thought of everything.

"I really loved being with him, and then it happened all over again, he got pulled into work and I got left."

"It has been a crazy time at work though." Dionne adds.

"I know, and I feel like I am being a bit crazy-needy about it but the nature of the job means there will always be something that comes up. And I surely deserve better or am I just living in a dreamworld? Is it too much to ask?" I look round the group. "It's a genuine question, is it too much to ask or is that not reality?"

"I don't think it should be too much to ask. It's a partnership and one person's needs shouldn't go above the other's all the time. It's a balancing act really," Beth explains.

"That's why me and Jonathan fell apart, it was all one-sided. But it's different now, we found a way to balance it, but it took us being separated to work that out, and also the communication. Look at the differences with Emma's relationships."

"Yes, I mean with my ex David, it was all one-sided, but now with Ben we are a partnership. But it started with him giving it all up for me."

"What do you actually want Megan? From life?" Lizzie asks.

"I want someone who is there for me when I need them, that I don't need to ask for their love and support. But I also want the freedom to be able to make my own way without decisions being made for me. I told Myles than I want to be the main character in someone's love story?"

"I want to be someone's plot twist." Says Dionne and everyone look at her for a moment and she just shrugs.

"Megan I think maybe you are still mindful of what happened with Darren. You need some closure on it." Emma grabs my hand and gives it a little squeeze, drawing my attention back.

"But will I ever get that though?"

"Maybe you need some kind of therapy?"

"Where does Myles come into your life plan?" Lizzie pulls the conversation back on track.

"You see the thing is, Myles is really two people, Myles and Mr Beckett CEO. I absolutely adore Myles, but I'm not keen on Mr Beckett. But I can't have one without the other."

"What about the sex?" Beth asks, which is very un-Beth like.

"The sex is next level. I think he's ruined me for all other men."

"Can you imagine having sex with anyone that isn't Myles?"

"No."

"Well that is a dilemma." Their faces become passive as they think about how to help me sort out my thoughts.

"Right, well. I'll go ask Mitch for some more drinks." I get up and head to the bar, my head is spinning with thoughts about how this would all work out. I ask Mitch to drop the drinks off and I head to the bathroom, just to get some time to breathe.

After a few deep breaths and a splash of water on my face, I leave the bathroom and head back to my friends.

"Hey Megan, someone wants you outside." It's a man who I don't know and he walks past me and back into the bar. Now there's some massive red flags going off, but my curiosity gets the better of me and I step outside.

There's a little lit up courtyard out back, mainly where people come and smoke, with a picnic bench to sit on. It's closed off to the rest of the street with walls surrounding it, but people easily access it through a little gate, to get in the pub from the back. Tonight it's pretty deserted.

"Megan!" The familiar voice has the hairs on the back of my neck standing to attention. Anxiety hits me, and I can't move.

"What do you want Darren?"

"I wanted to tell you that your little game of *go tell* won't make you feel any better. You'll still be that dumb little girl. Just because your friends believe your pathetic stories, doesn't mean anyone else will believe you." My brain is going round and round fighting the instinct to believe what I'm being told, one half saying, it's just words the other wondering if there is just a little bit of truth behind them.

But he continues, "you'll be that stupid little slag, bitter because you were dumped. You are nothing, and no one will ever love you. You are damaged goods, and no-one wants damaged goods." His words are spat out, meant only to harm me.

My head snaps out of the haze and I know for sure that it's all him. "Is that it? Is that all you have? You're pathetic!" I don't know where the courage comes from and I stop to think how proud of myself I am. But while I'm focusing on my success, Darren has moved forwards, so close that I can smell the alcohol on his breath and see the blood shot whites of his eyes.

"You'll regret saying that!" He grabs me by the throat, but my instincts kick in and I lash out. As I manoeuvre him, his centre of gravity is compromised and he stumbles and falls on the picnic table, the plant pot that houses all the dead cigarette butts catapults through the air and smashes on the floor. The noise is tremendous.

I stand there taking in the scene for a moment. "No Darren, YOU will regret that! And FYI, you have a tiny dick!" I say, just to be petty.

People have heard the noise and have made their way outside to check out the chaos. Mitch pushes himself through the crowd, followed by my friends.

"Are you okay Megan?" Mitch asks.

"I think you're gonna need a new ashtray," I say, arms folded across my chest as I look down at the pathetic excuse for a man. "Not only did he break his restraining order, but he also assaulted me."

"Lizzie, call the police!"

I look at Dionne. "I told you self-defence classes were a good idea."

"Everyone back inside, show's over!" Mitch shouts to everyone. "Megan, take yourself and the girls up to the function room. I'll deal with him." Darren is rolling around on the floor moaning, completely winded by the force of his fall.

"There's a function room?" Beth questions.

"I know, that's what I said when I first found out." Lizzie smirks.

"It'll give you a bit of space, and the police will want to see you away from the crowd." Mitch suggests.

I gather the girls and our drinks and head up the stairs to the function room. The smell of beer and musty air fills my nostrils and I realise I'm the only one of us to have been up here before, and pretty much for the same reasons. I make my way behind the bar and flick on the lights. The place is illuminated, and everyone looks round.

"Do you think, next time we come out, it might be drama free?" Emma asks.

"Where's the fun in that?" Lizzie smiles.

We all get settled at a table by the bar and I can feel the adrenaline starting to leave my body. My hands begin to shake.

"What happened? One minute you were going to the bar, the next all hell had broken loose," Lizzie asks.

"I don't actually know. It all happened so fast. Someone told me someone was outside and wanted to see me, so I went out and he was there, spouting all sorts about stuff about how I'm damaged goods."

"You know that's not true, right?"

"I know, so I stood up for myself and he went for the jugular, literally. Next thing I know he's on the floor with a bang."

"Good for you. I'm telling the guys." Dionne pulls out her phone and types a message.

The door to the function room flies open and in rushes Jonathan.

"I thought you were at work?" Is the first thing Lizzie comes out with.

"*Hi Jon it's great that you came over so quickly...*" He mimics.

"Yeah, that. But we didn't expect you here."

"I wanted to see if Megan was okay."

"Jonathan's always wanting in on the action." Lizzie laughs.

"Megan, you okay? You're shaking." Beth looks at me and grabs my hand.

"I think it's just all caught up with me."

Mitch walks through the door. "Heating's on." He takes one look at me and continues. "I'll get you a jumper." The girls huddle up beside me with their arms wrapped round my body.

"We've got you!"

And they really have. We just sit, wrapped around each other, everyone else fussing around us but we don't break our bond until we really have to. What would I do without this bunch of crazy, unique, perfect women in my life?

Chapter Thirty-Eight

Myles

It's late night in the office again, paperwork is piling high and I feel like I'm drowning. It didn't help that we had the police here most of the day and were sorting out what happens next with Fawcett. HR have officially suspended him with a view to firing him, so we just need to tick all the relevant boxes.

Not helping my work situation is the fact that I'm absolutely devastated at the way things are going with Megan. I totally understand I've been completely absent for her, and as if proving a point, I had to leave her to go straight into another meeting, just as she was letting me know how she was feeling.

There's a knock on my door and it edges open. "I have food for you Mr Myles!"

"Kateryna! Am I glad to see a friendly face."

"What's happening?"

"I don't know! No, I really have no clue what's going on."

"How did it go with Megan?"

"It went really well, up until the point where I had to leave for a work, AGAIN!" I rub my hand over my face. "Loads of shit went down today and it's been taking up all my time. She deserves someone who can be with her when she needs them."

"What about you? What do you deserve? What would you like?"

"I wouldn't be here, that's for sure."

"Then why are you here?"

"Because I have a duty to fulfil."

"What about the duty to yourself, to be happy?"

"I don't even know how to be happy."

"Forget about family, forget work or expectations. If it for you, what would you be working?"

"Well, I trained as a lawyer. My parents were fine with that because they thought I could be an asset with the business law side of it, but I wanted to do something that would help people. Like stand up for the underdog-type law, whether it be family law or criminal law I wasn't that bothered. At least I'd know I was making a difference."

"That seems like good career. And what about personal life?"

"Well I'd have time for my friends and I'd be sharing it with someone I loved."

"That doesn't seem too much to ask."

"I don't suppose."

"Instead you going to live miserable life, no friends, no girlfriend and a job you hate."

"That's a bit harsh."

"But truth."

"But I can't change my job."

"Why not."

"Because it's a family business."

"Why not Sebastian?"

"Because I'm the eldest."

"Your point is?"

"Is it fair on Seb to pass this burden on to him?"

"Is it fair on you?"

"What do I do, just quit?"

"No it's family! You say you need a break to sort your mental." She taps the side of her head with her finger.

"Hmm. I'll think about it." It's only then I notice Kateryna's sunken eyes. She doesn't look like she's been sleeping enough, and she looks thinner than usual. I've been a total arse, consumed in my own life, and not thought about anyone else. "What's going on with you?"

She does that overly expressive shrug that she does. "Same."

"Tell!"

"I just realise I'm not going back home. At least not soon. I feel sad, but also boy is settled and loves his friends and his school. Everything else is temporary. House, job, everything."

"Maybe it's time to make everything a bit more permanent then."

"But how?"

"Come work here."

"Not possible."

"Don't be mad but I looked into it. We can make it work. We can sponsor any residence applications, we could fund courses to get the correct qualifications in place. Actually, a job became available today, in finance."

"You'd do that?"

"Of course. Where's this food then?"

Her eyes fill will with tears, but she pulls herself back together quickly. This was what she was meant to do. I will do everything in my power to help my friend settle into a new, more permanent life.

Chapter Thirty-Nine

Megan

Things aren't done in half measures around here. After Friday night, actually the whole of Friday, which was particularly eventful, the police came and took my statement once they had carted Darren back to the station.

The whole crew were round at mine on Saturday, fussing. I had Sean constantly on the phone checking I hadn't had some kind of mental breakdown, but I actually felt kind of good. Darren doesn't hold any power over me anymore, he is just a pathetic low life who prays on innocent, vulnerable women.

By the end of the day I'd had enough of everyone and ordered them to go home, which they took absolutely no notice of. That was until they knew that Darren would be kept in custody this time. Dionne went back home so she could get ready for her new exciting job opportunity, and so I could spend Sunday catching up on sleep and watching rom-coms back-to-back.

Unfortunately, that gave me time to think about Myles. He's given me some space to think about what I want and I'm no further forward. I keep flip-flopping between how much I like Myles and the time we have spent together and then back to his work and how I wouldn't be able to cope with the constant let down and missed meetings. I would end up resenting him and I don't want that to happen.

Which is the best situation to be in? Be together and end up hating each other, or not be together and have to see him at work and wonder what could have been?

And then an awful thought pops into my head, what happens when he starts seeing someone else? I will be devasted. Oh god, I feel like I'm in a no-win situation. I need to pull myself together and get ready for work, focus on my job, rather than my love life.

As I push through the revolving doors and into the foyer, the energy in the building seems different. Or is it that I'm different. As I tap my ID on the scanner to let me through the small turnstile-type doors, I see members of the board coming out of the lifts. That's unusual for first thing on a Monday morning. They all stand around the foyer chatting. Marcus Beckett is standing with his arms crossed, not looking too pleased, with the head of HR talking at him, rather than to him. I push it out of my mind. It must be this whole thing with Fawcett. I make my way upstairs and settle in at my desk.

Everyone has been at my desk this morning for one thing or another, and to be fair it's made the morning go a lot faster and I haven't had time to dwell on everything. Lunch can't come soon enough, so that I can catch up with Dionne and her new job. I'm so excited for her, even if it's just temporary until they find a new CFO. My phone beeps so I pull it out of my pocket.

> **Dionne**
> Sorry, can't do lunch, in a meeting

> **Me**
> No worries

Well that's put the kybosh on a lunch catch-up. My mind drift back to Myles and I wonder if I should go and tell him about Friday night. I remember Dionne saying he has a law degree, maybe he could talk me through what happens next. But let's face facts, it would be just an excuse to see him again. And I'm not sure I can give him any answer yet, either.

I shout over to Imogen who is sitting at her desk, "I'm going on lunch, want anything?"

"No, I'm good thanks," she shouts back.

I grab my bag and head for the lifts and instead of hitting the ground floor button I press for the fifth floor. I don't know what's come over me, but I may as well go with it. I exit the lift and follow the corridor down towards the PA's desk. There's no sign of Eric and Myles' door is closed. I take a deep breath, not knowing what I'm even going to say. I raise my hand and knock.

"Come in!" The voice is familiar but not quite Myles. I push the door open to see Sebastian Beckett sitting at Myles' desk.

"Erm, I wasn't expecting to see you here." He looks up at me, his face like thunder.

"Really?" His tone is a bit hostile, not the usual carefree Seb. Maybe it's that chair and this office that makes everyone who sits there a moody arsehole.

"Yes, really. Where's Myles?"

He stares at me for a moment then answers in a clipped tone. "He's gone!"

"What do you mean, gone?"

"Gone! Left the company."

"He can't have left the company. He's CEO."

"Not anymore."

My head is spinning. Has Myles quit his job? Why would he do that? Why wouldn't he tell me? Has he had some kind of nervous breakdown? Have I pushed him over the edge?

"Where is he now?" I ask in a desperate tone.

"Probably packing!"

"Packing!" I shriek.

"If you don't mind, Megan, I have loads of work to get on with." I'm totally frozen to the spot. I don't know what to do next, my brain is misfiring and I have a million things running through my mind all at once. I can't focus on one solid thing.

Seb waves me out of the door and I turn to leave. On autopilot I head to the lift and travel down to the ground floor. I pull my phone out and order an Uber. I head out the door ignoring calls from Annabel the receptionist. I'm only focused on one thing and that's finding Myles.

I bite my nails the whole journey, a habit I thought I had overcome. It seems to take forever, but it's really only ten minutes. Jumping out of the car, I head straight for his building. My heart hammers as I press the buzzer. No answer. I press again, the anxiety washing over me, I feel like I might pass out. Eventually I hear him answer and the relief is unreal. "Hi! It's me!" He doesn't answer, but eventually the door clicks open and I pull on the handle.

As I get out of the lift onto his floor, I see he has left the door open for me again and instead of loitering like last time I barge right in. I'm shocked to see suitcases, open and spread over the floor. I'm totally dumbstruck and he just watches me taking in the scene.

"What's going on?" I eventually muster.

"Shouldn't you be at work?"

"Shouldn't you? Seb said you'd left."

"Seb is always very dramatic."

"But you're packing."

"I am!"

I can feel my eyes filling with tears. "You're going away? Why didn't you tell me?"

"You didn't give me chance. I left a message at work and I sent you a message asking to meet up for a chat." I take out my phone, and yes, he's sent that message.

"So, what does this mean?"

"Well, when I said for you to think about what you wanted, I did the same. And I decided I don't want this life. I'm taking some time out, a sabbatical, to think about what I want from life. Seb is interim CEO."

"When are you going?"

"Tomorrow."

"Right!" Tears fill my eyes. He's leaving me!

He goes over to the kitchen island, picks something up and brings it over to me. I take it automatically, not even registering what it is.

"I want you to come with me."

"What?"

"I heard what you said about not liking me as CEO and in all honesty, I don't like me either. I never chose this job and it brings out the worst in me."

I feel a splash on my hand and look down to see the tears have silently fallen. Then I notice the ticket in my hand. A flight to Thailand, dated for tomorrow. It has my name on.

"I don't understand."

"Come with me! I know this is a lot of pressure and I don't want to be THAT guy. But I need you to choose.

"We can try being together, in this same situation, me trying to do a job I don't like while you try not to be pissed off at my lack of engagement. We could see what happens. Going around in circles, not knowing how to love each other the way we both deserve.

"Or! We can try being us, Megan and Myles, and see what it's like to be together, doing new things, getting to know each other, loving each other. We could spend time away from this crazy world to see how we can work together."

I'm lost for words. I keep staring at the ticket with my name on. I look up at this beautiful man. A few minutes ago I thought he was walking out of my life. Instead he wants to take a chance.

"And if I don't say yes, what happens then?"

"Maybe I can get a refund on the ticket, maybe not. Either way I have to leave, for my own sake."

"I don't have a passport!" Is the only thing I can muster.

"Erm actually you do."

"What?"

"Okay, it wasn't me. I know I'm a bit much but I'm not deranged. Sean applied for a passport for you, he thought you may want to spread your wings eventually, maybe escape from the ex situation."

"I don't know what to say." Myles' face drops.

"Let me ask you one thing." I nod. "Why did you come over in a panic?"

"I..."

"It shows you care about me, surely?"

"You know I do."

"So just for a moment, forget about everything else, any of the consequences and of the all the arrangements. If you had to make a choice right now, on the spot, no thinking, what would you choose? Go with me or stay here?"

"I would choose... You! I would always choose you!"

Myles' body seems to fall in on itself. All the tension from the past few weeks pours out of him and he puts his hands on his knees, bent as if winded.

"Thank god! I wasn't 100 percent sure I was gonna be able to leave without you."

I laugh through my tears. He stands up, steadies himself, takes the few steps toward me and envelops me in his strong arms.

"We do need to sort things out though," I say into his chest.

"First things first." He leans down to kiss me, and I open my mouth to let him in. He bends putting his hands just under my thighs and lifts me off the ground, wrapping my legs around him, as he sets off up the stairs.

Chapter Forty

All our friends are gathered in Myles' flat. They think it's a celebration of us getting together. There is chatter between them all. Dionne is standing at the kitchen island talking to Seb, probably about work. Emma is sitting chatting to Lizzie while Ben sits on the arm of the chair, one arm wrapped around her. Sean is chatting with Jonathan and they are both full-on laughing. Beth is deep in conversation with Kateryna on the other end of the L shaped sofa. I love this bunch of people.

Myles comes up behind me and wraps his arms around my waist, pulling me back to his chest.

"It's time!" He whispers in my ear, and I nod.

"Hey!" Everyone ignores me and continues whatever they are doing. "HEY EVERYONE!" I shout louder and they all stop and look at me. "We have something to tell you all. This isn't just a *get to know my friends* drink. It's a goodbye drink." Everyone stares in shock. "Chill your boots." I laugh. "We are going away for six months, travelling and seeing where things take us."

There's a muttering of congratulations but I know the girls will have questions.

"What am I gonna do without you?" Beth speaks up with a quiver in her voice.

"You've still got us," Emma says.

"You're planning on moving up to Edinburgh!" Beth answers and Emma pulls a face and mouths *sorry*. "Looks like it's just you and me Lizzie!"

"And me," says Dionne

"I'm here too," Kateryna says. "I need friends."

"Well that's okay then, you're allowed to go," states Beth with a smile.

"What about the trial?" Jonathan asks. After we had some time getting acquainted with each other again, I talked to Myles about what happened with Darren and that having a law degree would come in really handy.

"Well now she has her own legal team." Myles grins back. "Plus, I expect we'll be back way before anything happens."

"A toast then." Sean lifts his glass. "To Megan and Myles, happy travels. And don't get married in Vegas without us!"

Everybody laughs as if it's a completely ridiculous suggestion and Myles just shrugs. I'm going to be sad to leave this lot, but I'm excited to see what life brings for me and Myles. This isn't the end of anything, it's just the beginning!

Epilogue

Megan

Six Months Later

Looking out at the white sandy beach and the crystal-clear sea from my sun lounger, big floppy hat and sunglasses, Mojito in hand, I'm contemplating the past six months. It started with a relaxing beach scene and its ending with a relaxing beach scene. Except I'm a lot more tanned and a lot more relaxed than I was at the start.

I watch him as he walks out of the sea, like some kind of god. Pushing wet hair off his face, longer now, more carefree. The sea water rolling down his toned chest and stomach, it's like the scene out of a movie, walking out in slow motion. He still makes my stomach have a little flutter every time I see him. He strides over to the sun lounger and squeezes the water from his shorts onto my legs and shakes himself like a wet dog. I shriek, nearly spilling my cocktail.

"It was funny the first time you did that in Thailand! Not so much now…"

"You love it!"

And in all honesty, I love him more and more as the weeks have gone on. We've been through so many adventures together and we've been with each other pretty much 24/7 and never once regretted the decision.

He sits himself down on the sun lounger next to me and dries himself off. We have pushed the decisions about our future to the back of our minds, but we have been constantly talking about what we want for our new life together. The idea was that our last stop here in Santa Monica would be the time for decisions and relaxation.

Myles doesn't want to go back to his corporate job at Beck, and I don't blame him. We talked about it and he hated every minute. He's been talking to Seb a lot while we've been away. Seb's stepped up and doing a really good job at being CEO. And the best thing is, he's loving it. I did have to get a second opinion from Dionne though, because the Beckett men like to hide their real feelings deep, deep down. She confirmed that he's absolutely smashing the job and seems as happy as anything.

Instead, Myles wants to focus on a career in law, helping people, whether it be domestic abuse or miscarriages of justice. And I know he will just be great at it. He needs to work at something he's truly passionate about.

Me? Although I was mad at being moved departments, it was the best thing that could have happened. I took a six-month sabbatical and although Imogen wasn't too happy, she understood. But I was on strict instructions to come back to work because the place wouldn't run properly without me.

We've talked a little bit while I've been away, just catching up, and she also floated the idea of me having a more creative, as well as leadership role on the team. I spoke to Emma about what that would entail, and I think it's something I could really get into.

Despite missing everyone while we've been away, we've managed to keep in contact. I send Poppy and Jonah a postcard twice a week, although at first, they had no clue what they were. And we have a video call every Sunday. I didn't want to miss any more of their lives while we are away.

"Myles. It's our last few days. We need to start making plans."

"I know. Kat is a little apprehensive." Kateryna and Tomasz moved into Myles' flat. She wanted to pay rent, but I told her she was doing him a favour, housesitting. Dionne loved my house so much, she moved in there and still has Sean as a house guest. But that leaves us with the question of where we set up home, which is equal amounts scary and exciting.

"Are we moving back to the flat?"

"Well I told Kat, even if we did, we'd not move back in straightaway. We'd give her time to find somewhere. But it's really up to you. I don't care where we live as long as we are together."

"I think we should find somewhere that we choose together. Nothing too clinical." I laugh, because Myles has a touch of OCD about things having a place. "But in the meantime, Ben has found somewhere we can go to straight off the flight."

It will be weird going back to our old life because we've both changed so much. We've visited some amazing places I never in my wildest dreams imagined I'd see. We've done things that were way out of my comfort zone, like jumping off big rocks into the sea and riding scooters round the Amalfi coast. I did enjoy that, but now Myles is talking about giving me driving lessons when we get back.

"Are you looking forward to getting back?" He asks.

"I have missed everyone terribly. My friends are my family, so yes." We even met up with my parents while we've been away. They were on a stop off on their Mediterranean cruise, so we dropped into Sicily to see them. They met Myles for the first time and, as he does with everyone, he charmed the pants off them. I think his magic started when he shut them down as they started to criticise something I had done.

"What about you?" I ask.

"Same, I'm looking forward to seeing Seb and my parents I suppose. I'm not looking forward to having to share you with others. I know Sean and Beth will want to spend all their free time with you when we get back. I just want to keep you all to myself."

"At least we didn't get married in Vegas!"

"They'd never find out!" he jokes. In all honesty we did consider it, but we knew that this trip was something out of the ordinary and we needed to work out how we navigated real life before we had the added pressure of marriage. Plus, our friends would never have spoken to us again. Poppy has already made her feelings perfectly clear about wanting to be a bridesmaid.

So this isn't really the end. This is just the beginning of a new adventure for me and Myles.

The end.

Not quite, you can read what happens next in the Bonus Epilogue.....

Afterword

Thanks for reading my book, I hope you enjoyed it. It would be just awesome if you could put a review over on Amazon and Goodreads. Reviews are like little tips that keeps us authors motivated to write more stories.

But its doesn't have to end just yet. If you would like to read more of Megan and Myles you can download a copy of the Bonus Epilogue, by going to this link and a copy will be emailed to you www.carriemcgovern.com/beckettbonus

Hello Mr Handsome is the next book in the series. Find out what life has in store for the rest of the friends.

If you would like to follow updates on my work follow me on **Instagram** and **Facebook** at **@carriemcgovernauthor** , or find me on www.carriemcgovern.com/socials

The Hello Series

This series of books focus on a strong friendship group. The books are individual stories with interconnected characters.

Hello Happiness
Emma's story
Hello Mr Beckett
Megan's story
Hello Handsome
Coming 2024
The Other Mr Beckett
Coming 2024

Acknowledgements

There are loads of people to thank who have supported this journey. Thanks to my friends and family who have supported me and put up with my constant talk about *The Book*. Thanks to Emma and Marian my first Beta Readers, Helen for being a very patient editor, Lauren for being so patient with changes to my artwork.

I want to thank my author mentors, Cygnets, without you guys for support, this book would never have been published. I also want to acknowledge the support from an amazing group of women who empower and support each other and have been my biggest cheerleaders and support, **The Northern Lass Lounge,** you have kept me sane and motivated, thank you.

About the Author

Carrie McGovern

Carrie is a contemporary romance author based in the UK. She writes relatable romantic fiction with strong female characters. Her books have a strong emphasis on friendship and female empowerment.

Carrie has been writing since the age of sixteen and has a BA(Hons) in Communication Studies, specialising in Journalism. It is only recently, through the love of reading, that she has taken up writing again.

She is married with two boys and a cat.

As well as reading she enjoys binge watching crime dramas and growing random plants.